I0591374

The Century's Last Word

Brendan Walsh

Black Rose Writing | Texas

First printing

This is a work of fiction. Names, characters, businesses, places, events, and
incidents are either the products of the author's imagination or used in a
fictitious manner. Any resemblance to actual persons, living or dead, or
actual events is purely coincidental.

ISBN: 978-1-68433-756-9
PUBLISHED BY BLACK ROSE WRITING
www.blackrosewriting.com

Printed in the United States of America
Suggested Retail Price (SRP) $18.95

The Century's Last Word is printed in Garamond

*As a planet-friendly publisher, Black Rose Writing does its best to eliminate
unnecessary waste to reduce paper usage and energy costs, while never
compromising the reading experience. As a result, the final word count vs. page count
may not meet common expectations.

*This book is dedicated to Richard Thompson and Ethan Ibsen,
friends and coworkers taken too soon.*

This is my fifth time doing one of these, so I think I've got the formula down. I laid it on pretty thick in *The Century's Scribe* how much this story means to me, so I'll just say that I'm extremely happy I can be satisfied writing something I consider to be so personal and to have others get enjoyment from it. My time writing *The Century's Scribe* and *The Century's Last Word* wasn't easy. I was going through the roughest time of my life, but I believe I'm a better human because of it.

I want to thank my brother, Robert, for being my first fan and never getting tired of reading my work. If I didn't have you, I probably would have given up writing long ago, or never even began. You are a kind, intelligent, and sympathetic presence in my life, even when you're thousands of miles away. I want to thank my dear friend Scott Wagner for being my second fan, and for still being my friend after all these years. You're one of the best and smartest people I've ever come across, and I am still surprised that it's me who's been lucky to be one of your closest friends. Of course, my parents as well. I love you both, and thank you for traumatizing me just enough to get that writer's spark going into adulthood (haha). It would be wrong of me not to also mention some of my other close supportive friends, Ransom, Kevin, Debby, and my new friend Jake, also a Black Rose Writing fantasy author. It's been awesome connecting with you and reading your work, and I think you have an excellent gift for characters and world-building.

Lastly, I'd like to thank everyone at Black Rose Writing for believing in my work, and for being great people to work with. More than ever before, I feel like I am a part of a great community of writers.

The Century's Last Word

CHAPTER 1

Dreden found a note waiting for him under the door. It didn't have a name on the front, but he figured it could only be from one person.

It was well after midnight. On any of the previous nights in the strange, wonderful city of Brunswald, he would have been with Morell and a new roster of his wealthy, accomplished friends.

He pulled the thin piece of paper out of the envelope. The black ink was still fresh.

Dreden,

I'm sorry if you were hurt tonight, or if I was needlessly harsh to you. I'll admit, you were probably right. I should have told you about my relationship with Davon. I made an unpleasant assumption about you, since you come from such a different place. I should have been better than that.

Maybe tomorrow we can go out for cocktails after lunch. I'll buy. I don't want this lingering between us for much longer. The longer it takes us to address it, the more uncomfortable it will get, and it really isn't the kind of thing that justifies more drama than it has already produced.

Oh, and bring Gerry with you. I still regret the way we poked fun at him at The Royal a few nights ago. I want him to know I'm not such a boor all the time, and I'd love to hear how a creature like him is dealing with his newfound fame. I'll be staying over at Davon's tonight, so don't expect me back.

The Best,

Morell

Shutting the door to the flat, which was really Morell's flat, he lazily tossed the note to the side of the bed. He knew Morell was trying to cheer him up, or at least do something that would improve his mood, but it had the opposite effect. It just reminded him of all the things he was dealing with.

Now, having spent days in Brunswald, the events that led him and his friends there seemed like weeks and weeks ago. Back in their hometown of Kroonsaed, he, Chanin, and Gerrika had been ambushed by strange men who used weapons they had never seen before. Dreden now knew those weapons were called 'guns', and had to be reminded of them a second time as several more men had attacked him and his father in his own home, which sent him hotheadedly on his crusade to find the truth about his attackers, resulting in his and his friends' arrival in Brunswald via the mysterious Sunitian Sea.

His father…

Dreden's heart tightened.

He hadn't seen his father in days. It was the longest they had ever been apart in their entire lives. Since the death of his mother, Dreden was most of what his father had. As a poor professor in a poor town, they didn't have many possessions.

I'm selfish, Dreden thought. *I'm so selfish for leaving him for Morell, a handsome, deep-pocketed man who I suspect doesn't care for me nearly as much as I care for him.*

Even then, he had to ask himself: Did he love Morell?

Infatuation was a better word. Morell represented something to him that he never thought he would have. Freedom. Success. Money. And what did that all get him? It had him thinking he didn't need his friends, the people who stood by his side for years. Now that he knew Morell was seeing someone else besides him, the illusory spell cast by the man was beginning to fade. Perhaps this young rich man wasn't all he was cracked up to be?

Dreden shook his head. He couldn't be thinking about that now. He had more pressing things to worry about.

Like the new revelation about Mick Jowns, he remembered, *about how the bright, world-shattering philosopher he was reading had been the very man to attack them back in Kroonsaed. What kind of sense did that make? Could it be true? Could the worlds of Kroonsaed and Brunswald truly be one in the same?*

That begged too many questions that he and his friends simply couldn't have answers to. He felt like a fruit fly in a closed glass jar, having a cloudy vision of the room around him, yet not being able to see anything for the shapes they were.

They would get to the bottom of it. He just needed to get some sleep.

As he put his head down on the pillow of his vacant bed, he heard a familiar pair of footsteps trudge up the stairway.

"You still don't want to talk about it?"

Gerrika ignored her question, even though it was eating him up inside.

"Fine. You don't have to." Chanin said. "I just feel bad, since we let Dreden go on his own because you said you wanted to talk to me alone. I want to help you, my friend."

"It's a lot. I'm sorry." the aveho said. "I…seem to only be able to make stupid choices. I did something dumb. That's it. I don't want to say any more."

"You're anxious about your performances, aren't you?"

They made it to the top of the stairs, to the floor with both their flats. Gerrika felt a sour taste in his mouth as he remembered who was letting them use the rooms. Morell Edland.

"Take a few days off." she added. "There's no harm in it. Besides, singing can take a lot out of someone, even if they're an aveho."

"Chanin," he made a fist against his head in frustration. "I appreciate you. I appreciate you more than I can show right now, but I don't trust myself to have this discussion and not snap at you again. I'm sorry."

The human put her hand on his shoulder. He successfully fought the urge to brush her away, not wanting her to feel bad.

"You know where to find me when you need me." She slipped her key into the hole, giving him a halfhearted wave as she entered the darkness. "Get some rest. I'll see you at the library."

Sighing, the aveho entered his flat. He didn't want to. He *really* didn't want to, but they had no other choice. The questions posed by the revelation about Jowns's presence in Kroonsaed were disturbing at their mildest. The entire reason they had ended up in Brunswald was to find out why they were attacked back home, and that turned into a whole drama about how he and Dreden needed to stay there, since their lives were so stagnant back home.

Except Chanin, Gerrika remembered. *She actually wants to go back home. Knowing my luck, she will go back tomorrow and not come back for me.*

It was a bitter thought, and a part of him knew it was ridiculous, but in his current mental state, it made sense. Even if it was only going to be a temporary thing, the possibility of her returning to classes and her parents and deciding not to come back was too daunting a thought for the aveho to process. She wouldn't have been the first major presence in his life to leave and never come back.

He couldn't bring himself to tell her about his visit to Winds Wilk. It was, in a unique way, one of the most disillusioning things that had happened to him. Wilk wasn't a childhood hero, not even someone Gerrika had read as a teenager. He was a writer Gerrika had been reading for only a week.

I'm not like Dreden. I'm not an academic guy. Winds was supposed to be the writer that taught me it's okay not to be the brightest, it's okay not to be the best. That writing from what's in your heart, expertly done or not, is fulfilling and something others could appreciate. But he wasn't. He's not that kind of guy…

And that's what attracted him to Winds, and why Winds's words stung him like a wasp. He told Gerrika to give up.

What will I have if I give up? I'll be nothing. My whole trip to this stinking place would have had no point. I would have come to escape only to be shot out of the sky like a hunted duck.

He knew he couldn't give up. Giving up would require him to go back home and face his father again. And *that* he couldn't do.

Gerrika flopped himself sloppily onto his bedsheets, not even taking off his boots. He closed his eyes and waited for sleep to come, but it never did.

CHAPTER 2

He was exhausted and without sleep for close to twenty-four hours, but the Prime Minister needed to keep reading. With how much he had been reading, and how much he had to stop and consider the weight of what he read, it was only another few hours until sunrise.

The elimination of creatures called avehos...

That final line had stung him. Even though the Edland gang had already told him the awful truth about the first Prime Minister of Skaltbard, reading it from the man himself was a whole other beast. Now, knowing he had no other option, he had to finish the documents given to him. A large, messy group of notebooks that made up Jowns's Final Testaments.

The Edlands' revelation was the cherry on top of an unwanted dessert. Earlier in the week tensions were rising between Skalbard's neighbors, followed by an earthquake that killed dozens and injured hundreds in the center of Brunswald. With Andayt and Borgetta sharing more explosive incidents, no one was willing to give anyone any sympathy. Except for the Edlands, who had set up shop among the newly homeless to recruit cheap labor. In hindsight, as he continued reading Jowns's testaments, he wondered how he couldn't have seen the revelation of the Edlands' evil coming.

Charles hadn't expected there to be so much storytelling in the testaments, but it was clear after reading how important they were to how Jowns came to be. Some of the stories unnerved him so much that he felt the need to shut his window so he wouldn't be spooked by any passing wind or animal sounds.

Jowns's work on his testaments was admirable. There was an order to all the books. In *WHAT I DID TO THE OLD WORLD OF MAGIC AND*

SORCERY AND WHY, it even transitioned after the introduction to a glued-in journal entry that was apparently written by his mother, Alene Jowns.

It had read: *I don't know if this will ever be read, but I am frequently asked about Mick's upbringing and I can't bring myself to talk to anyone about it. Writing is all I'm willing to do, and hopefully, if I am deserving, it will give me some peace.*

My baby Mickeel Rippler Jowns had problems from birth. The doctors say that something happened in the womb. There was a defect in his right leg. They said it would always be shorter than the other, and that he would likely have to walk with a cane his whole life. He said there was not much he could do, but welcomed me to turn to magical remedies. I didn't want to. My baby Mick was perfect, or so I thought. Isn't that the thought of all mothers? Has any mother ever taken a look at their helpless, wide-eyed infant and felt that they would grow up to be a monster?

As far as I can recall, Mickeel's first encounter with an aveho was Boreno, our groundskeeper. We didn't have a lot of money, but we weren't poor. The middle-class Chammeter District of Brunswald was where I and his long dead father grew up and fell in love, and I wanted to give my son the same life. His father, Raley Jowns, was an assistant in a bank with close ties to the monarchy who died of tuberculosis months before Mickeel was born. His position allowed us to receive a lot of money in the years following his death, so I was able to afford a groundskeeper.

Boreno was very pleasant. He always wore simple clothes and had white feathers on his chest and on the top of his head that made him look like an eagle. He always offered to do more than what I hired him to, and he was always sweet with Mick. I remember the first time they met Mick was maybe three or four years old. Boreno had gotten him some chocolates from the nearby store. My son took them with a glazed, stupefied look in his eyes. It was as if, even at that age, the first sight of a talking non-human had challenged his whole worldview.

A few years later, while Boreno was out in the yard working on the hedges, I caught my seven-year-old son staring out the kitchen window, leaning on his cane for support.

"Come back to the table, Mick," I said to him. "your turkey is getting cold."

He didn't do anything for another few moments, just staring out the window and watching Boreno work. When he finally sat down at the table, I had long finished eating, and he stared at his meat for minutes as if expecting it to start moving. He sliced the turkey into even pieces, using his knife to eat them instead of his fork.

"Mother?" he asked.

"Yes, Mick?"

"Does everyone feel pain?"

It didn't strike me as a strange question. He was only a child.

"Yes. Everyone feels pain."

"Even turkey?"

It seemed he was thinking about the meat in front of him.

"I think it's reasonable to assume that they do."

"Does that mean Boreno does too?"

I remembered him staring out the window. *"Of course he does."*

"Why do we eat some birds but not others?"

"If you're asking about Boreno, it's because avehos are creatures like us. They're our equals. They're civilized."

"But we eat birds."

"And mammals too. Remember the bacon you had at breakfast today? That came from a pig."

"Who feels more pain? Mammals or birds?"

"I don't think it's a contest."

"Does Boreno feel more pain than a pig?"

"That's a rude question, Mick. You can ask that to me but don't go asking anyone else anything like that."

I didn't care to give my son any profound answers to his questions. He was only a small child for damnation's sake. Besides, I was never much of a philosopher myself, and I did not feel I had good answers to begin with.

Looking back, I can't escape the guilt I feel about what my son would end up doing, but a part of me feels that there was nothing I could have done to change him. My son was born deeply broken.

Despite his growing knowledge, Charles didn't find reading about the existence of avehos any less unsettling, especially seeing how they used to be everywhere in the city. What *truly* happened? The Prime Minister's eyes couldn't read fast enough. He had to know the truth, even if the truth would cost him countless more sleepless nights.

Alene Jowns's first entry ended there and was succeeded by another piece from her son. Thankfully, it had still been chronological: *I consider my questioning to my mother on that day to have been the moment my true thirst for knowledge began. After school, for years to come, I would spend hours at the library, hoping to learn everything I could about the study of animals. But the information I desired was sorely lacking. I didn't even attend a magic or wizarding school, yet the library was suffocated with books on magic.*

It was already as if the whole world were trying to work against me.

Having nothing else to read, I turned to my study of magic, which quickly led to my hatred of it. One cannot study magic without also studying its history, and one cannot study magic without studying the history of avehos.

It all seemed to happen so quickly. I had always been a bright boy, that much has never been disputed, but I was subjected to daily torment by my fellow classmates for my leg and the cane I used to walk. I intended to try remembering how many times I had been tripped or shoved, but they became too many to count. In hindsight, what angers me more than anything was the audacity of my aveho classmates to make fun of me, a member of a superior species. But I would have the last laugh, as is nature's way.

After that, his mother's journal continued, still in continuity: *My boy didn't have any friends as a kid. As far as I ever knew, he only ever had one friend as a young adult, but I'll get to that later. I was concerned. Locking oneself away with books for hours a day in a library couldn't have been good for a developing boy. I never knew specifically what he was reading, but I had some hints at what he would sometimes talk about. Philosophy, history, science, but I never wanted to hear it. He was only eleven years old when the incident happened. Those aren't things boys that age should be talking about. He should have been playing sports or spending time with his friends, anything that would allow a child to enjoy their youth.*

I think it was always because of the way he was born, the way he always had to use that cane to walk. I think he felt he always had to prove himself. Not to himself, I don't think he ever doubted who he was or what he could become, but he needed to show everyone else what he knew. He had to change the world. In a way, I consider it supremely selfless of him.

But his first act of his philosophy wasn't selfless. It was horrifying, and I wouldn't have believed it if I hadn't seen it for myself.

Boreno the groundkeeper was out in the yard. Summer was approaching and the plants needed to be watered. The aveho was standing out by the hedges, not paying mind to the sound of labored walking behind him. And why would he have? He had known Mickeel for many years.

I regret not screaming when I saw the butcher knife behind my son's back.

***

"I'm sure you're all happy that we're finally going to be finished with this book." Renny said, finishing some notes at his desk. "I know its climax didn't exactly deliver on all the action-packed adventure that came before, but rest assured that you may never have to study *The Mage Unlimited* anymore."

The professor's joke earned a few light laughs from his class. He knew that some of them weren't genuine. None of his students had any idea why his son hadn't been in class for the last few lectures, and the fact that he never mentioned it made the whole thing even more mysterious. Dreden was one of the best if not *the* best in the class. It was way out of character for him to miss any lecture.

He saw in his students' eyes as they watched him at his desk like snakes. They all wanted to know what he wasn't telling them. Odds were bigger that a giant whale would plow through the classroom than the odds he would tell them even if they asked.

The classroom clock struck 3. It was his last class of the day.

"I'll see you all in a couple days," he told them over the scuffle of books being put in bags. "Remember, no exam on this text, but if I were you, I would start thinking about what I want the focus of the final essay to be. If it's any help, I always commend any student brave enough to tackle *The Mage Unlimited*. Even if your work ends up being terrible, you join the ranks of many scholars who failed at properly grasping it."

He sat at his desk as his students shuffled out the door, on to whatever they usually did in the afternoon of the day before the weekend. He knew what Dreden and his friends always did. They always went out at night to Heathback Caverns, not coming back until late at night, or more accurately, early in the morning.

It had now been days since he'd last seen his son, but with times being what they were, it felt like more than two weeks to him.

The classroom door closed, and he was left to himself. He had nothing to do at the moment, so he decided to start on his next lesson plan for a different class the following day. He didn't get far into it. Three calm but strong knocks called to him from the door.

"Coming,"

He slid himself out of his desk. It was probably a student who left a book or a notepad. Opening the door, he realized that couldn't be so, since he didn't have any avehos in his class.

"Honja," He gave Gerrika's father a smile. "haven't seen you in a long time."

"Likewise." the aveho nodded. The large avian was wearing a light grey shirt. For all the help of his memory, Renny couldn't remember a time he'd ever seen dark-colored avehos like Honja and Gerrika wearing bright colors.

"I mean, that would be weird, right? If you'd been seeing me when I haven't seen you?"

"May I come in?"

"Yes. Sorry."

Honja came in, pausing in the middle of the room, taking in everything from the desks to the notes on the chalkboard.

"Never been here before."

"Where?" asked the professor. "Faeriebridge?"

"No. Never been inside a classroom."

"Is that right?"

Honja looked back to him. "Can't say I like it too much. Feel too cramped, like my arms have no space."

"It's a space for the mind, my friend. We forget our physical limitations in pursuit of knowledge here."

The professor sensed that even though Honja knew he was trying for a joke, he wouldn't give him the satisfaction of a hint of a smile in either his beak or eyes.

"What brings you to the campus for the first time? Can I get you something? I have tea, coffee, a couple kinds of ale."

"I don't drink alcohol." he said sternly. "Tea would be good, thank you."

Renny opened the door between his home and the classroom to retrieve the tea. When he came back with a full mug, Honja continued: "I think you know why I've come, professor. It concerns our sons. I suspect yours, like mine, has vanished."

"You would be correct. I can't say I'm surprised Gerrika is gone too. Despite everything, those two along with Chanin don't seem to do anything without each other."

"Am I also correct in assuming that your son told you a sensational story about a new world he visited?"

"It was rather difficult to believe, but my son has never lied to me about anything like that."

The aveho took a sip of his tea, raising his red-colored brow at the professor's words. "I know you have obligations to your students, but I consider my son being gone for days something that I ought to take seriously. I'm going to find this place Gerrika told me about, and I'd like you to come with me."

"Look, I try not to presume too much about people I don't know well, but why would you want me to go with you when you've tried making a life of avoiding contact with humans?"

"A fair question." Honja took a seat at the closest desk to the professor's, sipping his tea again. "My son told me that this other world was only populated with humans. No avehos. I think it would give me an advantage to have a human partner. Besides, your son has left you, just like mine."

"My son hasn't left me." He raised a finger at the aveho. "He's only been gone a few days. He's just taking some personal time after everything."

Honja gave him his first smile from the edge of his yellow beak, but it wasn't friendly. "That's an awfully foolish thing to believe."

"I know my son, Honja. Do you know yours?"

The aveho let out a long breath. "The implications of your question don't go over my head. Come now, professor, you're a smart man. Your job is basically teaching the psychology of fictional people. How many ways do you think this can play out? Surely you know that we never truly know everything about those close to us. A part of you is aware of the idea that you'll never see your son again."

The professor wanted to pound a fist against his desk or do anything to give away his feelings about what Honja was saying, but he knew he was better than that. Fist tightened on the top of his desk, he allowed himself another moment before responding.

"I am aware of it." he said. "I don't think it's likely. My son and I have always been close. Barring tragedy, there's no reason why he won't be home any moment."

"There's a way to ease that anxiety. Come with me."

He paused for another moment, just staring at Honja. From a certain angle, he didn't look that much different from his son. They both had the same black pattern that ran along their feathers from their chest downward with a splash of color around the collar. The biggest differences were his cold stare with eyes that could be still as stalagmites and the weight around his shoulders that came from a vastly different life.

Honja was trying to do right by his son. He knew he had to help him.

"Alright, but I have some meetings to attend to this evening."

"Not a problem. I'll be back here a couple hours to midnight." The aveho took another sip of tea, this time seeming to enjoy it a lot more. "I would bring clothes that you wouldn't mind sleeping in, and any weapons that you have."

CHAPTER 3

Questions were asked. How could they not be? Coming up with an explanation for Boreno's disappearance wasn't the hardest task. Luckily enough, Boreno had been thinking about moving out of the country for some time. Telling people he left for Andayt only earned thoughtful nods.

I became paranoid that a neighbor would see me digging in the yard to bury the body, so until I was sure I could do it, I hid the body in a locked concrete case in the cellar. In the moments that followed the murder I couldn't find my voice or even the right things to ask my son. I don't remember exactly what I asked him, so this part here might not be correct, but I remember what Mickeel said.

"I did nothing wrong."

At this point I grabbed the bloody knife out of his hand. "You murdered him!"

I remember rushing out to the yard. It was no use calling for help. No doctor or wizard could have saved him.

"He did nothing for us that we couldn't have done ourselves." He told me, unblinking like a shark. "I've been reading, Mother, reading way more than you ever have. This has been the way of history. Animals kill each other, eat each other, and sometimes a whole species may die out. Why wouldn't God save them?"

"You are not an animal, and neither was he! Murder is never acceptable!"

"I don't believe in murder, and neither would you if not for your religion. Besides, more humans and avehos have died in the name of religion throughout history than for any other reason."

He claimed to know all about the violent history of humans and avehos before we finally became one civilization, calling it "unnatural", also bringing magic into his argument and calling it the "tool of the weak". In anger I called him evil, trying to overcompensate for his bad leg, but he just laughed, telling me that if it was so bad, why could he kill Boreno so easily?

In the years that followed he didn't get any better, and there is a heaviness in my neck as I write this because I wouldn't do anything, because even after the horror, he was my son and I loved him.

Even after what I had found days after hiding the body.

The neighbors were out for the night, having a party that I didn't attend because of what I had to do. When I went down to get the body, I had to cover my mouth with a gasp. Parts around Boreno's arms, legs, and chest had been cleaned of feathers, with large chunks of skin gone as if a wolf had gone to work eating him.

I remember what my son said about animals eating each other.

Only my son knew where I had put the key.

The last line made Charles curse. Mick Jowns was eleven years old here. What could possibly possess a child to have such brutality? He knew that trying to answer that would send him down a metaphysical rabbit hole that would have him confront the very question of evil, which no philosopher or priest, genius or not, had ever solved.

Morning was quickly approaching. He could hear nearby doors of businesses open and close, with their owners starting early days and setting up shop for the day. Even then, he knew he couldn't stop. Jowns's testaments still beckoned more questions than they answered.

The next part wasn't from Jowns or his mother. The name at the top of the page was Rommuel Ashing. In reading the first sentence, it appeared there was a bit of a leap in time to where the new character's story began.

I met Mick Jowns on the first day of secondary school. I was a troubled child who hadn't had a friend before in his life. More than anything, as I prepared myself for the first day of school as a fourteen-year-old, I just wanted to feel like a part of something. I sat next to him in a history class, where he frequently remarked to me that our teacher was lying to us. I was relieved that someone had reached out to me, even if it was just in class. A few days later, I felt like I had a friend.

He taught me everything he knew. In my young mind, Jowns represented everything I wanted to see in myself. He was confident, good-looking, extremely charming and always said exactly what was on his mind without pause or stutter. It was something I desperately wanted, and I can't say that it didn't soon rub off on me. He taught me to hate avehos and magic, as well as the system that kept them among us: the monarchy. For over a thousand years either a human or an aveho occupied the throne, a concept that would sometimes send Mick into a shouting frenzy. You see, whenever there was a human king, there had to be an aveho queen, and the other way around. It was a way to be fair, so the government wouldn't favor one species over the other, and perhaps if it hadn't done such a good job at it, a man like Jowns would never have come to power.

It was his idea, the first time we started attacking people. The two of us would hide behind bushes or around the corners of buildings and throw stones at passing avehos. Some of the ones we hurt were certainly important people. Some of them dressed so sharp with their ties and caps that they could have passed for humans in the corner of your eye. To my knowledge, and to Jowns's disappointment, I don't believe we ever permanently injured any. We lived in a busy metropolis, and it would have been impossible to get away with murder, but I saw it in Jowns's eyes with every stone he threw. When I learned later that he had personally killed one before, I wasn't surprised.

What scares me the most was how I never felt guilt. I was so happy to have a close friend with a seductive philosophy that I never regretted hurting anyone. It is so easy to not care about the welfare of others when you are not the one with something to lose.

In reading about the years that followed, the Prime Minister couldn't help but pity Rommuel, even though he knew his pity was misplaced. All these records were slowly building up to the revelation of something terrible. They had to. He tried speeding through the rest of the account of Jowns and Rommuel's four years of secondary school, but he knew he had to focus again when Jowns's Theory of Evolution was mentioned for the first time, right at the end of the secondary school account.

"I'm about to figure something out." Jowns said to me, on the day of our graduation party, nearly leaping with his walking cane. "Obviously, the creation myths we were taught in primary and secondary school are nonsense."

"Obviously," I smiled at him. "is this another speech about killing God?"

"Something like that. I refuse to believe that the natural events that led to the rise of humans were in any way influenced by magic. I believe it was some kind of process that took more years than most people think have even occurred in our universe. Some kind of evolution."

"What do you think came first, humans or avehos?"

"It would make more sense for avehos. They've been leeches to the accomplishments of humans since recorded history. It doesn't take a bright mind to compare their place in society to that of a terminal old man."

We had to hail a carriage to the school for the party an hour later. An aveho couple was already in the carriage, and Jowns went manic at the idea of sharing a ride with them. At the time, I wasn't any happier than him, but I convinced him that it wouldn't be too unpleasant and that he could close his eyes the whole way if he wanted. I almost had to take his cane away before he hurt himself with it.

During the entire ride he had a hand behind his back and made a closed grip a few times every minute. It was later when I learned about the incident with the groundskeeper and the butcher knife that I made the connection.

That appeared to be all from Ashing, at least for that part of Jowns's life. The following pages transitioned into Jowns's university life. It seemed nothing changed for him personally, except his obsession with finding the 'Truth' about the origin of humans.

It quickly became my life's purpose. I knew that if I didn't succeed while at the University of Hinbarg, then I would spend the minutes until my last breath in pursuit of the Truth. Luckily I didn't have to wait that long. It was at the end of my third year that I published my Theory of Evolution by Natural Selection. It was the very first academic paper to deal with the origin of life as we know it without once mentioning magic. Needless to say, it turned everyone's heads.

Had it not been for my dear friend Rommuel, I'm not sure I would have been able to get through it. I was attacked on all sides, many demanding my expulsion from the University, not to mention half the scientific community called me a madman. But in the years that followed, I gained more converts. The next thing I knew, my greatest work was being taught in schools before I hit the age of 25. Now that I had the world's attention, I intended to seize it. I intended to prove through science that magic and avehos were inhibiting mankind.

The road before me grew easier with every year. My theory, at least as I wanted to use it, left no room for entertaining the possibility of old creation myths. It showed that even humans and avehos were as bound to the unchanging laws of nature as any other animal. It also meant that one of us had to be the superior species, and looking at history, it wasn't the hardest riddle to solve.

Invertebrate life came first, followed by fish-amphibians-lizards-birds-mammals. Avehos are birds, and, with the help of my work, anthropologists have been able to estimate that the modern aveho has been around for up to fifty million years, making them many millions of years older than humans, further indicating that they probably should have died off first. But they didn't. Magic and ancient humans saw to their survival.

***

"Did you guys get any sleep last night?" Dreden asked.

Both of them said they hadn't. Neither had he. There was too much going on in his mind to allow for more than a couple hours of rest. Besides, they agreed to meet at the University of Brunswald library as soon as it opened to do research. Trying to force yourself to sleep knowing you would be waking up early in the morning was never very effective.

The university library was at least three times as large as the Faeriebridge Library. Dreden's inner booklover wanted to spend hours in the place, but they didn't have that kind of time. Instead they went straight to the geography section, searching for anything they could find on the Deadlands. It was easy. Everything was alphabetized, and since it was so early in the morning there weren't many people around. Dreden, Chanin, and Gerrika grabbed as many books on the subject as they could and carried them to a private study room in the corner of the first floor.

"These all just have words." Gerrika flipped through a hefty one-thousand-page book. "We can't possibly go through all of these today."

"Some of these must have photos." Dreden said, taking a glimpse through the table of contents of another book, still looking like it would be no help. "If there are photos, maybe there's a chance we could recognize something we see."

They knew it was probably a longshot. If it was true that their home was the Deadlands here, it covered a *lot* of land. In all their lives, none of the friends had gone more than ten miles away from Kroonsaed. The odds that they would catch something they recognized were slim.

"I think one of us should go get food." Chanin said. "Neither of you ate this morning, right?" They both shook their heads. "I think a bit of food and coffee would make this less miserable."

"I don't have any money on me." Dreden replied.

They both looked at Gerrika, who had previously bragged about all the dollars he received from singing.

"*Fine.* I'll be back shortly."

"No rush." Chanin told him. "Take your time. We'll just be busy with these."

"Yeah. Don't worry. I'm not going to leave and not come back."

"Neither of us suggested you would." said Dreden.

"I know, but you never know about some people."

As he left the room, Dreden gave Chanin a quizzical look, but she didn't appear to be as clueless as he was.

"Something happen between you two?"

"No. It's just Gerrika overreacting again, and he's very tired." She wiped the hair out of her eyes, returning her focus to the books spread out on the table like a puzzle. "He'll figure it out. Let's get back to work."

Most of what they found dealt with the communities and societies living right outside the Deadlands, and the economic effect of the lands being so close to their homes. Apparently, it was true the Deadlands were entirely unpopulated, even by any animals. According to their readings, even plants had trouble growing near them. Living next to such a spot would make maintaining natural resources difficult. It was a great read, but definitely a read for when they didn't have a mystery hanging over their heads.

Gerrika returned with the food forty minutes later. Even with all the time that had passed, he and Chanin didn't feel they made any developments.

"Damnit," the aveho sighed. "I was hoping you two would have cracked the case while I was out."

"Sorry we haven't," Chanin gave him a weak smirk. "now sit your ass down and read. It's all we've been doing."

Gerrika plopped the bags on the table, almost knocking out all their contents. He bought three cases of coffee and three dozen assorted breakfast pies from Spetter's. It was very early in the morning and they were tired and starving, so Dreden and Chanin thanked him profusely.

In the following hour, now that they had food in their stomachs and the open eyes that three cups of coffee provided, their productivity grew.

It was only moments later when Chanin slammed a back of a book flat on the table.

"I found something!"

The book she had was a photo book. Like the others, it was mostly dedicated to the lands surrounding the Deadlands, but this one had some of the supposed uninhabited parts as well.

"Here. I think you guys will recognize this."

Dreden and Gerrika looked. They only needed a glimpse to see what Chanin saw.

"Heathback Caverns." Gerrika said. "Where are all the trees?"

"Dead, I guess." Dreden looked closer into the photo, as if expecting to suddenly feel the cavern breeze and the dirt under his boots. "There's no question about it."

Chanin nodded. "That's our home."

***

Now approaching the end of the testaments, Charles still hadn't moved from his desk. He thought about asking his assistant Jess to bring him food or a drink, but he didn't want to risk anyone seeing what was on his desk.

Jowns's handwriting grew more rapid and excited as the ending approached: *By the time I was 29, I had a rabid following. My work had influenced every other branch of science there was, leading to a growth of understanding of the secrets of the universe like there had never been before. In just short of ten years since the publication of my greatest work, science was what everyone was talking about. There was a drop in enrollment in wizarding schools, and magical businesses were losing money every week.*

And it wasn't just that magic was losing its utility. People stopped trusting it, blaming it for the fact that we had never had such a surge of knowledge before.

I was a hero.

How I wish I could say that my dear friend Rommuel was at my side the entire time, but he decided his life was going to go a different way. It would all be for nothing eventually, but he didn't know it at the time.

Rommuel Ashing betrayed me. He might have been playing me the entire time after what I discovered. It happened when I caught him degrading himself with an aveho.

Flipping the next page, it became an entry from Ashing: *Looking back, I wanted to get caught. Jowns had been my best friend for fifteen years, but I didn't want to share his beliefs anymore. Months before the ending of our friendship was when I met Morina. She didn't know who I was, and didn't until I had the courage to tell her, amidst a shower of tears and sobbing from me. It was a lot for her to digest, considering how things were now in the country, but she forgave me for everything, telling me that she was happy there were still humans out there with hearts.*

In a wasted effort, after I put my clothes back on, I tried to tell Jowns the error of his thinking, telling him that even if everything he thought was true, it was no reason to treat 'inferiors' with such cruelty. Our argument went on for an hour, even after he whacked me in the head with his cane twice to try to "get my mind back". I told him I was in love with her and that we intended to marry, and that was the end of it. As he left my house, he told me that I better pray he would show me mercy when everything came to an end.

I don't believe I'm a good man. I'd like to believe that I would have left Jowns's madness one day even had I not met Morina, but there's no way to know for sure. All I know is that after that day, I was happier than I had ever been.

To the Prime Minister's surprise, the next passage came from someone he had heard of. It was written by King Madan, the last king of Skaltbard: *For a time, there were riots outside the castle on a daily basis. The public and the scientific community had grown to love Mick Jowns so much that they demanded he be allowed to speak before Parliament. Queen Sirram, the aveho, and I fought back until people were actually dying in the riots. What could we do? Despite our contempt for Jowns, we let him in.*

On the day he was finally going to speak before us and the hundreds of members of Parliament, the castle became so crowded that our guards had to stop letting people in. But they wouldn't leave, they stayed outside the castle, hoping to still be able to hear Jowns speak.

There was no room on the floor for anyone else. It was completely packed, and the sound was deafening. They only shut up when Jowns took to the stand. There, leaning on his cane and swinging his fist through the air as if bludgeoning an invisible man, he made his speech. For what he lacked physically he made up with his volume and passion, as well as the fact that most of what he said was factually true, even if Sirram and I detested his conclusions.

He denounced everything from magic, avehos, to myself and the Queen, seemingly enjoying condemning us while pointing at us with his cane. When he finally finished, he grabbed his cane and raised it high in the air, as if wanting to prove to us that he didn't need it to stand up tall, and shouted "Hail Humanity!", and, to my horror, nearly everyone on the floor and half of parliament followed the gesture, repeating the chant.

I couldn't breathe, and sought the Queen's hand for comfort.

The next one was the first and only account from an aveho in the books. It was from Queen Sirram: *It was that day we knew it was over. The monarchy's days were numbered, all because of one broken little man, who, in a strange way, I pity.*

What followed was madness. Ten people died in the room after a fight broke out on the floor. Our guards did everything they could, but seven avehos and three humans were beyond help. The strangest part of the whole Jowns situation is that I am very much a fan of his work, and so is my husband Madan. His work on evolution is brilliant, and it is true no matter what he went on to use it for. Reading his scientific work is like sneaking a peek at history while its clothes are off. Initially the King and I were so taken by his work that we were inspired to invest in scientific education in schools across the country. But now, considering the political climate caused by a man as charming as a wolf from a fairy tale, it's like offering a gun to someone who wants to shoot you. More than anything, I hate Mick Jowns for taking the joy of discovery, something that should be so wonderful and beautiful, and turning it into a tool for hate.

After that, it was continued by Jowns: *It would only be months after my speech before Parliament until the coup. It would have happened on the spot, but I needed to build a proper army. They ended up calling us "the Rebellion" but I would argue that we represented the true force of nature, and that the monarchy was the real rebel, as it served to preserve things that shouldn't be preserved.*

It was a final bloody battle, and the King and Queen were executed. I can still feel a thrill deep in my bones as the crowd chanted my name. My first order as the new leader of Skaltbard was the exiling of all avehos and every human who had fought for them. I wanted them far away, so I put all the ones that had survived the changing tides on ships and sent them to another continent, to a settlement called Kroonsaed, near a common fishing port called Sunitia.

But I wasn't satisfied with that.

They should all be dead. I was going to send warships over to Kroonsaed to finish the job for good, but a better solution was brought to my attention, by a group of wizards of all people!

That gave me an excellent idea.

The problem was that magic was still around. Despite my hatred of the practice, I knew a lot about magic. I had to, in order to make the kind of arguments about it that I did. Everyone knows stories about little magic tricks, about making things disappear. Ironically, I found myself with big magical aspirations. I wanted the most powerful spell of all time to occur.

The wizards were desperate. They knew that I was going to do away with them at one point or another, so they felt they needed to make themselves useful. I went with an army and dozens of the world's most powerful wizards to Kroonsaed for the end. Every other nation on the planet tried to fight us, as we didn't want to just get rid of OUR avehos, but all of them. They didn't seem to like that.

When it became evident what was going to happen, the indigenous inhabitants of Kroonsaed along with the new settlers fought back, and there was another battle. We won it, obviously, but not before draining their whole little nations of guns and most of their resources before unmaking them from existence. I watched as the wizards did all the work, writing their spells in a large book before casting them into reality.

That's right, they all became UNMADE, and so was magic, sent into some other plane of existence. It meant that history was now back on its proper course. Even after the victory, I knew it wasn't over. As the wizards and I stood out, casting the spell to unmake Kroonsaed and everything around it, something was born. No one knew what it was, but just the sight of it was enough to give a man many sleepless nights. I am not sure exactly the nature of the creature, but it was a color darker than the human eye could perceive, vibrating and formless, and hostile to matter. I went on to name this thing "The Unmaker".

Besides the book with the spell that the wizards used, and this enigmatic new creature called The Unmaker, there is no other evidence that magic and avehos ever existed. After the spell, since it was suddenly as if magic and avehos never were, no one on the planet could remember them. That, and there were still the wizards who casted the spell who remembered, so I had them all killed once it was done.

There was a massive economic recession. One cannot just rid the world of millions and have things go on as they were. To make up for everything lost, I set my ambitions for an empire. I sent Skaltbard's soldiers all over the world, increasing conquest in the developing nations for all their precious metals, spices, and cheap labor. It wasn't long before we were back on our feet.

Before you finish reading this and think I'm some kind of monster as my dear friend Rommuel and my own mother believed, let me ask you something: why should humanity have to carry the burden of a parasitic species? No serious advancement in technology, philosophy, or culture had ever come from an aveho. They had never done anything for us, WE had only ever done things for THEM. They would have died off thousands of years ago if not for the advancements in medicine and, yes, I admit it, magic, to eventually give rise to the world we currently inhabit. Keeping them around was like having some cute little puppy-faced animal that people have affection for that happens to be naturally dying off, and people feel irrationally responsible for keeping that species alive, even though it's simply ending up like thousands upon thousands of creatures that have come before. There is no utility to it, nothing except soft humans being unwilling to accept the way of nature and assigning value to a creature where none actually exists. If they are truly our equals, why have we been the ones doing all the real work? Skaltbard didn't become the most powerful nation in the world because of human and aveho equality, it became that IN SPITE of it, and because of the brilliant humans who have gone on to prove to the world the superiority of our culture.

There is an argument religious people make, an argument that I happen to agree with in a different context. They say that even if God doesn't exist, we should pretend that He does, because if people believed there was no eventual punishment or reward for their actions, then society would crumble into lawlessness. I am not saying that my studies are infallible. I have probably made many errors in my life, but I stand by the Theory of Evolution by Natural Selection. If, somehow, it turns out I was wrong and magic did play a role in the making of mankind, I believe it is best to pretend that it didn't. Incalculable progress can be made by believing this lie. A noble lie.

Humans are certainly not the end of this story. One day, something beyond mammals will rise, and we will die out, and they will become the dominant creatures. To them I say, "Good luck" because that is just the way things are.

But until then: Hail Humanity.

CHAPTER 4

"That would explain the time difference." Dreden said, as they hovered around the photo book. "The distance on the map between Skaltbard and Kroonsaed is enough to cause the night and day difference."

"I think this still raises more questions than it answers." Gerrika replied. "If where we are right now, our home doesn't exist, then that must mean we came from a different time."

Chanin agreed. "At least with this confirmation there are some things that are settled, like the fact we speak the same language and everything, but the aveho mystery is still one of the most damning things here."

With the confirmation that their home existed in the world of Brunswald, the three went back out onto the library floor. They couldn't find Kroonsaed under 'K' anywhere, and any other book that dealt in some way with the Deadlands never mentioned it.

Chanin skimmed through another book and put it back. "If we're going to solve this, we need to find out how our home became the Deadlands."

"We probably won't have a lot of luck with that." Gerrika opened another book before tossing it away. "In everything we've read here, they only ever talk about the mysteries of the Deadlands. It's just like the Sunitian Sea."

Dreden stopped in his place, book in hand. "Gerrika, you're a genius."

Chanin and Gerrika followed him as he rushed into the 'Local History' section of the library, finding everything the library had on the Sunitian Sea. It wasn't nearly as loaded as the material on the Deadlands, so at least going through them wouldn't take as long.

"Think for a second," Dreden said, already two new books in hand. "we need to go back to the starting line, to the thing that brought us here in the first place. There's no way that the Sea isn't somehow connected to this."

He took the rest of the books on the Sea and handed them to Chanin and Gerrika, returning back to their private room to set their new literature on the table.

The following hour saw the rest of the coffee and food go empty. Then if they wanted anything to give them a bit more energy they would have to drink from a public fountain, but all the coffee seemed like it would hold them for a while. It made them able to go through the Sunitian Sea texts three times as quickly as anything on the Deadlands.

"Nothing here is outright saying it," Chanin said, sloppily reclining on her chair. "but it seems like the Sea hasn't been around forever. There is no account here that mentions it before the year 1000."

"That can't be right...or, maybe it's a clue." Dreden scratched his head, poking his face with the edge of a pencil. "According to all records back home, the Sea has always existed."

Gerrika let out a loud sigh, stealing his friends' attention from their research. "Ugh, this has been a lot of fun, guys, but I need to be heading out."

Dreden stood up, catching Chanin's eyes on the way. "Where the hell are you going?"

"I have a meeting. I have another appointment with Errick Lesting from the Lesting Theater."

"You are in absolutely no shape for that." Chanin said. "Look at yourself, Gerrika. You are a mess. When was the last time you slept?"

"A bit this morning. Look, I'm fine. I've survived so far like this."

"Barely!" Dreden laughed. "You have been drunk almost every hour since we first came to this city."

"You're not one to lecture me, Dreden." The aveho sharpened his eyes. "We've both been the drunks around here. You think I'm not aware how much you and Morell and his uptight friends have been drinking every night at The Royal? For your own sake, contain yourself a bit more, and at least *try* to look a bit better. You're wearing the same clothes you wore yesterday."

"I didn't really think I needed to get all dressed up for going to the library."

"Having decent personal hygiene is not 'getting all dressed up'."

"Regardless, you can forget about them for now. I'm with you two at the moment." Dreden raised his hand, stopping his reply. "What exactly do you mean by *try* looking a bit better? Forgive Chanin and I for not becoming as obsessed with our appearances as you have."

"You're both missing the point here." Chanin swooped in, separating them. "Gerrika, it would be good for you to rest today. You shouldn't be doing any more meetings or singing until you're back to normal."

The aveho made a fist against his head, eyes shut. "I don't have time to rest. I need this."

"What are you so afraid of?" Chanin asked.

"I don't see why I'm being picked on. Dreden is the one who has been unable to deal with things *way* before we ever even heard of Brunswald."

Dreden blinked. "Excuse me?"

"This is not the time or the place for this discussion." Chanin warned. "And I won't be having it here, especially not when we're trying to solve something serious here."

"Then I'll do it."

Gerrika took a seat on the edge of the table, almost hovering over Dreden in his seat. All Dreden could think about doing was passing his eyes from Chanin back to Gerrika as the aveho cleared his thoughts.

"Dreden, you've been our friend for years, but sometimes you can be one of the biggest bastards I've known."

"Where is this coming from?" Dreden leaned back, defensively.

"From *always*. How do you think it makes me and Chanin feel when you act so condescendingly about what you do? How you talk about the things we enjoy?"

"Is this still about that Winds Wilk comment I made after we saw that play?" he asked. "I was just joking."

"I'm not so sure you were. To answer your other question, this is also about those terrible people you've been getting chummy with. Dreden, I think they're the worst, especially Morell. Are you going to tell me next that Morell was just playing around when he made those awful comments about Winds?"

Dreden sat up, not losing the aveho's glare. "I am sorry if you were hurt by that, but I don't think Morell meant anything by it. That's just who he is, and his sense of humor."

"It's not funny. Winds doesn't deserve to be talked about that way by rich children who've never suffered for their work before like he has, and if you continue sticking with those people, you're only going to become more like them."

"Maybe if you'd try challenging yourselves a bit more, I wouldn't have said those things." He turned to Chanin, waving his hand to show he was including her. "I'm sorry if you've been bothered by me trying to enrich you with new ideas."

Gerrika pounded the table. "Are you shitting me?"

"Guys, this is pointless." Chanin pushed herself in between them, trying to stop the argument again. "You both have a lot of other things bothering you that you're keeping to yourselves. Can we please start by sharing that, and then maybe you two can be friends for the rest of the day?"

"You don't have to say it, Dreden. Chanin and I know how you feel. You think you're above us. You know what hurts? What hurts is that you can't help it, and soon you'll realize that no one will ever meet your standards. I think you'll soon hate Morell because he didn't live up to your expectations, and then you'll hate yourself for being unable to break your pitiful cycle."

"Think that's right?" Dreden raised his voice, stirring in his seat. "Even if what you're saying is true, I'm not the one who has made an ass of himself the entire time we've been here. Oh, you put on a good performance for these people here, but that's all it is. It's just a play. It's not real. There is not one aveho you could pluck from Kroonsaed who couldn't do what you're doing. I'm sorry, Gerrika, but none of the people you perform for actually gives a crap about you."

"And Morell is somehow different from them?" The aveho asked, talking with a strong enough bite to crack his beak. "He and his friends are nothing but empty shells. They have such easy lives, so they have the luxury of not needing convictions. Society has taken care of them fine, so they can live just talking about whatever knew idea some horseshit philosopher has come up with, without ever having the misfortune of seeing how their 'fun little ideas' can impact real people."

"Just because you don't have the best grasp of what they're talking about doesn't mean that what we talk about isn't meaningful in an important way." Dreden looked over to Chanin, who looked resigned, standing in the corner of the room, waiting for them to finish. "You're wrong to assume that everything is always easy for him. He has a lot weighing on him, both creatively and with his parents' business enterprises. You've had two real interactions with him, and you think you're an expert on him? Fine, I'll admit it, there are things that I talk to him about that I don't talk to either of you about. It's okay that the way we think about things is similar, and it's okay that I can turn to him for it. It doesn't mean you're an idiot."

Dreden felt something being turned inside of him. He didn't know how much he believed his own words. Prior to their argument, he was in no mood to defend Morell, but Gerrika's tirade against him burned away all reluctance he had. He wondered if it told him who he was more committed to, and after the argument his friend had started, he didn't feel he cared.

"I'm not saying it isn't okay. What isn't okay is how you've known him for a few days and that's enough to justify you ditching us at every turn."

"To be fair," Chanin's eyes looked heavy, making her seem more tired than she was after waking up. "you've been doing a lot of that too. You both have been drinking way too much. It can't be heathy for your current mental states."

"Relax, Chanin, I'm not the one who needs to worry about it. It wasn't my father who had the problem here."

It took the comment about his father to get Dreden on his feet. Even Chanin looked like she couldn't believe what she had just heard, as her palm flew to her mouth, as still as a statue.

"I cannot believe you just used that against me!" Dreden raised his arm, looking as if he were about to strike the aveho. "Why the fuck would you say that to me?"

Gerrika's head fell. He gave Dreden his back, turning to the door. As he stood there, with Dreden's question still in the air, he shook himself off as if finally trying to get rid of all the tension he had been feeling all morning. Gerrika's normal, less hostile soul seemed to fall back down behind his eyes. They both felt the tension evaporate.

"I'm sorry." he said. "That was intensely awful of me."

Gerrika walked away, leaving the table full of open and unreviewed books as he exited the room. Chanin caught the door before he had gotten far.

"Where do you think you're going?" she asked.

"I have a meeting to go to." He answered, continuing down the aisle. "I think I'm getting really tired of humans."

***

He felt dead. The Prime Minister spent the entire night reading through the texts the Edlands had given him, and now he couldn't even bring himself to sleep. He knew too much, and now he was being thrust into a situation in which he had to continue as if nothing happened.

His eyes were closed as he was spread out on his living room couch, lying on his stomach like a tired sea lion. As he heard someone enter the room, he couldn't bring himself to lift his head. Pretending to be asleep was a much better alternative.

All he could see of his visitor were the shoes, but that was enough, along with the sound of the man's small frame being moved as he walked, to know that it was his lead aide.

"Now you really look like you're the Prime Minister of Skaltbard." He could tell Skitt was smirking. "I always thought you had too much energy, Charles. Looks like things are as they should be."

"What do you want from me?" Charles moaned.

"There's work to do today." Skitt pulled up a chair by the coffee table and made himself comfortable. "You have another meeting with the ambassadors in an hour. You're going to need to look a lot better than you do right now if you're going to have a shot at solving anything."

The Prime Minister winced. "The world is going down the drain, Skitt. I'm not even sure why I should care about this stuff anymore."

"You should care because Skaltbard is the most powerful nation in the world. As you've read, we've done more for the progression of our species than any other civilization, and your obligations to the people don't cease simply because your modern sensibilities are sickened by Jowns's accomplishments."

"I'm a puppet, you cow's ass. By what I've read, I haven't had any real power in my whole life in politics. People like you have kept the truth to yourselves." With every bit of will he had left, he lifted himself upright onto the couch, fixing his hair. "Now that I know everything, what was the point of it? You, my friend Loid, the Edlands and all those other people in your little gang have been looking for something. You searched my home and the library for it, and clearly you don't have it yet."

"That's right. We don't. You may not be feeling well now, Charles, but we actually told you a bit about it yesterday at the Edland Estate. Either you weren't paying attention, or you forgot."

"I'm going to snap if you speak down to me one more time, little man." growled the Prime Minister. "Tell me what it is."

Skitt smiled, his rodent-like face looking more punchable than ever. "No. Later. I think it's better for you to go into the meeting without that knowledge." He rose out of his chair, walking away without putting it back in place. "Good luck, Charles."

The Prime Minister buried his face in his hands. He heard the front door open, followed by a 'Hello, Venka' from the exiting Skitt. She gave him a 'hello' back and entered the room.

After what he read, he couldn't bring himself to look at her the same way. His wife of over ten years had known the truth about Jowns for years. She and the Edland gang could almost be family.

"I can't believe you knew. You knew about Jowns and magic and avehos and everything and kept it all to yourself."

"What did you expect me to do? Even if I wanted to tell you, you would have thought I was making something up."

"You don't think you had any moral obligation to me? To the Saedians? To the visitors?"

"Morality had nothing to do with it." she answered. "and it's not about to start. We're on the brink of war. Are you really prepared to let something that happened a hundred years ago interfere with problems that innocent people are dealing with right now?"

"No," he softened his voice, shaking his head. "I don't think I will."

She paused, smiling at him before sitting herself on the couch next to him and giving him a hug. He was too tired to wrap his arms around her.

"Just try to relax. Take deep breaths. If things go Skitt and the Edlands' way, it won't even come to war."

"That's what I'm trying to do, Venka. I've done the best I can with these people, but I've got to defend Skaltbard's interests. I must consider those who still need help here after the disaster."

"I know, but that's not what I'm talking about."

He just looked at her. "What do you mean?"

"Skitt said not to say anything to you, so I won't. All I'll say is that, if they end up finding what they're looking for, all those other countries won't be a problem anymore."

"You think they can just-" Charles was going to say, 'magically fix them', but thought better of it after what he read from Jowns.

"All I know is what I've been told. There's a good chance our problems will just disappear. If you really want advice from me, I would tell you that you need to have the visitors and the bird locked up for what's coming."

CHAPTER 5

The bar was full.

Gerrika didn't know why Errick Lesting had insisted on meeting at Keethkay's. It seemed like the entire city revolved around bars. Keethkay's was one of the more popular and classier bars in the area, but that didn't do anything to negate the existence of a normal office meeting.

He took a couple trips around the inside and passed through the middle twice, but he couldn't find him. The aveho picked an empty table and sat there with a glass of gin for twenty minutes before getting out of his seat and heading to the bar counter.

"Excuse me?"

Behind the counter was a bartender he hadn't seen before. She was a woman with curly hair and darker-than-normal eyelashes.

"Ah, songbird. What can I do for you?"

"I was supposed to have a meeting with an older gentleman here. Errick Lesting. Heard of him?" She shook her head. "He's about eight inches taller than me, around fifty-years-old, probably wearing a suit, brown goatee?"

Recognition lit in her eyes. "I think I saw him earlier. He was here for about fifteen minutes before he left. You sure you got to the meeting on time?"

"No. No." He cursed to himself and shook his head. "I was a little late. I had other things to deal with."

"Sorry to hear that. Hey, if you're still here in ten, the pianist should be coming in. Maybe you can sing again. It's all everyone here talks about, and I've been on vacation, so I missed it!"

He didn't mean to, but the aveho was so tired and angry with himself that he didn't realize what he was doing with his face. Based on the bartender's reaction he thought he must have given her the kind of look an owl gives to a fleeing chipmunk. She almost dropped the glass she was cleaning, which made him go upright.

"I'm sorry." he told her.

She seemed to quickly sense that he meant it, continuing back to work as if it hadn't happened. "I've never seen anything like you before, but you seriously look like crap."

"I feel like it."

"Believe me, you don't drink in a bar after feeling worse than you felt when you arrived. You're supposed to feel the worst when you enter. If you don't, then that's an uphill battle you're not going to win."

"We'll see about that." He plopped down a ten dollar note on the counter. "Another gin and tonic, please."

He knew he shouldn't. A little voice in his head was telling him to stop spending money and ask for just a glass of water. Gerrika wasn't strong enough. The last week had seen him drink more hard liquor than ever before. He needed it to sleep, to talk to people, to not talk to people, and to forget for at least a single moment what he was. An aveho. A poor student. No one's favorite.

The following hour went by in almost a haze. Gerrika drank his refill in minutes before getting another one, and another after that one. When the pianist showed up, management told him not to play, since the bar already had enough entertainment. The aveho was spreading himself out around the bar like a plague, making conversation with everyone and acting as if he were some discount court jester.

After finishing his fourth cocktail, he threw the glass on the floor, shattering it to bits followed by a cheer as if everyone were watching a sporting event. He couldn't remember any of the names of the people he spoke to and could hardly remember what they talked about. All he knew for sure was that he had just leaped onto a table surrounded by a crowd that had become way more intoxicated than anyone had expected for noon.

"Sing!" Shouted some funny bearded man he had spoken to.

"Sing!" Came from a woman who he let touch his feathered arm.

"Sing! Sing! Sing!"

"Alright!" Gerrika groaned for a successful comedic effect. "This one is a personal favorite," He wobbled on the center of the table, causing some of the staff to watch him more intently. "I know it is because of how damn miserable it makes me. My mother used to sing it to me before she left me!" Applause and whistling followed, and he spread out his arms as if trying to grab the sun. "It's called Sky Man."

Knowing the song well, the pianist gave the aveho a nod as he made his way to the piano, playing the first notes of the song before the vocals came in. It was a slow, pause-inducing blend of an upbeat finger-dancing tune and a song that could cause rain to fall.

The wind is alive, tonight, no clouds
Telling me I'm the only one around
My legs hurt, but my wings are fine
It's funny, but I don't need to fly

Nobody has to walk, nobody has to fly
Nobody has to ask me why
I am the bird I am, but nobody knows
Who I really am after I've left the ground

When all the shadows are the night
And the moon can't cough another light
There's one thing no one knows,
I won't mind. I won't mind.

I can run without sound
I can fly without sight
And when there is no one around,
I will fall to the ground.

My god took my eyes
My god took my voice
And took them above the clouds
And left the rest to the flies

I won't mind. I won't mind.
They saw my eyes and heard my voice
In the clouds, and I sang my choice
And the world was never so kind.

It sounded as if another earthquake had hit the city, but it was just the entire tavern erupting in cheers. Gerrika wasn't sure what to do with himself, since every time before there had been a lot of room between his stage and the crowd. It didn't need to be extravagant. He just smiled and bowed, leaping off the table and somehow landing evenly on his boots.

He threw himself back, bellowing a cheer that echoed as everyone imitated it. When he was back upright and steady, he noticed a familiar face in the front of the crowd.

A very concerned-looking close friend of his stood in front of everyone.

"Chanin!" He rushed over to her, shaking her hand in a lighted frenzy. "Oh, you saw my song! I'm so glad you did."

She didn't look much better than she had in the morning, as if she had tried to get some rest but failed even at just easy breaths.

"Gerrika," she said softly, her loose brown hair appeared to have lost some color in the last few hours. "did you see Winds Wilk last night?"

"I did," He shut his eyes, shaking his feelings away. "guess I forgot to mention it. You know what? I'm over it. That guy can't write for shit." He turned around, back to the attentive crowd. "Am I right?"

They answered him with a resounding cheer, and he threw his fist into the air in appreciation.

"I am right! See, Chanin, that's all in the past. I'm completely over him."

"Gerrika," He caught a change in her breathing. "I'm so sorry. He was found this morning. He killed himself last night."

All signs of inebriation were flushed out of his eyes, and suddenly the ground felt wobblier than before. "He's dead? Winds is dead?"

She didn't reply. Chanin wrapped her arms around him, locking him tight against her. The aveho raised his arms slowly under hers, unable to move more quickly with the weight of the news inside him.

The crowd around him had grown silent, watching the pair like characters at the end of a play.

"How did it happen?"

33

"They say he overdosed. Based on the scene, it was a combination of alcohol, pain killers, and cocaine."

"I can't take this right now, Chanin." He sniffed, burying his beak into her shoulder. "I can't take this. I'm not strong enough for this."

"May he rot in his grave!"

Gerrika and Chanin turned around to a man who had his pint raised up in a toast. He was a short man with a fat, beaming smile under a brown cap.

"What did you say?" the aveho asked.

"I run a theater, one of the only ones that would do his plays." He turned around to the crowd, looking as if he'd just been named a lottery winner. "I may never get all the money he owed me now, but glad that burden has been sent back to the Creator."

He laughed, his whole body shaking as he took a swing of his beer.

Chanin returned to her friend. There was something else in his eyes now. Something that made the aveho look as if he hadn't eaten in days.

"I'm going to kill him."

And he dashed at the man before anyone could move. His brown cap and his unscarred face were in the past.

***

"That can't be right." Morell said. "I don't think any of it is right."

"How can it not be?"

"Dreden," he scratched his head. "I don't think some page you ripped out of my novel is evidence of anything. Besides, how can you tell for sure that the photo you found in the book is..."

"Heathback Caverns."

"Heathback. Right. How can you be sure? Every cavern looks the same, even on the outside."

Dreden wasn't feeling much better after leaving the library. He hadn't expected Morell back in the flat so early, but he would have to face him again at some point. After the way he ended things with Chanin and Gerrika in the morning, he needed to feel like he had someone.

"You're completely ignoring the most damning evidence. After everything I've laid out for you, how could you not think this is my world too? What are the odds we're not from the Deadlands, or any place here? We even speak with the same accent!"

"There are still too many gaps in your hypothesis. There is absolutely no record of anything that could suggest Kroonsaed's existence and disappearance anywhere in history. Nothing. And the nonexistence of Gerry's species is like a nail in the coffin. The Deadlands have been the Deadlands for as long as anyone can remember."

Dreden fought a frustrated growl. "How about the Sea then? Hmm? You all seem to think that it's been some pretty tourist trap forever, but we could find nothing to verify its existence before the last hundred years."

"Why is this so important to you?" Morell asked. "Do you think you're in danger or something? Is your home in danger? What?"

"I don't know."

"Then until then, just let it alone." Morell sighed, reaching over and brushing the side of Dreden's neck with his hand. "Have you even looked in the mirror this morning? You look awful, and you need a bath."

"I can't. I feel like I can't do anything." He took a seat on the bed and buried his face in his hands. "Morell, even before I knew you were fucking Davon, I was still feeling horrible. What you've been doing with me is maddening. How do you live like this? I see the way you're looking at me, and I don't want to fight again, but I'm not sure I can do this for much longer."

"And why do you think that is?" Morell couldn't hide a smile in the corner of his mouth.

"Because I want *you*, Morell. I want just you, but apparently that's completely out of the question."

"Good answer." He got up from his seat and went over to the faucet. He poured a glass of water for Dreden and himself and returned with them, handing Dreden his glass. "Dreden, I've had many physical partners before. Women too, if you can believe it. You are the odd one out in all of them. Know why? Because you're not rich."

"Is this about what you said to me last night? That I feel entitled to you? That I believe I deserve you?"

"Yes," he said, after a moment's thought. "but it's more complicated than that. You're bright, sweet Dreden, but you're very predictable. You know what your problem is?"

"I am seriously tired of being lectured to."

"Your problem," continued Morell. "is that you think so highly and so poorly of yourself at once. You have so big an ego, yet you make yourself miserable because you feel as if you have nothing to show for it. If you're in a bar or a classroom, you think you're the smartest person there, and sometimes you might be, but how do you prove it? How do you prove it to yourself? You've never written a book. Never received acclaim outside of a few good grades in school. But you're not going to brag about that? Many people get good grades. You feel that you not only need to be the smartest, but you have to have the work to show for it, otherwise how can you justify your behavior and, yes, sometimes the way you treat your friends?"

"I know, I know." Dreden took a few sips of water. "I can't help it. I've been alone most of my life. Never had friends until I found a couple people who could tolerate me every day at Faeriebridge. I've kept so much to myself for so long," He grunted, shaking the emotional weight in his head away. "yet I hold it against people when I feel they don't understand me, and I keep everything to myself because I think I weigh people down with my imaginary problems. There are some people in Kroonsaed who don't know where their next meal is coming from, and I have the arrogance to be unhappy when I think the people closest to me don't think of me as being as smart or creative as I believe myself to be, and then I hate them for it."

Morell nodded, sitting against his arm on his chair, looking almost more fascinated than empathetic. "But you don't hate them for long, do you? Then it goes back to yourself. You hate yourself because you've spent so much time with those people when you could be with others: People who will see you for who you've built yourself up to be in your mind."

He looked away from him, wiping away a tear in the middle of his cheek. "I have this fantasy where I accomplish something, maybe it's writing a book or creating a new kind of philosophy, and that's forever all I need to be happy. I've proved myself to the world, and most importantly, to myself, and then I can be a proud bastard for the rest of my life, and then all the times I've been alone or felt uncared for would be justified. I'm not sure I have it in me to be happy if it doesn't come true. It would mean that I threw away people and my friends over something that I never had in the first place."

"And that's all it is. It's just a fantasy. You have a lot of issues, Dreden. You're smart, you have potential, and I like sleeping with you. I don't walk away from people who meet those criteria." He smiled at own jest. "But that doesn't mean I'm the person you've been looking for all your life to make you happy, it just doesn't work that way. You need to finally learn how to adapt, sweetheart. In the future, please don't get angry with my friends for just doing what I've asked of them. I'm not changing my relationship with Davon just for you. I understand the part of you that makes you want to latch on to me and not let go, and now it's your turn. Write, read, do something today that makes you happy. You should be your own primary source of happiness."

Morell rose out of his seat, shooting Dreden a sympathetic smile as he leaned forward and wiped Dreden's eyes and fixed his hair. He turned for the door, leaving his half-filled glass of water on the arm of his chair.

"I'll see you later."

"Don't go." Dreden begged, sniffing. "I haven't had a good day, and it's been all downhill between my friends and me since we came here. Please, I need someone right now."

"I'm sorry." Morell said. "I have places to be. You need to speak to yourself. You need to decide what you really want from people before it's too late."

He didn't reply. Even if he did, Morell was too far out the door to know what he would have said. He had prayed for Morell to tell him what he wanted to hear when he was opening himself up. He prayed Morell would tell him he was smart enough, tell him he belonged with him, tell him that he meant more to him than his friends, tell him that things would get better.

When the footsteps down the hallway faded, he threw himself down on his back and closed his eyes, still unable to rest.

***

Gerrika and Chanin dashed down the alleyway. In the last six minutes they had run almost a mile. It didn't sound like they were being chased anymore, but they wanted to be safe. They didn't know the city as well as some of the people in pursuit of them, so it was best to just keep running and running.

Looking behind her, Chanin grabbed Gerrika's arm and tugged him into the corner of an alleyway. A few random pedestrians saw them go down the alley, but it was expected. Two people running down the street in the middle of the day were going to turn some heads, especially if one was an aveho.

"I think we're good." Gerrika caught his breath, putting his hands on his knees. "That was fun, wasn't it?"

"*No.* No it definitely wasn't fun."

She sat herself down against the back wall. The aveho followed her. There was a mountain of trash bags lining the alley, which kept them out of view, in case any of the people from Keethkay's were still chasing them.

"I don't know about you, but I've never been chased out of a bar before."

"That man nearly lost an eye! Not to mention you clawed off part of his ear. You'll be lucky if all they ask you to do is pay a fine."

The aveho rested his arms on his legs as he sat, wiping the rest of the man's blood that was on his talon-hands on the concrete ground. "I know it's bad. I know. How did you find out about Winds?"

"His death made the afternoon newspaper." she told him. "The article claimed that a neighbor saw you go into his flat yesterday, and since you're the only aveho here, it's not hard to put together."

"They don't think I killed him, do they?"

She shook her head. "Unless you force-fed him liquor and pills, you didn't kill him."

"Maybe I did, Chanin. Just maybe I did." Gerrika softly banged his head against the wall. "If I didn't go see him, maybe he would still be alive. Our meeting didn't go well."

"It's not your fault." Chanin told him firmly. "Maybe some people can't be helped. Maybe there are some people that have dealt with things for so long that every dark thought is no longer a bad day, but as much a part of them as their lungs and heart. Maybe if you went to see him on a different day, he would still be alive. We can play 'maybe' games all day, but that doesn't change the fact that it was Winds who chose to kill himself."

"I could have done more. I could have left him with some kinder words. I could have hugged him."

She closed her eyes, putting her hand back on his arm. "I can only imagine how you feel, but you need use everything in yourself right now to calm down. You could have killed someone today. The Gerrika I knew two weeks ago would never have done that."

"I've done a lot of growing up." he said sourly.

"Listen to me. I understand what's been bothering you and Dreden, but you two need to do better. Despite how the two of you feel right now, you are *good* friends. You can't be inciting arguments anymore like you did, and if you have something to say, there is a way to say it that doesn't involve the mauling of a complete stranger."

Gerrika opened his beak to interrupt her, but she raised a hand to silence him. "I've been trying to keep myself afloat this last week. It hasn't been easy, and I've been so glad to have met the Gumarys, since they've been extremely nice, but it's hard. It's really fucking hard watching what the two of you are doing to yourselves." She wiped the corners of both her eyes with her sleeve. "And I can't do it. I can't do what you're doing, because one of us *has* to be the stable one. One of us has to be the middle."

Gerrika threw his head back again, taking a few quiet moments between himself and Chanin before bringing it level again and let out a tired breath.

"Damnit, Chanin, you're right. I've been an absolute prick this last week, haven't I?"

"You've been dealing with a lot, but it's mostly not been pretty."

"I need help. I want it. I never want to feel this way again. I think Dreden was right. These people don't actually care about me. Shit, I'd never thought I'd turn into a hawk on a guy."

Chanin wrapped her arms around him, and this time Gerrika returned the embrace. He could feel through her breathing that she was fighting more tears. It made him keep himself still, to show that even though he felt as if he had never been so depressed, that he was about to keep himself steady. If not, he would have ended up breaking apart in her arms.

"What do I do now?" he asked into her ear.

"You need to just forget about yourself for a while." She let go of him, and they shared eye contact again. "Come on, I want to take you to my friends. The Gumarys. They've been great at cheering me up. I promise they won't ask you to sing."

"That sounds almost too good to be true." The aveho smiled.

"It's not." She stood up, getting back on her feet. Gerrika's hand was locked in hers as she helped him up. "Maybe now they will stop bothering me with tedious aveho questions."

CHAPTER 6

The meeting was a nightmare. It was as if Charles could show everyone how weak he felt just by walking into the room.

He didn't think it was possible. Then again, he didn't think that anything he had learned or that had happened in the last week were possible. Disasters plagued the most powerful nations in the world, on top of the fact that he now had to deal with the evil past of the nation he led. The worst part was that he couldn't tell anyone about it. Who would believe him?

A hundred years of armistice between Skaltbard, Andayt, Borgetta, and Gontland was about to go down the drain. In wake of the thousands dead across the countries, new alliances were formed. Warring Andayt and Borgetta had issued ceasefires on all fronts, eventually leading to Gontland giving aid to Andayt when it had been promised to Skaltbard and had even become an expectation over the course of the last hundred years.

The Prime Minister had been tossed around like a ragdoll in the meeting. Skitt was no help. If anything, he made him look even worse.

That little man and his gang are ruining everything. I've done all I could to prevent war, and to help those still hurt by the earthquake. What do they want? It seems like one minute they want chaos and the next they want peace. How am I supposed to deal with it?

There was too much brewing inside him to sit about and do nothing. He couldn't even talk to his wife anymore. She may as well have been one of them.

The Edlands said they might have plans for the visitors, but Venka said she would have them locked up. He clenched his teeth in frustration as he thought. *My wife isn't one of them. She knew about Jowns and everything, but she's not a part of the group. If the Edlands are coming after the visitors, I need to do something about it. I need to keep them out of their hands. The least I can do is keep the Saedians free of whatever evil those monsters are cooking up.*

An idea came to him. It wasn't great, and it made him feel even more sick than he already did, but he didn't know what else he could do.

He darted out of his office, out into the lobby.

"Jess?" he called.

His young assistant came out from behind her desk. Charles suddenly felt like he was looking at her for the first time. She was probably half his age, definitely not older than twenty-five. She knew nothing of the world of Skaltbard that had existed a hundred years ago. Her ancestors might have been wizards or witches. They might have had aveho friends, or they might have been Jowns supporters. There was no way to know for sure. Either way, he knew she was living a life that would have been completely different had Jowns never come to power, and she had no idea. In that moment, she was the face of innocence.

"Yes, sir?" she asked.

From the look on her face, he knew she wanted to ask about his poor appearance. He knew he had the baggy eyes of a fresh cadaver.

"Jess, I need you to hook up the telegraph. I need you to send a message to the chief of police. Chief Milbrey."

"What do you want me to tell him?"

"Tell him I want Dreden Sharpstand, Chanin Adderfoth, and Gerrika the aveho arrested."

She cocked her head, letting out a smile. But apparently he wasn't joking. "Did they do anything wrong?"

"That's none of your concern."

"It's going to be Milbrey's." she said. "I don't think he can do anything if they're not breaking any laws."

"Tell him to find anything on them. Absolutely anything. They need to be locked up."

***

A pounding on the door woke Dreden up. It did nothing for his head, which felt like it was being struck from the inside.

Looking at the bedside clock, he had gotten just over an hour of sleep. He tried sitting up, bringing a hand to his forehead as another series of banging came from behind the door.

Who the hell could that be?

Couldn't be Morell. He had a key to the flat. It could have been one or more of Morell's friends, or it could have been Chanin and Gerrika. Whoever it was, their pounding of the door beckoned energy from Dreden that he wasn't willing to provide. He took his time to the door, buttoning his top button and fixing his hair to look as presentable as possible.

He opened the door to see two men in black uniforms and large round hats to match. Both looked to be around thirty years old. Dreden remembered seeing men in those uniforms before, back when he and his friends had first arrived in Brunswald and had almost instantly been detained.

They were policemen.

"Are you Dreden Sharpstand?" asked the officer on the left.

"I am." He blinked. "What is this about?"

"Do you have any form of identification with you?"

Dreden gave them a shrug. "I don't. I didn't think that would be necessary. Many people already know who me and my friends are."

"We're just following protocol, son." the officer on the right said. He took a notepad out of his breast pocket and began writing Dreden's responses down. "Do you know where you are?"

"Morell Edland's flat… *one* of his flats, at least."

"How long have you been sharing it with him?"

"A week. I'm sorry, I don't see what this has to do with anything. Is he in trouble?"

Neither officer replied. The other one simply stood still, watching what the other was writing.

"Do you have any legal agreement that is allowing you to stay with him?"

"No, I've been here a week. What's going on?"

"Hands behind your back, please." The officer returned the notepad to his pocket as the other one took out a pair of handcuffs.

"What am I being charged with?"

"Suspicion of homosexuality."

"You must be joking."

The officer grabbed his arms and locked the cuffs on them. "You will have time to fight the charges at a later date."

"I'm not going to fight the charges." Dreden said. "I'm crooked. There you go."

"In the future, son, I advise you not to confess before the hearing. It won't look good to the judge."

The officer grabbed his arm, and the two of them escorted him down the stairs and out of the building. A police carriage was waiting at the curb for him.

"You people are pathetic." Dreden entered as they opened the door for him. "Where I come from, we would kill for the technology and resources you have, yet somehow we're so far ahead of you in easy psychology."

"That's the world that includes murderous bird-people?" The officer smirked. "Don't worry, your fellow aliens will be joining you."

***

Thankfully for Chanin and Gerrika's tired legs, it wasn't much of a walk to the Gumary's garage. They talked about going to get Dreden to join them, but that would have required them to go back through the part of town they had run away from after the bar brawl, and things probably hadn't completely settled back down yet.

"I'm already bored." Gerrika teased.

"Quiet," Chanin said as they rounded the corner for the garage. "you'll never get anywhere with that attitude. Besides, I promise you'll learn something new."

"They got food here?"

"More than they know what to do with. You don't even have to ask," Chanin smiled. "I guarantee they're going to offer you everything they have, including the kitchen sink."

The aveho put a talon on his stomach. "Good. I might need to use it after all the running and all the gin I've had. Drinking and exercise do not mix."

Chanin knocked on the garage door. They could hear a shuffling sound coming from inside, along with a clatter of something metallic, followed by a woman cursing.

"Come in!" came a man's voice.

At his permission, Chanin bent over and lifted the garage door from the bottom, holding it until it folded itself into the ceiling like a turtle's head.

The scene was a mess. Even Gerrika could tell. The smell of smoke was potent, causing both the human and the aveho to start coughing.

"Chanin!" Sidra Gumary cheered after the smoke cleared enough for her to be able to see. "We weren't expecting you today, but we could sure use your help. Oh," she noticed Gerrika standing shyly behind her. "Gerrika, right? Good to have you again!"

"It's nice to be here again, Mrs. Gumary." he said, hands tucked at his waist.

"Please, call me Sidra. Chanin and everyone do. Besides, we're not that old."

From behind the motor-horse came Allin in the midst of taking off his soot-covered shirt. "Why do I keep wearing a white shirt while working? Hello gang! Can you keep the door open? It's about time we had some fresh air."

"Good afternoon, Allin!" Chanin said, rushing up to him and giving him a hug.

"Hello…ugh…Chanin." He smiled, awkwardly accepting the hug without his shirt on. "And a good afternoon to you, Gerrika. We're happy to finally have one of Chanin's friends over. You're all she talks about."

"That right, Chanin?" The aveho brushed her on the elbow. "We're all you talk about?"

"I'm afraid it is," She said, jovially. "but it's not my fault. These gossipy geese are always asking about you."

Sidra and Allin smiled awkwardly, as Allin remembered to find another shirt to put on. "In our defense," Sidra said. "you can't blame us for our curiosity. It's not often we get non-human visitors."

"Besides the raccoon that lives in the alley that we sometimes leave leftovers for." Allin laughed.

"I can't promise I'll be more interesting than that guy." Gerrika said, coming out of Chanin's shadow. "If it's no bother to you, can you guys forget for now that I'm not human? I really just kind of want to forget myself for a moment."

"It's been a long day for us already." Chanin told them.

"Absolutely no problem." Sidra approached him, extending her hand. "It's a pleasure to have you here, pal."

Gerrika shook her hand. Allin came around after putting on a fresh flannel shirt and they shook hands as well, leaving the aveho with a warmth in him that he knew wasn't from the gin.

"I want to thank you guys for putting up with her this past week." Gerrika said. "It's good that some other people can."

"You kidding? We love Chanin. She's like the daughter we never had." Allin shot her a look from the other side of the motor-horse. "I mean...the daughter we don't have *yet*."

"Hey, Chanin," Allin called from behind the metal monstrosity. "I think we're going to have to cut the cord on the motor-horse for today. The damn thing isn't capable of *not* combusting."

She walked over to him and looked through the exhaust port, where a dark cloud was still being emitted. "Damn, and I thought we made such great progress the other day."

"What's the matter with it?" Gerrika asked.

Allin turned to Gerrika, unable to hide a glow on his face that the aveho had taken an interest in the work. "The problem is I think we're going to need to continue looking for a different kind of fuel. If not, then we're going to have to make this out of something that isn't metal."

"You have any ideas?" Gerrika asked Chanin.

"A few, but it was nothing that either Sidra or Allin hadn't thought of before." She put her hand on his shoulder, eyes bulging in excitement. "Oh! I want to show you something I'm working on with their help."

She showed him to the other side of the garage, where a large bin filled to the brink of old metal trash was stationed. Taking note of Chanin's excitement, the Gumarys followed her lead.

"There are probably a lot of people working on something like this right now," she told him. "but I thought it was a cool little idea."

Chanin handed him a small device. The aveho flipped it around in his grasp, getting a good look all around. There was a small round lens in the center of the device, which made him recall their first night in the city. While they were at Keethkay's a swarm of journalists had brought large devices in to take their pictures. Gerrika remembered that well.

"Is this one of those things? A camera?"

"Yes, though it's a little different." She touched the lens with her finger, opening up a slot on the side where a tiny wheel was inserted, rolled in a film. "With the cameras that are on the market now, you can't take more than one photo at a time. You have to reset the machine each time, which could waste good seconds. We haven't gotten the thing to work yet, but we think it's promising. Our goal is a camera that can take multiple photos within a second. This would revolutionize photography."

"Chanin, that is incredible."

"It was her idea." Sidra cheered. "She came up with the design model too. We've done what we could to help in the mechanics."

Allin sidled next to his wife. "Sadly, we have way too many projects here and not enough results. We're hoping this delightful hand that is Chanin can help turn the tide for us."

"I'm still in disbelief." Gerrika flipped the camera around in his hands more before putting it back in the bin. "You study history! You're a character of many surprises."

"Hear that, guys?" Chanin stood up straight with pride. "I'm a character of many surprises."

Sidra and Allin shared a laugh. That was when Gerrika noticed the opposite corner of the garage for the first time. There was a massive tarp covering something that was even bigger than the motor-horse in the center of the room. It rivaled a carriage in its size, and he could also see the bottoms of wheels peeking out from below the tarp.

"What's that?"

The Gumarys followed his finger to the object. "That?" Sidra asked. "That, my dear Gerrika, is both our biggest accomplishment and our biggest failure. Chanin, want to tell him about it?"

"I got it." She said. "Remember days ago when we first came here and they told us the reason they were building the motor-horse? Remember what they said about the horse shortage because of the war effort?" Gerrika nodded. "At the same time, they realized there was another way to solve the problem. They *could* make metal horses to pull carriages, or they could make carriages without the need for horses."

"How would that be possible?" Gerrika asked.

"The mechanics would be similar to the motor-horse." Sidra said. "The difference is just that we're making the entire thing run on steam."

"So, it's a motor-carriage?"

"That's the idea." replied Sidra.

Allin approached the metal beast, putting a hand on the tarp and exhaling in disappointment. "Amazing enough, we have actually gotten it to move. It's just very unstable. We're having trouble with the math for the size of the engine."

"In other words," Sidra continued. "like the motor-horse, it is a serious explosion hazard."

The sound of a quick clattering of horse hooves stopped everyone still. The garage door was wide open, so they had a clear view of the speeding carriage that was barreling down the street. Several pedestrians who were walking in the middle of the road dashed out of the way just in time as the pair of horses were ordered to a halt.

Gerrika and Chanin remembered the symbol on the side of the carriage. They had ridden in one of them before.

"The police?" Allin stepped forward. "What are they doing here?"

A pair of officers exited the front, holding things in their hands that the two friends had seen in action once before.

Things that they knew were called guns.

"You!" screamed one of the officers. As the man pointed the gun at Gerrika, his hands instinctually went into the air. "Claws behind your back. You're being taken in, by order of the Prime Minister."

"What is this about?" Sidra stormed forward. "There's no need to point a weapon at anyone!"

The other officer's hands were also on his gun, but he was much more relaxed. "The two of you realize you're hiding fugitives here? This fucking crow tried to kill someone today."

"That's not true!" Gerrika protested. "Come on, guys, it was just a bar fight. That's a normal Tuesday for me."

The aveho's joke didn't lighten either officers' temper. "And you, girl, you're under arrest too."

"What did *I* do?"

"Failure to turn in a violent offender. Now come on. Turn around." The other officer tucked his gun under his arm as he locked the cuffs on Chanin's hands.

Gerrika winced as his restraints were clicked on. "Do they have to be so tight?"

"You're lucky that's all you're getting. You might have fooled everyone else with your pretty voice, but not us. We knew you were just an animal."

"This is ridiculous." Allin said, getting right up against the young officer who had the aveho restrained. "I don't care what you think these kids did, you can't just come into our home and forcefully take our guests!"

"Want us to come after you next?" the officer showed him some teeth. "You and your little wife here violate safety codes in this shithole you call a home every single day. Interfere here anymore than you already have, and we'll have you shut down for good. You and your useless inventions will be out on the street."

With that threat, Chanin turned back to the engineers. They read her gaze well. She was telling them to stay out of it, that she could take care of herself. But Gerrika didn't look so certain.

All they could do was stand under the open garage door as the pair was shoved into the carriage and taken down to the station.

CHAPTER 7

Renny's meeting had been finished, he had eaten dinner, and now he was ready for whatever was about to happen.

He was too nervous to do anything. For the last half hour, he had just been sitting on his bed, waiting for Honja to come knocking. It was one of those moments where he was both waiting for time to go by faster and not wanting it to come. He wanted to make sure his son was alright and that there was nothing to worry about, but if it turned out something bad happened, he would have longed for a time of ignorance.

The knock came. Perfect timing. Two hours until midnight.

He got out of his bed, trying not to sound too rushed, since he knew Honja could hear him from the other side of the wooden door. As the professor opened the door, he felt as if he had just laid eyes on an entire armory.

"Good. You're awake." Honja said. "Where are your things?"

"Hello to you too. What do you mean?"

"Your supplies and weapons. Where are they?"

He picked up a small satchel from the edge of the door and put it over his shoulder. "I've got everything right here."

The professor had known many avehos in his life, but none before that moment had ever captured such a perfectly human look of disappointment as Honja had upon seeing the small bag under his arm.

"Very well." The avian said, after a pause. "If anything happens, I'm sure I have enough for the two of us."

Honja shrugged his shoulder, tossing his massive leather bag over his arm for the professor to see. Judging by its size, there probably wasn't much that couldn't be found inside. At least thirty arrows were sticking out of the top. In his free hand was his bow.

"What do you think we'll be running into?" asked the professor.

"Could be anything. That's why it's always good to prepare for the worst." Honja turned around and gestured for the human to follow. "Let's go."

The professor wanted to get a carriage to take them to the edge of town, but Honja said it would take too long, and there was no reason why the two of them couldn't make the full walk themselves. He knew he had no reason to complain, since he was the one with the light bag while the aveho was packing at least twenty pounds in his, so despite the fact that he hadn't had so much exercise in a while, he kept his hardening breaths to himself.

Their first ten minutes of walking were done in silence. The two of them had nothing in common, but Renny's nerves prevented him from keeping quiet any longer.

"Don't you think we should tell the Adderfoths about this? Their child is gone too."

"I did go to them. I went to them right after I came to you."

"Oh. What did they say?"

"They said there was nothing to worry about. Their daughter would come back once she was done playing her silly games."

The professor shook his head. "That's horrible. No one as sweet as Chanin deserves parents who would talk about her that way. What did you say after that?"

"Nothing. I left. I don't give fools my company longer than is necessary, professor."

"In that case, thank you for bringing me along with you."

He smiled at his own joke. Since Honja was in front of him, he couldn't tell if he had any reaction to his jest. Odds were he could guess, however.

Since his response didn't end with a question, it was almost another ten minutes before either of them had spoken again. Their walking led them to the edge of town, not far from the path through the woods that their sons always took to get to Heathback Caverns.

"What if it doesn't work?" asked the human. "The Sea. What if it doesn't take us like it took them?"

"Let's just focus on the present, professor."

"I've never been out this way before. Are there dangerous animals in these woods?"

Honja stopped, waiting for his partner to catch up to him. "Sometimes. That's why arrows are good tools out here." When the professor sheepishly continued along the path, the aveho shot him an amused leer. "Relax, professor, your son takes this path every week."

That did make him feel a bit better. "You know, Honja, you don't have to be so formal with me. I don't call you 'hunter', so there's no need to call me 'professor'."

"It's just a habit." answered the aveho.

"Before today, we hadn't spoken in years. I'm pretty sure I only introduced myself to you one time." The human stopped his walking, making Honja pause on the path as well. "Do you remember my name?"

The aveho looked like he was debating in his head whether or not to give the human the satisfaction of either a yes or no answer. "Hmm. I believe I do, Renfield."

"I'm impressed." The professor laughed. "I wouldn't peg you as someone who cared enough to remember a stranger's name. Most people just call me 'Renny'."

"I can't help it. Maybe I made myself remember since our sons are such good friends."

Renny let a moment pass, remembering what Dreden had said about feeling distant from his friends on the night he left Kroonsaed. "I'm still impressed."

After another twenty minutes, they were within visual range of the caverns. It didn't take as long as the professor had feared, so he was thankful. He already felt like he needed a rest, and if they were successful in imitating what Dreden, Chanin, and Gerrika had done twice, he wouldn't have any time to rest.

"Do you have any water?" Renny asked.

"I do." Honja cocked his head to him, still several paces in front. "Thirsty?"

"Very."

"You couldn't even bring water with you?"

"I forgot how much I haven't walked in years."

The aveho dug into his bag and found a canteen, tossing it over to Renny. "What exactly *is* in your bag? Do you have *any* weapons?"

"In a way." Renny smiled, taking a gulp of water. "I brought a few books with me."

"You're going to tell me that books are the most dangerous weapons in the world, aren't you?"

"I take it you don't agree?"

Honja continued walking, which didn't stop the professor from seeing a smile form on the corner of his beak. "No. I agree. Surprised? An uneducated, illiterate aveho agrees with the bright Renny Sharpstand?"

"I didn't mean it that way." The human said, catching up to him.

"But *I* did." Honja paused again to let the human catch up, as if to let him know he wasn't irked. "I've seen what books have done to my son, and he's an average student at best. Books have made him into something that an aveho probably would never have become hundreds of years ago. I haven't decided if I'm okay with it or not. In everything but appearance, he's a human."

"Is he though?" As hard as it was, Renny kept pace with him. "I would argue that aveho and human culture has become essentially the same thing, and it's been that way for a while. Sure, there are some, like yourself, that maintain a kind of sovereignty, but you're a vanishing breed. Do you consider yourself some kind of proper model of your species?"

The aveho shook his head. "The point is that I know what I am. I am an aveho first, before a Saedian. As a father, I have an obligation to invite my son to my worldview. What he does outside I can't control, nor do I want to. He's chosen not to be like me, yet he's also chosen to not be someone like you. I know what my son thinks he is and what he wants to be, and he's setting himself up for failure."

The professor didn't want to give any sign to Honja, but he was enjoying their conversation. He thought that if it became obvious, there would be a chance the aveho wouldn't want to continue talking.

"I don't think that's right. I think the fact that Gerrika is different is going to open a lot of doors for him."

"It may, until those differences have been exploited to the point where there is nothing left of him."

"Honja," Renny said slowly. "I don't want to make any assumptions, but do you think that there's a bigger chance that your coldness is the reason your son isn't back yet, instead of him maybe being in danger?"

"I've considered it." the aveho answered.

The walk had become much more of an uphill trek for the past mile. Renny had to take another few sips out of the canteen. "You seem very composed. I'm sure it's obvious, but it's mostly your composure that's keeping me calm right now. Your son left you. Aren't you scared?"

"He gets it from his mother. Truthfully, I'm not. For a long time, I haven't felt much of anything. I've come to understand how the world works. Nothing surprises me. Those with overactive emotions are the same kind who are always surprised."

"Would you mind if I asked you something?"

"I've been letting you ask me things enough already."

"One more, and this will be it." He took another sip of water, as if preparing for the weight of the question. "You probably don't remember me, but I actually knew you while you were a kid. I'm probably almost ten years older than you, so I have that advantage of remembering. You couldn't have been more than nine or ten. You were, for a lack of a better word, a jester. A prankster. There was never a time you weren't laughing or getting into trouble. What happened to you to change it?"

"What do you want me to say?" Honja shrugged. "Want me to tell you a sad story? I don't have one. I just grew up and understood the way things work. I know you must be thinking of me right now as some character to analyze from one of those books you read, but I'm going to have to disappoint you. I'm afraid I don't have a tear-jerking story, or anything like what happened to you and your wife."

Renny shot him a sharp look, but the aveho wasn't looking at him. "Well, thanks. You didn't have to end by saying that though. In fact, I don't think-"

Honja's arm shot out in front of Renny, catching his chest and stopping him dead at the aveho's side. As soon as his hand had been on him, it was gone, and an arrow's tip sparkled in the moonlight as he tugged it into his bow.

"What's happening?" Renny asked.

A light rustling came through the bushes and the trees, accompanied by the chirping of crickets.

"We're being watched."

"By who?" Renny leaned into him in a whisper. "Who's there?"

"Quiet." Honja whispered back. "We're only a few hundred feet from the entrance to the caverns. This can't be coincidental."

"Okay, I'm going to get behind you. You seem to have this covered."

The aveho let out an amused grunt as they continued forward. Since Honja knew they were already being watched, being quiet wasn't their biggest priority. Honja's eyes snapped left and right like zaps of lightning.

A few sounds could be made out from nearby. Renny didn't have nearly the experience Honja had, but even he could sense that something wasn't right.

They made it out of the wood's clearance, passing the border of the caverns, which expanded all the way to the coast of the Sunitian Sea. There weren't many places for things to hide.

Renny and Honja paused at the clearing. The human was still behind him, with the aveho dragging back his bowstring.

Three figures came out from the side of the cavern, as if in a rehearsed motion. The one in the middle was the leader. As they approached, the professor could see they were humans. They were all cloaked in red, holding weapons that neither of them had seen before, but that Renny had seen the carnage of. He remembered the night the weapons popped holes in his home, nearly killing him and Dreden.

He sensed he was looking at the very same people.

"Well, if it isn't the parents." said the man in front, who lowered his weapon on the ground, leaning on it. "Two of six, at least."

"What do you people want?" Honja steadied his bow.

"Not much of anything. I'm very content, in fact. I must say, you're much different from your son. Gerrika is very…breakable."

Renny saw his partner's fingers loosen on the string. "Where did you come from?"

"My kind hails from the place you're about to enter." The man in the middle took some steps forward, using his weapon as a cane. "Let me introduce myself. My name in Mick Jowns."

"That means nothing to me."

"It *should*. I'm the reason you're here." His wolfish eyes turned to Renny. "You too, in fact."

Renny came out from behind the aveho. "You tried to kill them, and you and your goons tried to kill me too. You attacked us in our own home."

Mick showed his teeth, his canines shining. "If I wanted to kill you, you would be dead."

"That doesn't make you look any better."

"Go back a minute." Honja said. "What you said about where we're going. What did you mean?"

"The two of you are just what I need. I'm currently facing an enemy called The Unmaker, and if I want a shot at keeping my victory, I'm going to need the two of you."

"We're not doing anything for you. I just want to get my son back."

"That's not up to you." Mick crossed his arms, amused. "The two of you have no idea what's going to be waiting for you over there." He raised his brow, opening his eyes to the aveho as if they were trying to swallow him. "You're going to die. Both of you. And so are your sons. Want to know how your son is going to die, turkey? He's going to die because he can't fly. He can't *fly!*"

The arrow made a whistling sound as it was freed from Honja's grip. In the night it moved too quickly for Renny to follow, but he saw as the man on Mick Jowns's left swung his arm over in time to catch the arrow with his hand.

Honja reacted quickly, and another arrow was on his bow in the next second and sent whistling away.

It was caught by the hand of the man on his right, who proceeded to throw his head back in laughter.

The aveho let loose two more, which were both caught, but the fifth one got through.

None of them made an effort to catch it. The arrow sailed through Mick's chest, passing through completely untouched as it continued on and landed somewhere in the grass behind them.

Mick's chest was gone in a swirl of red-colored gas, as if he were a ghost.

Renny and Honja's mouths hung open at the sight. Mick looked down at the gas emanating from his chest, taking pleasure in the pair's reactions.

"That's not going to work." Mick raised a finger, taunting them. "This exchange is now pointless. Brace yourselves. The transportation can be painful to some."

Once the man's mouth finished his last word, the three gunmen disappeared. If there was still any rustling or crickets around, their sounds were drowned by the following thunder.

The sucking, swirling sound of the Sunitian Sea being rushed faster than a downhill carriage.

Honja and Renny dropped to their knees, grabbing at their throats. It felt like the air was being taken right out of their lungs. The professor could feel himself starting to go blue, and if the aveho weren't covered in black feathers, he would surely have looked the same.

Both of their bodies hit the ground, then disappeared under the command of the gaseous Sea just like Jowns and his men.

***

It turned out the officers weren't lying. Dreden wasn't alone in his cell for very long.

Sitting down on the floor of his cell, he saw the door open and three figures proceed down the hall. Chanin and Gerrika had their hands behind their backs with their heads down as they were escorted by one of the young officers who had brought in Dreden too.

As they raised their eyes and saw him, he smiled and lifted his hand in a somber wave. "Hello."

The pair nodded to him, not looking surprised to see him there.

"Alright," the officer opened the cell door and shoved Chanin and Gerrika inside after unlocking their cuffs. "Get in."

"You want the three of us to share a cell?" Chanin asked.

"I don't really care. Just get in."

The officer locked the door behind them, leaving them both dumbfounded. He was almost back at the door when Gerrika called for him.

"Hey! Can we get some food in here by chance?"

From the spontaneous look that formed on the officer's face, Dreden would have thought Gerrika had just insulted his mother.

"What did you say?" he demanded.

The aveho took a step back inside the cell. "You have anything you give prisoners? I haven't eaten in a while."

"Do you not understand your situation? Are you that stupid?"

Chanin joined his side. "No, you didn't explain anything to us besides the charges, sir, but continue to be an ass, please."

He didn't acknowledge her words, or even look at her. "You don't get anything, bird. You don't get anything because you have no legal rights. I could do anything I fucking wanted to you, and nothing would happen. I could keep you here forever, and there would be nothing anyone could do about it." The officer finally looked to Chanin and Dreden. "And that goes for you two as well.

As far as the law is concerned, none of you are people. You've never been people here."

The three of them stood still as the officer turned his back to them and exited the room, leaving them to themselves.

Gerrika glanced over to the two humans, rolling his eyes to the top of his brow. "Someone pissed in that guy's coffee this morning, huh?"

"Maybe not," Dreden said. "I'm sensing that that's going to be a common attitude towards us from now on."

"What are *you* doing here?" Chanin asked him.

"I'm crooked, and apparently that's against the law here."

"How could they have figured that out?"

"I'm clueless. My guess is that Morell might have a big mouth."

"Isn't he your lover?" Gerrika asked. "I would think you would know about the size of his mouth."

Dreden and Gerrika stared at each other for several seconds, as the weight of their situation and recent fight was still in the air around them. It had been days since the two of them felt as if they had a moment of the friendship they were used to, but they both broke their tone at the same time as Dreden tossed his head back in dry laughter.

"I miss you, Gerrika." he said. "Ugh, I feel like I haven't seen you in a month."

The aveho took a seat next to him on the floor and rested his arms on his legs. "I think we've both had that problem lately. I've missed you too."

"I want to be a part of this." Chanin smiled and took a seat on what could only loosely be described as a 'bed'. "I'm glad we're all here together. Better circumstances would have been ideal."

"Now tell me, what are the two of you doing here?" Dreden asked them.

"It wasn't one of my finest moments, but I nearly clawed a man's eyes out." Gerrika said.

"Shit. Damn, I would have loved to see that."

"I was there," Chanin frowned. "no, you wouldn't have. It was kind of scary."

Gerrika couldn't help but smirk. "Even now that I've sobered up a bit, I still think the guy was a complete ass." The look on his beak darkened as he turned to Dreden. "I had just heard Winds Wilk died."

"Are you serious?" He looked over to Chanin, whose soft nodding confirmed the aveho's words.

"I didn't tell you or Chanin, but I actually went to see him last night. He was a mess, and a bit cruel," the aveho looked away from them both. "and I think I was the last person to see him alive before he killed himself."

Dreden wrapped both his arms around Gerrika and put his head on his shoulder. "I'm sorry. I'm sorry for everything dumb I said about him. I can't imagine what that feels like."

The aveho looked to the two humans and took a deep breath. "Fuck, guys. I'm scared."

"What are you scared of?"

"What am I *not* scared of?" Gerrika ran his fingers through the feathers on his head. "I don't know what I'm going to do with myself. If I thought things were bad back home, things have gotten exponentially worse."

"You're not alone." Chanin leaned over. "That is, if I'm reading you right. Dreden and I have definitely been worried about what's going to happen to us next year once we've graduated from Faeriebridge."

"It was all I could think about." said Dreden. "It makes sense. I have the literature and philosophy focus, Chanin has the history."

Gerrika smiled bitterly. "And what did I have? Nothing. I never chose. Nothing ever interested me enough."

"That doesn't have to be a bad thing." Dreden replied. "Sometimes it's a lot easier to believe in the fortunes of others than your own." He put his hands together, which had turned clammy. "I've lost many hours of sleep these past months wondering what life is going to be like after school, and I can't shake the feeling that it's all downhill."

"*You* have?" asked the aveho.

Chanin brushed Gerrika's leg with her boot. "Me too. It's hard, really hard, to make a decent living in Kroonsaed now. Looking around the place, it seems like being a university graduate means less and less. Feels like you're bound to end up making the same amount of money as someone who didn't even graduate. Seeing how my parents and many of the adults back home are living, it's hard to kick the feeling that we've already peaked."

"The two of you are good students." Gerrika said. "You could both probably work at the university."

"With their budget?" Dreden shook his head. "No way. They can't even afford my father anymore."

Both his friends regarded him in surprised silence.

"Oh, I guess I never mentioned that. Last week he was told the most they could do for him was transfer him to a school on the edge of town. He's done after this semester."

"That's horrible." It was now the aveho's turn to embrace Dreden. "I can't believe it. That makes things look so much worse for all of us now. I've been…" He paused, getting his thoughts together. "I've been forcing myself to feel like I belong here. I've been forcing myself to feel like I'm loved and, damnit, I don't feel it. I felt like a nobody in Kroonsaed and now I feel like some caged animal here. If Winds Wilk couldn't get out of this place alive, then what chance do I have?"

"I don't presume to know him," Chanin got off the bed, taking a seat on the floor. "but you have something he didn't. You have the two of us."

At her words, Dreden and Gerrika got up on their knees, scooting over to her so they could grab her and lock themselves in a three-way hug.

"You two are wonderful." Chanin said, with her head in between theirs. "Now won't you two please stop worrying me to bits and try to keep yourselves on the ground?"

"I think we can do that." Gerrika said. "If we are wonderful, that makes you wonder-wonderful-ful."

"Poetic." Chanin laughed.

They released themselves from each other and sat back down on the cell floor. Dreden still regarded Chanin with eyes that sparkled from a moment of water.

"This past week, you've been who the two of us should have been." He told her. "I don't know how you did it, but we surely wouldn't be here as friends again if you had become like us. I've made a jackass of myself to you guys and to Morell. I've tried to put everything on him to make myself forget about all the real problems I have back home. It's not right. I've made him up to be something in my head that he isn't, and I got angry when I realized he couldn't help it. Gerrika may be right. Morell might be awful, but I don't think I'm a lot better."

"No matter what the truth is," Chanin said. "the fact that you realize it and want to make yourself better means that you're better than him."

She wasn't done yet, but Chanin fell silent as the hallway door opened. A new figure, tall and middle-aged, came to greet them. Dreden knew that his friends probably wouldn't recognize him, but he was a man that Dreden met on two occasions.

"Mister Sharpstand," the man said. "I'm sorry we're not meeting again in better circumstances."

The man was a wreck. He didn't look like he had been getting any more hours of sleep than the three of them had in the last couple days. In a better scene, Dreden would have pitied him.

"Who are you?" Chanin asked.

"That's Charles Dowlepot. The Prime Minister."

"You're the guy that had us arrested!" Gerrika got up on his toes.

"After what you did, son, things could have been a lot worse." He turned to the two humans. "As for you, I'm sorry about this. I promise I'll do everything I can to make this go away cleanly, but if I'm to be completely forthright, I don't know how much time I have left in power."

"What's going on?" Dreden asked. "What are you talking about? Why did you lock us up?"

Charles looked down the hallway, as if to make sure no one was eavesdropping. "It's for your own protection. I suspect that a dangerous group of people wants you. I'm trying to make sure that doesn't happen."

"Who?" Chanin asked. "Who would want us?"

"The group has many members, but Keeting and Janely Edland seem to be its leaders."

That got Dreden's attention. "What about their son? What about Morell?"

"He's not associated with them, as far as I can tell. I'm afraid I have the burden of giving the three of you some knowledge."

The Prime Minister reached into his bag and pulled out a fat stack of notebooks. There were loose pages sticking out in every corner of the books, as if someone had put them all together at the last minute.

He began separating the notebooks from each other and slipping them in between the cell bars.

"Dreden, I know you've read Mick Jowns, but I guarantee that you haven't read what I'm giving you."

"What does Mick Jowns have to do with Morell's parents?" Dreden asked.

"I'm sorry that you're about to find out." Charles put his hands together, sighing and lowering his head to them. "Before you read them, I just want the three of you to know that I had no idea about this. Very few people do, and I want to protect you from them. Those there? Those are Jowns's Final Testaments."

"What exactly is in these books?" Gerrika asked.

"Please, enough questions. I need to be off, but I'll be back shortly to answer any questions you might have. That should give you enough time to read through them." He turned away, adjusting his bag over his shoulder. "I would divide the reading. It'll go faster if you all do your part." Charles gave the aveho a final look. "I'm sorry about what happened. I truly am."

The Prime Minister retreated down the hall. The trio didn't stop watching him until he was out the door and his footsteps could no longer be heard.

Not having anything else to do, they each picked up one of the books, flipped open the cover, and began reading.

CHAPTER 8

Things were going too fast. Cipre knew it.

It had only been a day since she last visited Minkompa. No doubt the large, friendly dragon was expecting her to visit him again today. Ever since the earthquake put Mirthinout out of business for a while, and she hotheadedly tried to pursue the behemoth that caused it, she had been visiting Minkompa almost every day. Now it seemed like everything was moving on without her. Her boss's words stuck to her, even as she sat on her living room couch with a book in her hand. She couldn't get them out of her mind. The fact that attitudes about the three visitors had taken a turn didn't help her either.

What a wild week. she thought. *First an earthquake hits the city, then two humans and a bird-person appear out of the Sunitian Sea, and Andayt and Borgetta are hit too with thousands dead.*

The news was everywhere. It was being discussed on every street corner. With everything she was hearing, it was hard to believe anyone was ever fascinated by the three of them. Suddenly they were all violent and morally corrupt, and it was a good thing that they had been locked up before they could do any more damage to Skaltbard's culture.

Cipre didn't know what to think. She knew better than to believe everything she heard, but everyone's current feelings about the visitors didn't bode well for her plan for Minkompa. In her last meeting with the dragon, she told him she wanted to take him to her boss, thus introducing him to the world. He had written a book. It was a strange, unique, engaging narrative unlike anything she had ever read, and she wanted to give the gift of Minkompa's book to the world.

Surely those three kids couldn't have done anything that bad. I'm sure they're just people like the rest of us. With the exception of the bird, they look like us. If people can turn so quickly against those who they can see themselves in, how can they possibly react to the existence of a giant reptile?

It was troubling, and the situation wasn't going to end with her looking any better. It was getting nearer and nearer to the day where Morell Edland's *A Mad Past* was to be published, and here she was, still fighting it in favor of the dragon's book. If the problem continued for any longer than a few more days, that would be it. She would have to put Minkompa's *The Century* on hold.

A knock on the door interrupted her thoughts.

She let out a yip in surprise, hoping that whoever was behind the door didn't hear the embarrassing sound. She hadn't left the house all day and knew that she wasn't very presentable, but Cipre didn't care enough to change, no matter the guest.

Fixing her hair up a little, she opened the door to just the man she didn't want to see yet. The boss himself.

"Radoff!" she exclaimed. "Sorry, what are you doing here?"

The older gentleman smiled at the sight of her. She knew he was not used to seeing her in less-than-professional clothing. "No need to be worried, Cipre. I'm not here to tell you anything negative. You still have that book with you? *The Century?*"

"I do. Why?"

Radoff cleared his throat, narrowing his brow, making his eyes closer together. She had seen that look in his face before. It was the face of her boss about to admit a fault.

"I've never had something do this to me before," he said. "but that book has been stuck with me since our meeting. When my wife got home, I ended up telling her all about it, and she said I was a madman for telling you the things I did."

"I wouldn't go that far." Cipre laughed awkwardly.

"She does have a tendency to hyperbolize." Radoff relaxed his guilty look, giving her a comfortable smile. "That being said, if it is no trouble for you, I'm hoping to get the book back."

"You want to read it again?"

"Probably not the whole thing, but I would love to look over the parts I criticized. I think if I read them again, I might have a different takeaway this time around."

There was something about their conversation that didn't seem organic. Her boss had admitted fault before but had never come to her house for something that, in Radoff's mind, surely could have waited another day.

Maybe this is because of what happened to the visitors? Radoff has always been good about getting reads on what the public wants. Could there be a shift coming he sees that I don't?

She didn't want to dwell on it anymore. The point was that her boss wanted to see the book again.

"No problem." she said. "Let me go get it, or you can stay for a bit if you would like."

"No no no." Radoff shook his hand. "Got to get back home. The kids need help with schoolwork. Promised them daddy would all but do it for them."

Cipre retreated back into her home. She found the book on her kitchen table, right where she had left it. Dusting the cover off to make it look as best as it could, she returned to Radoff and gave it to him.

"I hope you like it more this time." Cipre shot him some teeth. "And I'm not just saying that because I keep proving to you that I'm the best at what I do."

"Remind me to soak myself in stale wine if I ever turn out to be wrong in front of you again."

He gave her a smile and a twinkle in the eyes as he turned away from her.

When he was halfway down the path to the street, she closed the door, happy that things seemed to be balancing each other out.

***

Radoff Dell hadn't gone to Cipre's house. The real Radoff Dell was still at home. The only truth to their interaction was that her real boss was indeed helping his kid with schoolwork.

The Unmaker allowed itself to smile. It had been doing that a lot lately. And what a feeling it was. Out of everything that existed in all of creation, what were the odds that something would become a thing that had the ability to feel happy? What were the odds that something would become anything at all?

Those were questions that only the Unmaker knew the answers to.

Now that its job was done and *The Century* was in its possession, it didn't need to look like Radoff Dell anymore.

Its body changed colors as the look of the middle-aged man was melted away. In its place became younger, fuller skin. Over the new skin appeared a layer of dark clothing and a cap manifested on the top of its head.

The cap was dark blue with a layer of black film above the visor.

It was the uniform the young man it was becoming always wore to his job.

The transformation was complete in two seconds, and if the Unmaker was right, which it always was, the young man's employers would be around the corner-

The clatter of hooves from around the street caught its ears. The carriage was slowing down, looking for it. The Unmaker raised a hand, hailing the cab so the driver knew where to go. It appeared that it was seen, since the horses picked back up speed again as they passed a few more homes before settling right in front of Cipre's.

The doors opened. Two armed security men leaped from the step, approaching the person the Unmaker now was.

"You've got it?" asked the first one, a muscled bald man.

The Unmaker nodded, proudly showing off *The Century* as if it were a trophy. "Told you I could do it. My people don't lie to me."

"Alright," said the other one, a pale, younger man, not unlike who the Unmaker was pretending to be. "so that's it? We take her in now?"

"Go for it. I'm done with her."

"Excellent, Mister Bair."

At that, the armed guards rushed to Cipre's porch and kicked her door down. The Unmaker heard Cipre scream, and it had to laugh.

The two guards were rushing themselves out of the home with Cipre, who now had her head covered with a bag. It was the middle of the day, so they had to take her as quickly and quietly as possible. Once she was secured inside, the bald guard came back to the young Bair and took *The Century* from him. The

Unmaker wasn't worried to be apart from the book. It knew what was going to happen next.

As the horses began to walk again, the Unmaker looked to the front seat of the carriage. Next to the driver were its two bosses, or, they were the bosses of the young Mister Bair.

The Unmaker gave Keeting and Janely Edland a pleased wave as they passed him by.

"I win." It said to itself. "I win, Minkompa, you bastard."

CHAPTER 9

I knew I would never be satisfied with sending the avehos and the rebels to another continent. It would have been a solution to a short-term problem, but what I was dealing with was more than hundreds of thousands of years old. Besides, the exiled could end up thriving among the Kroonsaed natives, and someone like me years down the road would have to deal with the same problem.

I am a practical man. I wasn't about to waste ammunition and labor. Besides, I still had the presence of wizards and witches to deal with.

Thankfully, it was the Wizard Laureate of Skaltbard who approached me with the idea. He told me that he and the entire wizard council would do everything to help me. He never outright said it, but I knew that it was just a last-ditch effort on their part to save themselves. To stay relevant and be useful. We went to Kroonsaed to complete the spell, knowing very well that it would be the last work of magic that any of them ever did. Spells involving the 'Unmaking' of things have long been considered unholy, and thus, very illegal. Not only that, they were exceptionally difficult, but I was confident that a handful of sorcerers fighting for their lives would be able to pull it off. You see, magic, like energy, cannot be created or destroyed, and an Unmaking spell would have to take an object and put it somewhere else. It would be gone, but still in a form in some kind of other reality. I knew nothing of how the spell would be done, but Brion, the Wizard Laureate, claimed all they really needed was a large book to record everything inside. It involved a lot of nonsense about tapping into the fabric of reality and existence, but I just shrugged and told him to do what was necessary.

And we absolutely needed it.

The entire world was at war with Skaltbard because of my vision. It was our goal to eliminate sorcerers and avehos all across the planet, so it would have been optimistic to assume other nations would simply allow us to do it. No matter how strong we were, the ENTIRE world fighting you is not easy. We needed to win quickly. We needed the weapons to end it all.

And we almost didn't do it. Somehow word got out about what we were planning, Thousands died that day, just in Kroonsaed itself, including my own men. But it was worth it. After six hours of fighting, we were successful, and all that was left in the wake of the Unmaking were barren lands where even oxygen felt difficult to find.

But that wasn't the end. What followed was the realization of my biggest mistake.

Once the spell was over, Kroonsaed gone and all of the magic with it, text filled the book as if I were watching an invisible speeding scribe. It was remarkable. It was the ultimate spell, and no one outside the nexus of the magical blast retained their memory of the war, the avehos, or even that magic had ever existed. I knew I was looking at the end of magic, which excited me even more. After the last page filled with text, something came OUT of the book.

As I write this, I can't remember what it looked like. I just remember feeling like I was being sucked dry, my body became dense, and solid objects were flickering on and off like a flame. Like I said in one of my other testaments, I named this thing 'The Unmaker'. I cursed my own stupidity. I, the mind behind the entire field of evolutionary biology, failed to realize that, like a liver, lung, or any body part, magic was a part of the universe, and the universe would need to ADAPT if suddenly all of it were gone.

Out of my arrogance, a monster was created.

I tried fighting it, and I believed that I gravely wounded it. With what magic was left, I cut a part of it off from the host body, but I fear it left to recover, and that one day it'll return. In that moment an image flashed in my eyes. It was of myself as a knight from a fairy tale, off to defeat an evil dragon. It was like a flicker of a distant star, and suddenly the wounded Unmaker seemed to suck that image out of me.

Perhaps the dragon just wanted to live.

Dreden looked up from his reading after every other page to see how his friends were faring. He had been given a notebook titled MY GREATEST FEAR while Chanin and Gerrika were given others with similar titles. They had been reading for almost an hour. When he was halfway through one called WHAT I DID TO THE OLD WORLD OF MAGIC AND SORCERY AND WHY, Gerrika had to get up off the floor and vomit in the toilet in the corner of the cell. He wasn't sure if it was because of what he was reading or if the gin was finally getting to him, but he and Chanin found themselves wishing they were in a different cell afterwards as the smell filled the room.

Part of him just wanted to keep reading. If he didn't, then he and the others would have to talk about what they read. Dreden wasn't ready for it. He knew something was off since discovering the Deadlands looked like Kroonsaed, but he could never have predicted a story about a genocidal madman and magic.

He continued to himself, as Chanin and Gerrika did the same.

The ordeal with the Unmaker made the following days rough for me. Even after I had the remaining sorcerers executed, I couldn't kick the feeling that there was more I could do to avoid a terrible fate of whatever the Unmaker was going to do, whatever its true purpose was.

I came up with a plan.

A contingency, more accurately. Since the magical book was still in my possession, I included a line at the end endowing myself and another with complete power to do whatever we wished to the contents of the book with my own blood. If someone who wasn't me or a chosen one tried to write inside, they would be killed instantly.

And I was glad that I did, because it was only days later when the book vanished.

The final section of the book was a glued-in section written by Brion Greyer, the Wizard Laureate of Skaltbard, on the day he was executed: *I couldn't believe the spell was a success. I was glad, but I couldn't believe it. Jowns promised that we would be spared if we went through with our promise, and I actually believed him.*

I have spent my entire life devoted to magic and furthering mankind's understanding of it. I do not share Jowns's opinions of avehos, and even many humans who he also deems inferior, but I and all of my fellow sorcerers just wanted to preserve ourselves, and if we couldn't preserve our titles as magicians, at least to save our lives. No spell of this caliber has ever been done before, going all the way back to about ten million years when we believe avehos first discovered and learned how to use magic. It was Jowns's idea that the only way to move forward was not only to eliminate a parasitic species that should have gone extinct thousands of years ago, but to ensure that no one remembered that they ever lived. He said that as long as people were able to mourn those who were lost, they would forever be clinging to the past, which was the opposite of what he wanted.

The war was over in the next instant. Skaltbard was victorious, with only the handful of us involved in the spell remembering both all the chaos that had happened along with all the death and destruction that would have occurred had the war gone on any longer.

That is the only good thing I can say about Mick Jowns.

I know how this makes me look, but I did want to spare as many avehos and humans as possible. Before I was preparing for the spell, I told Jowns that I was confident my collective of sorcerers could be able to turn every aveho left in the world into a human via magical metamorphosis. That way, they could live their lives as the 'superior' species and not have to die.

Jowns simply stared at me as if I had just combusted into flames, before he slapped his thighs and threw his head back in a raucous laughter that lasted at least two minutes. And that was the end of that.

"I don't think I care for Jowns anymore." Dreden said, as his two friends were nearing the end of their books.

"I'm going to throw up again." The aveho lifted himself up for a second, then sat back down slowly, feeling a little better after the admission.

Chanin closed her notebook. "What are we supposed to do now? What was the point of telling us the truth if the Prime Minister was just going to leave us in here anyway?"

"Maybe he just felt bad," Dreden said. "or maybe he's actually on our side."

The three of them remained alone for the next twenty minutes, exchanging Jowns's notebooks. Gerrika didn't want to read anymore, so he just closed his eyes and rested his head against the wall. So it was just Dreden and Chanin who traded off.

When the Prime Minister returned, they all rose to their feet and shoved the books away.

"Fat lot of good your gifts are going to be doing us." Dreden said. "How are we supposed to do anything about what Jowns did if we're locked up?"

"You got through them all already?" Charles's hands were in his pockets as he took slow steps to their cell.

"Some of them, but I think we get the big picture."

"Good. Now, as hard as this might be to believe, I think the situation can get much worse."

"For who? For *you*?" Chanin asked. "Are you sure it's your concern for us that made you lock us up, or are you afraid that we can actually fight you?"

"Now that's a really dumb idea." Charles bit his teeth. "The three of you against the most powerful people in the world? If what you were implying were correct, I would not be afraid of you."

Dreden fought the urge to kick the bars where he stood. "Then what was the point of you giving us the truth? What are you getting out of this?"

"As far as I know right now, the only thing I'm getting is probably killed." The Prime Minster lowered his head. "Please, judge me all you want, but I am in an impossible position here. I was deeply affected by the truth myself, and I have to continue doing my job as if I didn't know better."

"You're not going to help us?" Dreden asked.

Charles retreated a step, closing his eyes for a moment as if trying to phase them out. "No. I'm not going to help. That's why I gave you the truth. It was the least I could do."

"You fucking coward." Gerrika threw himself onto his feet, getting in between Chanin and Dreden. "There are people where we come from who are suffering right now. We get poorer every year and our resources are vanishing, and you say you don't have the balls to help us."

"That is not what I said." Charles countered. "This has nothing to do with me being afraid. Do you have any idea what trying to reverse what Jowns did could do to the world?"

"No." replied the aveho. "we couldn't possibly read everything in the time you gave us."

"Did you at least read about the Unmaker?" He took their attention as a 'yes'. "Jowns criticized his own arrogance that led to the creation of the Unmaker. In hindsight, he would indeed rather have used ammunition and other weaponry to wipe out the avehos, rebels, and sorcerers, and have burned all books on magic."

"Great. He had a conscience." Chanin said.

Charles ignored her. "Who's to say that something worse won't happen if the event is to be reversed? Who's to say that the Unmaker won't cause even more damage to the world if it knew what we were trying to do?"

"What are you talking about?" Dreden interrupted. "The earthquake? The disasters in the other countries? You think the Unmaker did that?"

"It's what the Edlands think. They've been in the business of the truth longer than I have, so I'm inclined to believe them. I am the Prime Minister of Skaltbard. I was appointed to do a job: to protect the interests, welfare, and lives of everyone in my country. Modern humans do not deserve to pay the price for the evils of their ancestors. I'm sorry, but it is what I must do. I will not risk lives, and no more will be lost if I have anything to say about it."

The Prime Minster cleared his throat. To the trio, the man looked like he had aged a few years since they had seen him earlier in the day. "Besides, there is no one alive who can reverse the spell. You read that Jowns had a contingency? Something that could reverse what he did to stop the Unmaker? That secret probably died with him."

Charles Dowlepot turned away, back down to the hallway door. He eased into a slow walk as he said to them: "I'm sorry. The three of you will have to learn to live with the truth."

***

Renny's breath returned to him as he felt his palms touch solid ground. Honja's returned at the same time, as Renny could hear the aveho's resumed labored breathing.

Daylight was the first thing he noticed. It had just been nighttime. It seemed that his son was right about the time difference.

"Are you alright?"

Honja gave a positive grunt. "We survived the trip."

The scene was like something the professor could only imagine out of an old fairy tale he was told as a child or that he told Dreden as a young boy. In the background, beyond a metal fence where a group of people had already started forming, were buildings more than twice as tall as anything found in Kroonsaed. Noises came from the surface beyond the shore of the Sunitian Sea behind him that he had never heard. They were ripping, pumping sounds of machines inside street-corner buildings along with the sounds of different shoes on different sidewalks, shoes that were made in a style and of a fabric not yet invented where he came from.

Renny had to wonder if anyone else could hear the sound like he did, or if they had become so commonplace in this strange city that everyone had long ago filtered them out like objects in the corners of their peripheral vision.

"This is incredible. We're in another world."

The aveho didn't look impressed, as he started for a rocky stairway on their right. "Let's go. There are people watching us."

A murmur swept through the crowd observing them. Renny couldn't make out anything they were saying, but he could tell that it was his language. He chose to keep himself behind Honja as they made their way up the stairs. None of the people watching them looked threatening, but one could never be sure.

Everyone backed away as the pair planted their boots on the street-level ground. A lone man broke from the pack and approached the two of them. He wore a tie and a kind of neat brown jacket that Renny had never seen before, but already envied.

"You two are new, aren't you?" The man asked, stopping in the way of their path.

Neither of them replied. Honja moved out of the man's way, but he rushed back in front of him.

"The two of you should go back to wherever you came from. If you think you can just come here and-"

Honja planted his yellow talon hand on the man's face, gripped the side of his head tight like a watermelon and threw him backwards. He landed on his elbow, and a gasp followed from the crowd as they watched the human and aveho in a threatened silence.

The fallen man stared at them in awe. Renny gave him a look of 'sorry about that' as the two of them proceeded down the street, ending their time with the crowd.

Going down the street, ignoring all the eyes and the sounds of stopping foot-traffic around them, there were many similarities between the structure of the buildings that reminded the professor of home. The architecture wasn't very different, just a lot more ambitious. Either the country was naturally rich with goods or they had relationships with other nations that Kroonsaed never could. For the first time in his life, Renny felt what it was like to be surrounded by wealth.

"What's our next move?" he asked.

"I'm thinking you could help me out with that."

"What do you want?"

They parked themselves on a bench a couple blocks away from the Sea. Honja slumped his massive bag down onto the bench and relaxed the bow in his grip, adjusting his loose grey shirt again, as if to hide his black and brown feathers from the gaze of the new city.

"Am I correct in assuming that the writing here is the same language as it is back home?" asked the aveho.

The professor stopped to read the writing on the signs above building doors. "Yes. It is exactly the same."

"Do you see anything that could be useful to us?"

Renny surveyed the shops and stations around them, ignoring everyone who was staring at the two of them. "There. Across the street has tourist information. Not sure if it'll be helpful to us. We're not tourists."

"It's worth a shot." Honja took a few arrows out of his quiver, putting them in his bow hand. "If my son is right about this place only having humans, then it shouldn't be hard to find him."

"Mind if I sit for a moment? I need to rest my legs."

"Fine. Stay here. I'll be back."

"Do you really have to bring arrows? I don't think you're going to be attacked in there."

"You never know." The aveho's eyes almost sparkled at the idea of a fight as he crossed the street.

Renny took a seat on the bench. It had been more than several thousand steps since he last had a sip of water. Honja had tucked the rest of the water near the bottom of the sack. He shuffled his hands between the myriad arrows, knives and other blades as he found the canteen.

The canteen was tucked between two other bottles. They were smaller than the canteen, but were made of glass, and he could see what they held. There was water in them. He wondered why Honja would put water in such small containers when using another canteen would have been more practical.

The professor raised the glass bottle to his head, eyeing the thin liquid inside as he put his hand on the lid.

"What are you doing!"

He turned to see Honja dashing across the street. A carriage had to come to a grinding halt as the horses almost didn't stop in time, and their wheels almost busted off. Renny fought the urge to back away at the sight of the aveho's speed, but he remained frozen with the glass bottle in his hand.

"Put that down! Why are you holding that?"

"I'm sorry." Renny sat up, alert. "I was thirsty."

"Don't you remember what the canteen looks like?" Honja dug into his bag and shoved the water container into the professor's hand and grabbed the glass bottle out of his clueless grip. "For being an intelligent man, I thought you would know better than to touch things you're unfamiliar with."

Renny let a moment pass and took a sip out of the canteen. "Sorry. Thanks again for the water. Did they tell you anything?"

"The humans there didn't want to help me. They wanted me to get out."

"Are we sure this is the right place then?" Renny wondered. "People here were flocking to Gerrika, according to Dreden."

"Yes. It is strange. I hope you've had enough water. We need to continue."

"We don't even know where to go."

"Then we'll go on until we figure it out."

The professor paused, wanting to give his legs just a few more seconds of rest before standing up. "Alright. Let's go. People are going to be staring at us the whole way though."

"Ignore them. Imagine they're all just snorting pigs. It's not hard."

"I'll give it a shot." He smiled as he put the canteen back in Honja's bag. "You know, with the way you talk about yourself not having much emotion, it was interesting to see you angry."

The aveho leveled his red feathery brow. "Trust me, Renny, you will know when I'm angry."

CHAPTER 10

"I don't think I can take much more of this." Gerrika said, pacing back and forth by the cell door. "How are they allowed to treat us like this?"

Dreden and Chanin were still sitting on the floor against the cold stone wall. All they had done in the last fifteen minutes was watch their friend walk back and forth, and that was losing its amusement.

"It's a mercy compared to what others got." Chanin sighed. "Please sit down."

"I'll tell you," the aveho obeyed her, sitting down with them. "if they don't give us food in the next hour, I'm going to eat one of you. It seems like the only reasonable course of action for me at this point."

"I'll scream." Chanin forced a smile. "Then they'll be forced to get you off me, then Dreden will run once no one is guarding the door."

"Dreden is actually the one I'm leaning towards. You're cute, Chanin, but I always thought he would taste better. All that meat of his getting tender from so much lack of activity while he's reading or locking himself away in the school library. Probably like the meat of a newborn calf."

Hearing this, Dreden shoved Chanin, making her fall on the aveho. She laughed as Gerrika had to readjust himself, with Dreden still trying to pin him against the wall using her.

"See?" Dreden said, glad to see a light had returned to their faces. "You weigh like eighty pounds, Gerrika. You're not getting me."

The silence of the cell room took over as the trio fixed themselves. Dreden could tell his friends wanted to continue talking, to talk about anything to cover the silence reminding them of the reality of their situation.

"I can't believe it." The aveho said, staring at the bars of their cage. "I can't believe it. My father was right. Those words taste so weird coming out of my mouth."

"Your father predicted this?" asked Dreden.

"In a way." Gerrika answered. "When we got back home after first seeing Brunswald, I told him that this world didn't have avehos, that it only had humans. Back then, we were still assuming that we had traveled to some other reality or at least just anywhere where avehos never existed. What he told me was 'they won', *they* being humans. I thought that was him just being his misanthropic self, but he was right. The humans won."

"Not all of us won." Chanin said. "You've seen how many humans there are back home. I can't imagine how you must feel now, Gerrika, but I certainly don't feel better about being a human in Kroonsaed after this. On behalf of my species, I fucking hate us right now."

The aveho blinked, leaning over her to look at Dreden. "You still remember the results of the latest Kroonsaed census?"

"I do."

"What was the population of Kroonsaed? No, wait, you remember the map from the library? Do you remember how big the Deadlands are?" Dreden nodded. "Do you know how many people back home make up Kroonsaed and *all* of the areas that have become unmade?"

He paused, doing the math in his head. "It's close to ten million people."

"And out of those ten million people, how many of them are avehos?"

The next pause was longer, both because of the additional math and the real weight of his friend's question. "Around one hundred thousand."

"That's how many avehos there are left in all of reality? Shit." Gerrika crossed his arms. "I've always known that we were outnumbered back home, but I assumed it just happened to be that way. I assumed there were many countries out there where the number was more balanced."

"You can't be angry at yourself for believing that." Dreden said. "There was no way we could have known that everything we knew was a lie."

Chanin's eyes went wide, as if just realizing the implications. "In that case, I have no regrets about abandoning my study of history. None of what we learned ever happened."

"Maybe some of it did." Dreden put his hand on her arm. "We don't have all the answers yet. Even if that's true, that doesn't mean we can't learn valuable lessons from things that never happened. As a culture, we tell stories all the time. They have morals, and they can inspire us. And the philosophy I've learned? As I see it, none of it has been nullified."

"What do your philosophers have to say about our situation?" the aveho asked. "Are there any who can help us figure out what we should do?"

"I can think of a few who might have some good advice, but right now, I think there are some things that I can say to help us."

"Do you plan on philosophizing the lock off the door?" Chanin asked.

"No," he pointed a finger at her jovially. "but I have a lot of things inside me right now that I want to get out, and I apologize in advance if I start crying."

"I think it's a good idea." The aveho put his talons behind his head. "No telling how long we're going to be in here, and with Dreden talking philosophy I may finally get some sleep."

The cell walls began to feel more compact as Dreden let out a breath. He could feel his two friends waiting for him to start talking. He still needed a few moments to get his thoughts together, but he decided it would be better to just start spewing out words and hope they made sense.

"I've been trying really hard to be a good person." he told them. "I've thought a lot about it, and I think it's harder than most people think it is. In my time at Faeriebridge, and as the son of Renny Sharpstand, I've been inclined to ask a lot of questions about morality."

"What have you discovered?" Chanin asked.

"I've read Jowns while I've been here, and I've read about who he really was while we've been sitting here. As evil as he was, there are some areas where he may be on the right track." He looked to Chanin and Gerrika, who were fixed on him after saying that. "His writings, the ones I read with Morell before I knew the truth, dealt with the reality of being human in a world where they were the only species to become 'rational' and to become 'civilized'. Of course, as we know, he's leaving out avehos, so there are two different species that carry the burden of being the shepherds of all life."

"But he makes it clear he doesn't think anything of aveho accomplishments throughout history." Gerrika said.

Dreden bit his lip. "And that's where he's wrong. There are moral philosophers throughout history who can't decide what makes a person a good person. They can't even decide if the same thing that makes a human good is the same thing that makes an aveho good. It's a fair question. What's good for a human isn't something that's automatically good for an aveho."

"Why do they have to be different?" Gerrika asked. "Back home there are hardly any problems between our species. It's not perfect, but compared to the manure heap that's Skaltbard, it's paradise."

Dreden felt a warmth from his friend's investment in the conversation. "I would argue they don't. In the thousands of years since humans and avehos have lived under the same laws and have lived as neighbors, it's become increasingly apparent that the things that make me tick in my monkey brain are a lot similar to those that make your crow brain squawk. I haven't known many avehos, and to be fair, I haven't known a ton of humans either. I'm shy and reserved and sometimes make stupid jokes for attention, but that's beside the point. If during our whole relationship you had a sack over your head, I wouldn't be able to tell if you're human or an aveho.

"All that is to say," he continued. "that despite the separation of our evolutionary ancestors millions of years ago, we are very much alike. Sure, throughout the history of our species, there were massive cultural differences, but look at what Kroonsaed has done. Even if everything we've known about history is a lie, the fact that our two species can currently live basically having the same lives is mind-blowing. What are the odds that it would happen? Astronomical, surely."

"That's all great and everything," Chanin replied. "but what does that have to do with you trying to be a better person?"

"Sorry, I'm getting there now. In the early stages of civilization, species-ethics was the dominant accepted morality."

"What's that?" asked the aveho.

"Philosophers, both human and aveho, argued that in order to be a good person, you needed to practice being one all the time, as if it were any other craft you were trying to learn, like reading or woodworking. They also believed that humans and avehos were intrinsically incapable of living together, due to their biological differences. Because of this, species-ethics creates a normative for humans and avehos. It tells us to imagine the ideal human and the ideal aveho and aim to emulate them. I'm not saying that we still can't learn from species-ethics, but after the thousands of years we've lived together, I think they need some adjusting, and that brings me to myself: I think Jowns is right at his start. I think in order to understand what makes someone good, the first step is to consider your place among every creature in the world. It may be just a random occurrence out of many possibilities that the three of us ended up here right now, or that humans and avehos came into existence at all. The first thing to do is to understand everything that led to our development, so we can better ourselves for thousands of years to come. We have the burden of being creatures that want to do good, and we would have died out long ago if we didn't have empathy."

"Don't forget," Chanin said. "especially in the example that you're talking about, there can be two kinds of empathy. The most powerful kind is selective empathy."

Gerrika cocked his head. "Selective empathy? Are you saying you think that people can just choose what they identify with?"

"It's an unconscious choosing." she answered. "For example, it's natural, and evolutionarily prudent to favor the well-being of a member of your species over a member of another. We don't exactly live in a 'state of nature' anymore, but that doesn't mean that it's gone."

"Exactly right." Dreden smiled. "That brings me to the meat of what I want to say. I think one of the most useful things in studying science with philosophy is that we can better understand what our limitations are. Jowns wrote that he was open to being proven completely wrong on his Theory of Evolution, but, even if it was all false, he thought that we ought to act as though its true for the bettering of society. That kind of reasoning is not new to him. It's used in a lot of religious contexts too, when talking about the afterlife. Many don't outright say it, but they basically say that we ought to believe in retribution in the afterlife so we can be good people while we live."

"That's a little depressing." Gerrika commented.

"I promise it's going to get better. We are all animals, and we need to understand and accept that, but we are unique too. We're capable of having these kinds of conversations, and we have the luxury of living in a civilization where we are free of natural predators, and thus we are likely to live long lives. Because of this, it's easy to build our personalities outside our identities as animals, so much so with technological developments that it can be easy to forget what we all really are. I don't think we should forget what we are, but it could be good to pretend that we are more than we are too."

"Are you talking about free will?" Chanin asked.

"Sort of, but I don't think the question of free will is very important."

"Why wouldn't it be?" asked the aveho. "I'm no expert, but isn't it free will that's supposed to give us the ability to decide right from wrong?"

"Some would say that. I don't. I think our conception of morality is a reflection of our evolutionary development, and that's not to say it's meaningless. I think it's a beautiful thing. I don't know about you guys, but I've tried praying before. No god has ever answered me in any way I'm aware of, and that's what's funny about our lives. We beg for meaning and understanding from the universe, and it answers us with silence. In a way, we are all condemned. Condemned to be inquisitive, intelligent beings that are forbidden from knowing the answer to the ultimate question of god and the universe. And even knowing how pointless the search for meaning is and the fact that we may never be satisfied, we must try to be happy, because we are also able to make our own meaning for ourselves."

"I think you lost me halfway through there." Gerrika shook his head, mirthfully.

Dreden paused for a second, trying to remember something his friend had told him days before.

"Let me put it this way, Gerrika, you remember what you told me about that Sky Man song?"

That was the name of the first song Gerrika had sung for the humans of Brunswald, days ago on the same day he met Morell. "I do, yes. I was quite drunk, but it was the truth."

"Let me see if I remember correctly, and please correct me if I'm wrong. It's an old aveho song about the loss of your wings. It deals with a narrator who, despite knowing that his flight will be his last, chooses to fly because that is what he loves to do. That's who he is."

"Correct."

"So, the sun ends up ruining his wings, and he falls to his death. I think we should interpret the sun in the song to be the inevitable failure of our search for meaning, but it's the aveho narrator's will to be true to himself that we should admire. He knows that it may all be for nothing, but he does it anyway, and enjoys what he loves, even though he has been condemned to death. It is my belief that we must imagine the Sky Man happy."

"We must imagine the Sky Man happy." Gerrika repeated, eyes steady as if in a trance.

"*Fuck...*" Chanin let a moment pass. "That's a deep cut."

"Therefore," Dreden continued. "I believe that most of the time, the right thing for someone, human or aveho, to do is to just be true to themselves. It's a tall task, but I think we ought to act as if we believe we have free will, and to try not to act in bad faith, meaning that we should try not to let outside factors impact our actions or our beliefs. If we can do this, then we can live authentically."

"In a very strange way, that is one of the most inspirational things I've ever heard." Chanin said.

"I…" Gerrika began, clearing his throat. "I agree. I think that that's something I really needed to be told right now. I'm not sure if I've ever made an authentic choice in my life."

Chanin said: "Are you kidding? Gerrika, you're one of the most authentic people I've ever known."

"Not all the time." he answered. "Ugh, most of the things I've done have probably been to avoid becoming my father. I've done everything humans are supposed to do in his eyes. I'm not an aveho to him, but maybe that's just who I am. Other motivations be damned, maybe I'm just a freak and I should be proud of it."

"I certainly haven't been authentic lately." Dreden shook his head. "I've been who I thought I wanted to be, and it's been eating me up inside. I'm not like Morell or his friends. I'm not really sure who I am."

"You're Dreden fucking Sharpstand." Chanin declared. "That's who you are, and you're one of the nicest people I've ever known."

"Honestly, friend." Gerrika leaned forward, cupping his hands at his lap. "I haven't been my best self lately, so I'm not going to judge you, but at this point in my life, I'm not sure what I would do without you. You've helped me think about things in ways that I never would have had I never met you. You've made me consider myself in ways I've never thought of before, and I am a better person because of it."

"Me too." Chanin said, wiping the corner of her eye. "None of us are the best people in Kroonsaed, or the happiest, but my life has improved in ways I can't put into words since I became your guys' friend. Sometimes I think my parents' care for me is a farce. I feel like in the last few years they've given up their jobs as my parent and don't even like having conversations with me or even scolding me. I would rather them shout at me than feel like they don't care enough to do it. It hasn't been easy, but I love you both so much."

"Let's all make a promise right now," Dreden said. "no matter what happens, no matter the horrible odds stacked against us, it's the three of us against the world."

"Three of us against the world." Chanin repeated.

"Three of us against the world." Gerrika joined in.

The door opened from down the hall, stopping the three of them as they were about to do another group hug. The footsteps that followed were slow and confident. Dreden had heard them many times in the last week.

"Morell?" He got to his feet. "What are you doing here?"

"What do you think I'm doing here?" The hair over his forehead was a mess, and he talked with a drag. "I'm here to bust the three of you out. Sorry, I would have done it sooner, but it sounded like you guys were having a moment. Didn't want to interrupt."

"*You* are going to let *us* out?" Dreden blinked. "Forgive us if we're wondering what kind of sense that makes."

"Do you know the truth?" Chanin asked, joining Dreden at his side. "You must, right? Considering your parents?"

Morell looked away from her, down at the floor. "You think I don't realize how this looks? How this makes *me* look? Dreden, I understand if you're not the biggest fan of me right now, but I promise that I knew nothing of the truth. Dowlepot told me everything. Gave me one of Jowns's testaments. I can't fucking believe it."

"I don't know, Morell. I don't know what to believe anymore." He turned to Chanin and Gerrika, who were watching him with full eyes, urging him to go on. "You just happen to meet me after we came out of the Sea and have a thing with me? Regardless if that's true or not, you haven't been a great person. You've been rude to my friends, and you've treated me as if I were one of your characters that you love to analyze. That is not okay, Morell, and the two of us are done."

Morell's hand flew to his face. He pressed his fingers against his closed eyelids in frustration. "Okay. I understand. I know I do not look well in this picture, but can we discuss this another time? We need to go."

"How did you get by the guards?" Gerrika asked.

"I'm very rich. I literally bought us time."

Morell put the key in the hole, turning it unlocked and opening the cell door with a click.

Since the door was open, and they didn't want to spend another second locked up, no matter who their savior was, Dreden, Chanin, and Gerrika shuffled themselves out of the cell.

"Great." Morell nodded. "I have a carriage waiting for us outside. We're going to need to move fast, since it won't be too long until the big dogs here get whiffs of you all being gone."

"What are we supposed to do afterwards?" Dreden asked, as they quickly started walking down the hallway. "Where are we going to hide from the police?"

"There's room for the three of you back at my house."

"You have a house too?" Chanin asked.

Morell ignored her. He guided them through several empty rooms until they made their way out of one of the emergency exits. As he promised, there was a carriage waiting for them, parked right outside in the alleyway behind the station.

"Come on," he said, ushering the three of them inside before jumping in himself. "something tells me time is of the essence here."

CHAPTER 11

The pair resumed their silence as they continued down the streets.

Honja was in front of him. Renny could see how little the aveho was turning his head to look at the structures around him, which was mind-blowing to the professor. Every other minute, he found himself falling behind Honja because of how much his eyes were swallowing up the city.

It was easier to ignore onlookers than he expected. About half of them didn't even make noise. They became silent as the two of them walked by. Renny had to fight the urge to stay a few extra feet behind Honja so people wouldn't think that they were together, but he wasn't going to let his partner down, whether or not his partner actually cared.

The aveho turned around, making sure the human was still behind him.

"I'm here. I'm here." Renny told him.

"Do you want to rest again?"

"No. Let's keep going." The professor stopped, resting a hand against the side of a brick building. "As interesting as this place is, I just want to find my son and get out of here as soon as possible."

Honja adjusted his bag back over his long shoulder. "Likewise. I don't think my nose can take much more of the smell of this city. It would smell better with fewer humans and more pigeon droppings."

Renny held his lip, trying not to laugh. "Right hand to the Creator, Honja, are you telling me that you're not joking right now?"

"I never said I didn't have a sense of humor. I believe you just inferred I didn't."

"Then I apologize." Renny kept his smile. "I didn't expect to find myself learning so much while being so far away from the university, outside of books."

Honja regarded him for a quiet second before turning back around and continuing his walk. The professor, fighting his exhaustion and thirst, kept up with the burly aveho's pace.

The streets became narrower, with fewer people going up and down to stare at them. He was new to the city, but Renny thought they had now crossed into a much less pretty part of the city. There was a heaviness in the air, and the sounds of machines grew three times as loud. The buildings weren't as tall, and many of them looked abandoned.

"Gerrika!" Came a woman's voice from ahead. "Hey, it's Gerrika. He's back!"

Renny paused. He could tell that Honja was caught off guard by the sudden shouting of his son's name. From a few buildings down the street, the figure of a woman came rushing up, shadowed by a man a few paces behind her.

The aveho pulled an arrow out of his quiver and tightened it against his bow as he watched the approaching strangers. Once they could be seen as having no weapons and having two of the most harmless faces Renny had ever seen, Honja relaxed the weapon in his grip.

He saw the woman's smile vanish as she paused several yards in front of them.

"Oh. You're not Gerrika." she said.

The man stopped at her side, turning his head in confusion.

"What are you talking about? Of course that's him."

She put her hand on the man's back. "Allin, do you seriously think that Gerrika, the walking twig, became this muscled condor in the past hour?"

"Gerrika is my son." Honja interrupted. "How do you know him? Where is he?"

The pair of humans straightened, looking at each other as if that were the last thing they expected to hear.

"No way!" The man approached Honja, extending his hand. "Nice to meet another one of you! I'm afraid we have some bad news though."

The aveho didn't even look at the man's hand. "What is it? Answer the question."

The human retracted his hand, awkwardly putting it at his hip, pretending it was never offered. "We met your son and his friend Chanin last week. We didn't get to talk to him much until earlier today about an hour ago."

"What about Dreden?" Renny asked. "Dreden Sharpstand?"

"We never met him," replied the woman. "but Chanin talked about him all the time. Are you his father?"

Renny nodded. "Me and the charming Honja here just came from the Sea. We're looking for our sons. Where are they now?"

"That's where the bad news comes in." the man said. "The police showed up an hour ago and took them away."

"Why did they do *that*?" asked the professor.

"Apparently Gerrika mauled someone earlier at a bar in the middle of town. They took Chanin away for trying to cover for him."

"*Really*?" Honja's feathered brow shrank as his eyes went wide. "Are you sure you're talking about my son? He's mostly black, a bit of blue around his collar, yellow beak, big yellow feet?"

"I think we've already established that they know your son, Honja." Renny said.

The aveho crossed his arms, smiling to himself. "I'm aware, but my son gags at the sight of blood. I'm surprised he attacked someone."

"You seem proud."

"Surprised, mostly, but a little proud too."

"It's alleged. It might not be true." The man told them. "Anyway, we've forgotten to introduce ourselves. I'm Allin Gumary, and this is my wife Sidra."

"Chanin has been spending a lot of time in our garage." Sidra said. "She's very bright, better than any assistant we've ever had to pay for."

Renny raised his hand in halt. "Wait, so if Chanin and Gerrika are in jail, is Dreden with them too?"

"I think he is." Allin said. "One of the arresting officers, a chimpanzee of a man, claimed that 'their friend' was going to be joining them. I'm not sure what he did to deserve to go there too, but I would say the odds he's with them are good."

"Then let's go get them!" the professor grabbed Honja's arm. "Those kids don't belong in jail. We need to get them out."

"I don't know how successful you'll be." Sidra said, before eyeing Honja's sack and the arrows sticking out of it. "The two of us can show you to the station."

The Gumarys guided the two of them down the street. As they were going to pass by their garage, a metallic, smoky scent filled Renny's nose. It wasn't offensive, but it wasn't like anything he ever smelled before.

The husband and wife suddenly burst into a sprint as they entered what was apparently their home, but to Renny it looked like a remnant of an old storage building.

"Crap!" Allin shouted.

His wife cut in front of him, and the two of them settled at the base of a giant horse. Only the horse was made completely out of metal.

"What's that?" Renny asked.

"It's a long story." Sidra sighed, burying her face in the steaming belly of the machine. "And I think it's a story that's finally over."

"Damnit!" Allin kicked the motor-horse in the leg. "All that work gone! Ugh…" He looked up to Renny and Honja, a guilty look in his wide brown eyes. "This was finally working. We were going to use this to take you to the station."

"Hey, don't worry about it. It's no problem." the professor assured. "We'll just walk."

Honja laughed, hiding it with a grunt. His brown chest feathers puffed in amusement.

"It's about an hour walk to the station." Sidra said. "I don't like the thought of the two of you out in the streets right now. There's something really fishy about how the police handled the situation earlier." She looked at the aveho. "Someone as noticeable as you might not get a lot farther, especially since you're packing all those weapons."

"That actually gives me an idea." Honja dug into his pack, taking out a blade long enough to cause the Gumarys to take a couple cautious steps back. "If I get arrested, then I'll be with them. Then I'll break us out."

"I don't know how the police are where you come from," Allin said, staring at the dagger nervously. "but you can easily get shot trying to do an operation like that."

The aveho was about to reply, but looking at Renny, he decided not to. The professor knew he didn't have to remind Honja about what guns could do.

"Fine." Honja said, tucking his dagger back in the bag. "While we're here, would you mind if my little friend had some water? He drank my share already."

"No problem." Sidra said. She went to the corner of the room, grabbing what Renny hoped was a clean glass and filled it with water from the faucet.

"Are you sure this is a heathy setup?" Renny asked. "Don't you guys have anyone else to help you tidy this place up? How old are you guys? Twenty-seven? Shouldn't you be living a little more?"

"Ha! We're thirty! Told you we still look good, Sid." He and his wife exchanged a high five, soot dissipating in the air after the smacking of their palms. Renny took the glass from Allin's hand and eyed it for cleanliness. "You're not the first person to tell us that. We live where we work, so we're pretty much working every hour we're awake. What do you do, if I may ask?"

"I'm a university professor." Renny answered.

"Nice! I remember school." Allin pulled up a stool and took a seat on it, wiping his brow of sweat. "Sadly weren't the best times of my life, or Sid's life. We weren't the greatest students, but look where we are. We're basically living the dream."

"Almost are living it." Sidra stood against her husband, putting her hand on his head. "We've had mild success, making small things and making small money. We've been trying to make something big for a while, and the motor-horse was our best bet. Sadly, looks like that dream is gone."

"Do you guys do this to everyone who crosses your path?" Renny smiled, sipping his glass. "Open yourselves up like this?"

"Pretty much." They both answered. Sidra continued: "We're dedicated, because we don't want to be people twenty years down the road looking back and wishing we did more of what we were passionate about. Our lives are our machines, and we like it."

Renny raised his glass in cheer. "Good on you then! I wish I could have lived more like that. I had a personal tragedy stop me for a while, even as I had a son to care for. I'm forty-three, and this is the first time I've ever left Kroonsaed. I've always wanted to see the world." He turned to Honja, who had been standing silently, hand on his bag, for the last two minutes. "How about you, friend? Do you have a dream?"

"I do." he answered. "I'd like my life to stay exactly the same as it is now until the day I die."

A loud ringing sounded from down the street. It grew louder as the rushing of hooves on the street followed.

Allin and Sidra rushed out of their garage, stopping at the edge of the sidewalk. Honja already had an arrow in his bow, as he took position in front of the Gumarys. Renny joined them at their side, and the gang watched as four carriages raced down the street, one after the other after the other. Each of them had a man extending his body out the window, his arm ringing a loud bell as they barreled down the street.

Renny felt the wind of the passing carriages swish his hair back. "The heck is going on?"

"Those are the emergency bells." Allin said, alert. "They do that when dangerous prisoners have escaped."

"Prisoners?" Renny turned to them. "You think our kids have gotten out?"

"Odds are they have." Sidra said. "Considering the latest police report, it was only the three of them that were being kept at the Central Station. From those logos, those were Central Station police carriages."

"Then we need to follow them!" The professor looked left to Honja, but found no one standing there. "Huh? Guys, did you see where Honja went?"

"No." The Gumarys and Renny looked around, and back into the garage, but there was no sign of the aveho.

As the sound of the rushing police horses faded, the smacking of lone hooves approaching made them all turn their heads.

A black horse came to a halt a few feet in front of them, and its rider had feathers that were a color to match.

"Hop on." Honja ordered.

"Where did you get this?" Renny asked. He backed away, anxiously as the horse swung its head and snorted.

"Just up the street."

"That's not a public horse!" Allin cried. "It belongs to someone up there. You can get into a lot of trouble!"

The aveho grabbed Renny's hand, ignoring him. "We need to go now, before we've lost them for good."

Before he could protest, Honja raised the human up by his arm. Renny let out a yip as the aveho was able to raise him all the way up with one hand over the horse's back.

"I can't do this! I've never ridden a horse before."

"Neither have I." Honja replied.

The aveho slapped the horse's side, and the animal sprang into a dash.

The professor fought the urge to scream and wrapped his arms tight around Honja's chest. "Do you mind if I hold onto you?"

"Yes, but if it'll stop you from dying, do it anyway."

***

The Gumarys watched as the horse ran away with Renny and Honja hanging on its back.

Just like when the police had taken Chanin and Gerrika away, they were stuck to the ground in silence, simply left to watch the action unfold in front of them.

Allin kicked the ground under himself, cursing as he walked back into the garage. His wife followed behind him. Her arms were crossed over her chest.

"I know. I know, but what can we do?"

"We've got to do *something*, Sid." He kicked some dirt up with his foot. "We didn't do anything when the kids were taken, and now that they've escaped, we're still finding ourselves not helping. We need to help. We've got to."

Sidra took the moment in, nodding to herself. "You're right. We must do something. Damnit, Allin," She slapped his arm. "our whole lives we've been playing it safe. Sure, we've tried to be new with our ideas, but we've never had lives like others."

"Isn't that a good thing?" he asked. "I know what you're always saying about being happy to be unusual."

"I am, but that doesn't mean I don't wish we weren't normal at least some of the time. We didn't do one illegal thing when we were in secondary school or in college. We've never been wild. That part of our lives just completely passed us by."

"We've never had the chance to be real heroes before." Allin said. "I always felt held back from doing what was right." He smiled, brushed the hair out of his wife's eyes. "You know what we're always telling each other about the day we met?"

He caught a spark in her eye. "My parents and my teachers told me no boy would want me if I was always covered in oil and grease."

"And they told me I would never get a girl if I never took my head out of an engine." Allin took her hands in his. "Yet here we are."

"Here we are." she repeated.

"It might be dangerous. We could get in serious legal trouble for what we're about to do."

"I say it's worth it. We can tell our kids that we did one crazy thing in our lives."

He looked over to the edge of the garage, where what he had told Chanin and Gerrika was their 'greatest failure' sat silent and unmoving. Sidra was already looking over there, and his smile grew to his ears.

"You're thinking what I'm thinking?"

"I am." She grabbed his arms and kissed him tight on the lips. "Let's let the motor-carriage loose on the world."

Rushing over, they pulled the massive tarp off the vehicle. It was beat up, wobbly, and stank of stale coal, but it was one of the most ambitious things they had ever thought of.

The Gumarys opened the doors, clicked the lever for ignition, and the car roared to life like a long-hibernating dragon.

"Alright," Sidra said, looking over her shoulder. "you're going to want to back the thing up slowly."

"No problem."

Sidra turned to the pair of straps in her husband's hands. Her mouth fell open.

"Allin! What is in your hands?"

"It's the steering apparatus." He blinked. "The reigns of the motor-carriage."

"They're completely impractical!"

"What would you have put?"

"A wheel!"

He rubbed his palms against his face, frustrated. "Right. Damn, I guess we'll have to do that later."

A few seconds later, after making sure there were no carriages or people coming down the street, the motor-carriage backed out of the garage, smoke already funneling out of the exhaust like a holiday stove.

CHAPTER 12

Dreden could hear a series of alarms go off as they escaped the center of the city.

Once they had traveled several miles, their carriage blended in easily with all the others on the street. There was no way to be sure if any of the officers pursuing them had gotten good looks at the carriage Morell was using to help them get away, but it became easier to not worry once the only sounds around them were the horses and the wheels on stone and brick.

"Where's your house?" Chanin asked.

"It's technically not mine." he answered. "I'm taking you to the Edland Estate. It's been my family's place of operations for about a hundred years."

The four of them were seated awkwardly in the back of the carriage. Morell was sitting on one bench by himself, where Chanin and Gerrika sat opposite him. Dreden, not wanting to sit next to him, found a seat on the floor to their right.

Dreden crossed his legs. "How do you know your parents won't be there?"

"They had somewhere to be earlier today." he answered. "It was way on the other side of town. They're not going to be back until the evening at least."

"You seem to be taking this new reality very well." Chanin said. "I don't mean to be insulting, but saving us is not the reaction I expected someone like you to have."

Morell shot eyes at her, pointing to himself. "Someone like me?" Looking to Dreden and Gerrika, seeing that they were thinking the same, he calmed down. "I already told you, I'm aware of how this makes me look. But I am not my parents. Dreden, I would have assumed after all our time together you would know better than to think I'd condone what Jowns did and what my parents may be trying to do."

"I don't know what to think anymore, Morell." Dreden shook his head, looking at him as if he were hundreds of feet away.

After the look in Dreden's eyes, he didn't want to continue the conversation.

Gerrika hadn't said anything the whole ride. Dreden was watching him more than anyone else in the carriage, even Morell. He spent most of the ride with his eyes closed, but the constant shifting of his tail in his seat and the movement of his hands on his lap showed Dreden that he was still awake.

Morell turned to the aveho, as if just noticing for the first time he was there. "I can't imagine how you must feel, Gerry."

"That's not my name." Gerrika grumbled.

"I'm sorry for everything." He stopped, looking around to all three of them. "Please, I don't want to fight with any of you. Any little bit that I can help until this is all over, I'm going to do."

Most of the rest of the trip was made in silence. When they were about a mile away from the Edland Estate, they ended up pulling over for a quick bite, since Gerrika was still hungry and they all felt that they could eat a little. Morell came back with a dozen meat biscuits that the three of them downed like a glass of water.

When the carriage came to a stop in front of the estate, Dreden looked out the window. From inside, he couldn't even see the top of the building. It wasn't long, as far as length, but getting out of the carriage, he could see that it was more than ten floors tall.

"*This* is the place?" He couldn't take his eyes off it.

Morell stopped at his side, waiting for the other two to get out of the carriage. "Tallest building along the peninsula. Lucky for you guys, the guest rooms are all the way on the top floor. The fifteenth floor."

"That'll be the closest to outer space we've ever been in our lives." Chanin laughed.

The trio followed Morell into the building. There were a couple armed guards standing outside the front door, but they just nodded and watched as the young Edland unlocked the door and let them inside.

The first floor wasn't much to look at. There were a few halls that looked like they led somewhere, but the center was reserved for a set of elevators. Morell took them to the left, and they all went inside the elevator after the heavy metal doors finished rumbling open.

When after what felt like two minutes to Dreden passed, the doors labored open, showing them to the top floor. It looked nothing like the first floor.

The biggest reason being the crowd that watched them as they stepped off the elevator.

All eyes were on them. By the looks of it, the entire top floor was just one big room, which felt much smaller with all the people. There were more than a dozen individuals standing up or enigmatically sitting in chairs, with at least eight armed guards as well.

Dreden didn't recognize any of the people in the room, but looking at the sullen, guilty expression that had taken over Morell's face, he could tell that he knew them.

One of the sitting men stood up, letting out a breath as he put his hands together. "Well done, son. Thank you."

"You're welcome, father."

Dreden couldn't even tell what he was doing with his face. Morell tucked his neck into his collar like a frightened turtle.

"I meant what I said to you three earlier." he said. "I am very sorry."

"The Prime Minister never gave you one of Jowns's testaments, did he?" Dreden asked.

"No, he did not." A woman stood up, taking Morell's father's side. "After Dowlepot had the three of you arrested, we knew what he was going to do. We figured it was time for our son to know the truth as well."

"See, I told you I wasn't lying." Morell said, voice tight in a beg.

The woman, Morell's mother, silenced him with a wave of her hand. "Enough out of you. We'll be dealing with you later, Morell."

"What the fuck is going on?" Gerrika asked, instinctively moving between Dreden and Chanin. "Who are you people?"

"It talks." Commented a rodent-faced man. "I had heard, but I wasn't sure I believed."

"Talks *and* sings, apparently." Came a new man, fat with thinning hair. "Word has it that it's very good at it. People really took to it, before it went savage on a poor theater owner."

Gerrika could tell it was not a verbal battle he was going to win. He shied away, tucking his talons in his pants.

"To answer its question," Morell's father approached the trio, a trace of a smile forming on his stiff lips. "we are the controllers of the present, and the controllers of the future. The perpetrators of the will of the great Mickeel Rippler Jowns, and you, poor Saedians, are going to help us with our most difficult challenge yet."

"Spare us a lecture," Chanin said. "we read the truth about Jowns. You're afraid the Unmaker is going to strike again."

"The Unmaker is a very real threat." said Morell's mother. "However, we're convinced that with the three of you, it is not something we're going to have to worry about after a few more minutes."

"You see," The rat-faced man rose to his feet, adjusting his small glasses. "what has been lost for a hundred years has finally been recovered. The book, the very book that Jowns and the last sorcerers in the world used in the Great Unmaking, has been found at last." The man swatted his hand carelessly at one of the guards. "Unmask the woman."

"Yes, Mister Skitt." answered the guard.

The guard lowered his weapon, freeing his hand so he could pull a sack off the head of the woman who was being held in the corner of the room. When the bag was off, Dreden could see the woman had a gag in her mouth. Her eyes were alert. There was a life in the way she showed her teeth through the gag that said she was more angry than afraid. She looked to be in her late twenties, and just about as confused as Dreden and his friends were.

The man who the guard had referred to as "Skitt" gestured to the bound woman. "We wouldn't have ended up with the book in our possession if this woman hadn't taken good care of it for us."

Another guard took the gag out of her mouth. When it came out, she looked like she wanted to bite the man's fingers off.

"You're all making idiots of yourselves!" she shouted. "You don't know what you're talking about!"

No one except Dreden and his friends paid her any mind as the obese man with the vanishing hairline turned around, picking up a book from the desk behind him. Holding it at its sides, he raised it up. Morell's parents, Skitt, and all the men and woman behind them watched as the man walked to Keeting Edland, looking almost reverently at the book in his hands, as if it were a religious artifact.

Morell's father took the book, bowing lightly. "Thank you, Loid."

The man called Loid nodded and went back to the middle of the gang.

Keeting looked at the book's cover and smiled, as if he were keeping a delicious secret to himself. "See this? This is it. This is Jowns's book. This is the last magical artifact in existence."

Dreden narrowed his eyes at it. It was clearly an old book, and the title on the front was hard to make out, but following the crease lines on the cover, he could read the title: *The Century.*

"And what are we supposed to do with this?" Dreden asked.

"You're supposed to write in it." answered Morell's mother. "We have reason to suspect the three of you are the only ones who can do it."

Dreden thought back to what he had read while they were in jail. After he met the Unmaker, Jowns created a contingency at the end of the book preventing everyone except himself and someone else from changing what he had done.

Chanin had remembered too. "His contingency. You think that the three of us are it?"

"That's all you can be. Why else would you be here?" Keeting asked. "The presence of Jowns's spell in Kroonsaed would never have let the three of you here if you didn't have a purpose."

"The men with guns?" Gerrika remembered. "The men in red back home are in contact with you?"

And they weren't just men in red, Dreden remembered. One of them was Jowns himself.

"Part of it." Loid answered. "Those beings aren't real people. They're just manifestations of the spell."

"The Sunitian Sea is the contingency." Janely Edland told them. "Its purpose is to allow whoever Jowns's spell chooses to come back from Kroonsaed and stop the Unmaker."

"You think that's us?" Dreden smirked. "You really think that we're going to help you?"

"I think you'll see that it's in your best interest to do so."

"War is imminent." Skitt said, standing up and beginning to join Keeting and Janely's side. He reminded Dreden a lot of a boring professor. "Even though Skaltbard has lived comfortably with the biggest powers, Andayt, Borgetta, and Gontland, since Jowns put an end to the great war, tensions over the last few years involving territorial disputes and growing nationalism have threatened to undo the harmony created by him."

"We wouldn't expect the three of you to understand." Loid laughed, arms crossed over his belly. "Coming from the biggest loser of Jowns's war, condemned to live in the poverty that you deserve, but the truth is that Jowns didn't go far enough. He lacked the vision to see past the end of magic and avehos. He couldn't truly see beyond the myth that all humans are created equal."

Dreden couldn't help but smile. "You people are pathetic. People like you thought that all of your problems could be solved if you eliminated magic and an entire species. How do you expect to survive like your precious Jowns promised you if you can't even get along with yourselves? You think that another war will be the answer to your problems?"

"It's exactly what we're trying to avoid." Janely said, through her teeth. "War is the last thing we want."

The meaning of her words swam through Chanin's head. Dreden could see it. "Right. Because what would happen if you lost the war? If they took you down, they could find out what Jowns did a hundred years ago, or worse, find a way to reverse it."

"It won't come to that, girl." Keeting frowned. "Thanks to the services of Miss Cipre Lane over there, you're going to win the war for us before it starts."

"The burdens of Skaltbard will be no more." Skitt raised his voice. "Andayt, Borgetta, and Gontland will join the fate of Kroonsaed a hundred years ago. You will have the honor of unmaking them, until there is only one nation left on top. One dominant culture of the dominant man."

Gerrika blinked, considering the weight of what the mousey man said. "How do you know it has to be us? Haven't any of you tried writing in the book?"

No one replied. Keeting dug into his breast pocket, taking out long white slips of paper.

They were things that none of the three had seen before, but they had seen the devices that produced them. Morell's father handed the photographs to them. The three Saedians recoiled at what the cameras had captured.

The bodies, of what they assumed were once living humans, looked charred beyond recognition. The areas along their arms, up to their heads and down to their chests were black, looking like they were a light tap away from falling apart into ash. The rest of their bodies looked normal, as if only their upper halves had combusted.

"What happened to them?" Gerrika asked.

"That's the result of trying to write in the book." Keeting said. "But you probably won't have to worry about that. If we're correct, the three of you won't have that problem. Who knows, if you do what we ask, the book might even make you a complete aveho."

"What the hell do you mean by that?"

Keeting lowered his head, confused, before throwing his head back with a smile. "Right! Right, you don't know!"

He opened *The Century*, flipping through a few pages before settling on the very last page of the book. There was an illustration of what Dreden thought was an angel, but the bird face and the dark-colored feathers told a much different story. It looked like an aveho. It was an aveho. The only difference was the long mass of feathers and muscle under its arms.

Dreden caught the look in his friend's eyes as he recognized what they were. They were wings.

Gerrika held the page open, frozen. "What are you saying?"

"You're a winged species." Janely answered. "At least you were before Jowns took your wings away."

"That's not possible!" Gerrika shouted at them. The Edlands simply watched him, unthreatened. "We never did. Our ancestors lost their wings millions of years ago. There was nothing in Jowns's Testaments that ever mentioned them."

Keeting smiled again, like a satisfied wolf. "It's right here in this book. When Jowns came to power, he made it illegal for avehos to have wings. Some gave in and had them removed, while others fought. He felt that, when the battle between the species finally came, flight would give avehos an undesired advantage."

Gerrika held the book, unmoving at the revelation. Dreden felt his heart fall at the look in his friend's face. He took the book out of the aveho's hands, so the attention could now be on himself.

"There, that's enough of that." Keeting said. "If you're going to-"

A seismic rumbling stopped him before he could finish. The fifteen-floor building began to shake like a leaf in a storm. Dreden and his friends looked to the Edland gang for answers in their expressions, but they clearly didn't know any more about what was happening than they did.

The next thing Dreden knew, he, Chanin, and Gerrika were forced to the floor. Every glass window in the room shattered, with shards littering the floor as if an explosion had gone off. Looking up, half the roof wasn't there anymore. It had collapsed into bits on the far side of the room. Everyone in the Edland gang who was under there needed to dodge out of the way before it all came down. Two middle-aged men, who looked like they were associates of Skitt, didn't make it in time. Their blood leaked like spilled juice under the wreckage.

When the trashing and scattering of glass and brick ceased, the sound of powerful beating wings, like a swishing of a great tarp over a field, was all that was left.

Dreden rolled onto his back, eyes and mouth agape at what he was seeing. An immense creature, settling its black wings at its sides, dug its claws into the floor. The room continued to wobble with each step of its four feet as it walked, its teeth fully bared at everyone in the room. Its dark red and black scales shined in the sunlight through the absent roof.

"Cipre!" it bellowed.

"Minkompa?" The previously gagged woman rushed forward to the creature, now that the guards had fallen on their backs. "What are you doing here?"

"You're in danger! I had to come save you. I wish I had known sooner."

"Is that a dragon?" Gerrika watched the creature, tucking himself next to some debris.

Dreden's elbows were planted on the floor. "I think that *is* a goddamn dragon."

"What is even happening now?" Chanin whispered.

They watched as the woman named Cipre grabbed the dragon by the arm, getting under its chest as the armed guards forced themselves back on their feet and leveled their guns to the giant reptile.

"Don't shoot!" she ordered. "You really think those are going to be effective against the dragon here? Let us leave." She looked over to the three Saedians, who were still cowered on the floor. "I'm taking the three of them with me. You're all lunatics. You don't even have the right book!"

Janely Edland, holding herself up against the trembling floor with one arm, didn't look as fazed by the surprise as her husband. "What are you talking about?"

"That Mick Jowns book that you're all obsessed with. That book isn't it! That book was made by my friend here." She rubbed the inside of the dragon's arm. He protectively lowered his head over her.

No one looked like they had any idea what to say. Keeting, Loid, and Skitt were still on the floor, looking at each other to see who would be the first to move. The dragon's eyes darted around the room, catching all their faces within a second, looking eager for one of them to be the first to move.

"I have a question." Came a new voice.

It came from one of the guards, still kneeling. He looked like a young man. Dreden noted that he didn't have a weapon on him.

Cipre faced him. He was looking at Minkompa, but she seemed to feel she could speak for him. "What is it?"

The guard got to his feet, a smile growing on his face. "You, dragon, how did you know she was in danger?"

The dragon snorted. "I heard her. I felt it, and I was right."

"Yeah, but where were you before all this started?"

The beast gave him eyes, as if to say, 'that's stupid'. "Under the city. I've been living down there forever, and now I've decided it's time for me to be in the light."

"That's so sweet." the guard said. "That's so sweet. I am so proud of you."

The guard approached the dragon as if it were a giant puppy, hands raised and a big smile on his youthful face. The massive beast snarled at him, baring his fangs, but that didn't faze the man as he continued and became within arm's reach of the dragon's nostrils.

"That's so sweet, but you didn't hear her, and you didn't feel anything. The only reason you are here is because I finally summoned you."

He raised a hand. At first Dreden thought it was some kind of illusion. The man's hand turned completely black, and as he touched the dragon's snout, the blackness spread over it like steam from a pot.

The dragon roared in apparent pain, throwing his head back. The force from his long neck caused one of the still-standing walls to crumble into bits, littering the ground far below with broken Edland relics.

"Minkompa?" Cipre got out from under him, retreating away to the middle of the room as she looked up, eyelids stapled open. "Minkompa? What's going on?"

"I've missed you, old friend." the guard said, almost singing.

Keeting Edland was on his feet in the next moment. "Mister Bair, what are you doing?"

"I'm not Mister Bair." he answered. "I am Mickeel Jowns's monster," He resumed rubbing the dragon's snout, who now appeared immobilized. "and so is Minkompa here."

Minkompa's once red-colored head had been swallowed by the blackness from the guard's hand. Every lamp and light that was still on in the room began to flicker on and off, and the one called Mister Bair began moving about the room like a light through a pool of water.

"The Unmaker!" Janely shouted.

The Unmaker paused, turning to Cipre as she watched what it did in stunned horror. "Sweet girl, did you really think that this dragon was real? That there ever were dragons? You're very kind, but very stupid."

Dreden didn't know what was happening, but he was just glad that all the attention was no longer on them, for however long that would last. He turned to Morell for the first time in minutes. He had taken refuge behind a chair, alone in the safest corner of the room.

It was small, but he could still see it. The black that had invaded the dragon's face started to recede. Its former glowing redness came back like a wave against a shore, and the Unmaker's hand twitched as it tried to maintain hold of the dragon's face.

"What?" The Unmaker's face grew long. Dreden could tell it wasn't used to not getting its way. "No. No no no no. You've changed. I knew, but you changed *too* much. What happened to you, Minkompa? What happened to me?"

Minkompa cocked his head to the left, then let loose and swung it around like a battering ram, smacking the Unmaker square in the chest as it went sailing against the wall.

The black was gone from the dragon's face, but based on the new color of its eyes, its fight with the Unmaker was far from over.

"I don't deserve this…" The dragon said. "I don't deserve to be you. I never did anything! I never hurt a single creature in my life, but now…" Minkompa shut his eyes, grinding his teeth loudly before opening them up. His eyes were completely gone, all that was left was the whitest color Dreden had ever seen. "Now I'm going to hurt *everyone!*"

The dragon reared around, throwing his head back and forth as if he were a bull trying to throw off its rider. He smashed his head into the ground several times, causing several gasps to echo through what was left of the room. Somehow, even with the tremendous beating, the floor hadn't given in yet.

Whatever was causing the beast to go wild, it looked like Minkompa was losing the fight. After three more smacks against the floor, the dragon stepped out into the massive open ledge he had caused, let out a roar that could have stopped every living thing in the world dead, and leaped off the ledge.

He didn't get very far. Dreden could hear his struggles continue as he tried to fly. It sounded as if he were getting tangled up in his own wings.

"Minkompa!"

Cipre ran over to the ledge. Her hand flew to her mouth as she watched her friend crash into the ground. The collision caused another quake to go through the Edland Estate.

Dreden and his friends grabbed onto each other. It wasn't as big as the first one, but with the structure's integrity being challenged the way it was, they wanted to be safe.

He looked over to the corner. The Unmaker was gone.

"What just happened?" Chanin asked.

Now that the dragon and the Unmaker were gone, everyone got back to their feet and the guards regained control of their weapons. The three Saedians were the center of attention yet again.

"This doesn't change anything." Keeting said, his voice tense from fright. "In fact, it just means we're going to have to work quicker. Unmake the nations. Unmake the Unmaker." Keeting took out a pen, looking at the aveho as if everything were Gerrika's fault, as he extended his arm. "Here. You first."

Gerrika was still struck, unmoving from the carnage. Together, with the help of his friends, the three of them stood back up and dusted themselves off.

The aveho cocked his head, fixing the dark feathers on his head. "Mick Jowns was a genocidal maniac." He said, looking at Keeting quizzically. "What could possess you to think that he would give an aveho the power to undo his work?"

Keeting and Janely considered his words, turning around to the others behind them. They all seemed content with his words.

"That's a good point." Keeting said. "Good point. Very well, we'll have another use for you."

He turned to a guard, gesturing to Gerrika with a cock of his head.

The guard came over, grabbing the aveho by the feathers of his collar. Being so light-weight, the man was able to pick up the aveho with ease off the floor.

"Hey!" Gerrika screamed. "Put me down!"

"Stop!" Dreden shouted. "What are you doing?"

"Just giving the two of you an extra incentive." Janely answered.

The guard walked to the edge of the room, still holding Gerrika above the floor by his neck. He stopped right at the edge of the room, at the gaping hole created by the dragon.

Dreden's heart was in his neck. With one hand, the guard was holding his friend out beyond the floor. At any second, even by accident, Gerrika could fall to his death.

"Stop!" Chanin shouted. "We'll do it. We'll do anything you want!"

"Let's see about that." Keeting said.

He picked the book off the floor, opening it to the last page and handing it to Dreden. "You first, boy."

"Don't do it!" Gerrika shouted, hovering over the edge. His protest caused the guard to tighten his grip on the aveho's neck.

Dreden's arms shook at the sound of his friend's labored breathing. "What do I do?"

"Just write." Keeting took a pen out of his pocket and handed it to him. "It'll be alright. Just do what we say. Be a good boy."

Dreden's mind was going everywhere. In his frenzy, he turned to Chanin, who was still as a portrait, not wanting to even move an eyelash out of fear of bringing harm to her friend. He couldn't tell if she wanted him to start fighting and call their bluff, or to try writing and see what would happen.

He caught Morell watching him. He had come out of his hiding spot, now standing in the open. He was visibly sweating as he watched the guard handle Gerrika. His softened brow and fallen eyes suggested he was considering protesting his parents, and Dreden had to fight the urge to beg him for help.

"Please, don't do it, Dreden! Don't touch the book!" The guard grinded his teeth, shaking Gerrika by the neck. The aveho's claws went wide, as he dragged the tip of his boot against the ledge for traction. He tried to swipe the guard but didn't want to be dropped accidentally.

"Hold on, Gerrika!" Dreden's wiped his forehead with his hand. "I'm thinking."

Dreden remembered the photos of the people killed trying to write in the book. A part of him knew that that would be him in the next second if the tip of the pen touched the book. He didn't want that, and he wanted to save his friend. Seeing him struggle for breath made Dreden bite his lip, to fight the heaviness building behind his eyes.

Gerrika was telling him not to do it. Gerrika was telling him to fight.

He had to fight.

The book was out of his hands. It struck Keeting in the nose.

"Ahh!"

The man recoiled back, recovering in time to see Dreden charge at him.

A shot stopped Dreden in his tracks, and he never made it to Keeting.

The pain exploded below his knee. He heard Chanin scream as he fell to the floor, flat on his stomach as the warm feeling of his own blood on his leg overcame his wound.

Looking back, he could see that Chanin almost dashed to Skitt and Loid. Luckily, she hadn't been shot. She got the pleasure of a warning shot.

He got the real thing.

"Coward." Keeting smiled behind his new bloody nose.

Morell's father turned to the guard, nodding.

The guard knew what to do. He looked Gerrika in the eyes, excitement in his face like a lion on a hunt. "Fly."

And the aveho fell.

***

He didn't scream. He didn't make any sound.

His brain was telling him to start flapping his wings, but he didn't have any. A part deep inside Gerrika's mind was ordering him to lay himself out in the air and spread his arms out for the thrill of the flight. Before today he would have attributed that urge of his to an ancient part of his psychology, something to be ignored now that his species had no use for wings.

But that was before.

Now he knew better. He knew the truth. Flying should have been as much a part of himself as his desire for companionship and his will to be different. His love of his friends and who he had become because of them. There was nothing unnatural about that. For as long as he could remember since the day he hatched, that had been who he was. But now he knew the truth. Something had been taken from him long ago.

The truth wasn't going to save him.

As the ground approached, his survival instinct kicked in and he began to flap his arms as hard as he could. Some feathers came off his arms in his manic swinging. At their loss, he could almost feel himself start to fall faster.

When he hit the ground, he no longer felt anything at all.

CHAPTER 13

He thought his heart exploded when he heard his friend hit the ground. Even after the sound of Gerrika's bones being broken against the solid ground, Dreden couldn't find it in himself to believe that he was dead.

There was no way that could happen. Gerrika had just been with him.

He turned to Chanin, who was standing to the side, now being held with her arms behind her back by one of the guards. She screamed, fighting her arms free so she could cover the horror washed over her face or to dry her tears, but the guard wouldn't let go.

Now the pain in his leg felt far away. All of his pain was in his chest.

He couldn't look at the Edlands or the guard who killed Gerrika. Dreden buried his face in his arms, splayed on the floor.

Morell rushed over to his side, putting a hand on his shoulder.

"Dreden," he said softly. "I didn't know they were going to do that. You need to believe me. I swear I didn't know they were going to do that."

"Leave him, son." Keeting said. "I think we now have his attention."

Morell's father picked up the book from the floor, approaching the bleeding Dreden and tossed it to him. *The Century* slid against his arm.

"Write," Keeting growled. "write or thousands more will die."

"Innocents." Loid added. "The Unmaker's rampage is beginning."

Dreden lifted his head, his eyes almost bulging out of their sockets. "I don't care."

"You *should*." Janely said. "You still have one other friend."

"You need her!"

Keeting looked to the guard who had Chanin restrained. At his gaze, the guard tightened his grip on her arms, making her wince. "We might, but there are many things we could do to her to make you comply without killing her." With a wave of his hand, he gestured for a guard to get behind Dreden. "Watch what he writes. If he writes anything deviant, break the girl's arms."

The guard grabbed Dreden by the shoulder, forcing him onto his knees. Dreden cried out in pain as he put pressure on his wounded leg. He had to rely only on his right leg for balance, as he opened the book in his hands, pen on his lips.

He wanted to write. He was going to. After Gerrika's death, a will was lost inside him. He meant it when he told them he didn't care how many people died. The people of Brunswald had done nothing for him and his friends. They had their attention, then completely shunned them away once it became convenient. Gerrika didn't deserve what he had gotten from them. He was worth more than all of them put together.

A tear fell down his cheek.

And he had never truly appreciated him when he was alive. He remembered what he had told his father his last night in Kroonsaed about wanting to meet people "more like him". Dreden grinded his teeth together, thinking about where that had gotten him. What Morell had done to them.

There was only one thing left to do. He felt it. Turning to Chanin, he could read it in her face. At his look, she lost the fear in her eyes. He remembered what the three of them had promised while they were locked in jail.

"The three of us against the world." Dreden said.

She sniffed, her cheeks shining with tears. "The three of us against the world."

The two of them against the world.

He moved quicker, but the back of Chanin's head hit her guard first.

Dreden felt the guard's grip on him loosen from the headbutt. The man let out a curse before falling on his rear.

As much pain as he was in, Dreden was full of adrenaline, his instincts kicking in to full-survival mode as he kicked the downed man as hard as he could in the groin with his uninjured leg. After that, the gun was easy to wrestle from the guard's grip.

No one knew what was happening. The rest of the guards in the room didn't know what to do. The one who had thrown Gerrika looked the most worried once the weapon was in Dreden's hands.

Dreden turned to him, gun steady in his hands as the guard tried to match him in time.

The sound of the blast filled the room, at least what was left of it. Dreden beat him to it. The blast from the rifle ended in a wet, pounding sound as the guard's stomach burst open, making him clutch himself as he fell off the edge of the building, eyes still fully aware.

Chanin had her gun in her hands, shooting the man behind her square in the chest as he tumbled over onto the floor, dying instantly.

With two guards down, the others were finally on the move, weapons level at the rushing Saedians who were readying their next shot.

"Stop!" Keeting shouted, hands raised at his men. "Don't shoot them! Don't shoot them! We need them!"

Dreden didn't know how many shots his gun would give before it had to be reloaded, but problems of the future were not on his mind. His heart raced back to his throat as the next shot from his rifle got the next guard in the chest. The man fell on his knees, blood coming out of his mouth as he fell flat on his face.

The odds were stacked against them. Despite his and Chanin's success in taking out three, there were still nine other guards in the room.

He earned a painful reminder of that fact as he felt a bullet enter his shoulder. It went cleanly through his body. He felt the explosion as the bullet and pieces of bone exited his wound. The guard who shot him was on the far, still-intact side of the room.

Another blast from Chanin's weapon to his head took care of him quickly.

It wasn't enough. The guard closest to him, camped in front of Loid and his remaining pals, leveled his gun to his chest and let loose a third blast to Dreden's body. This time it got him in the middle of his chest.

He couldn't stand anymore. He could feel his lungs and heart turn into soup. As hard as he tried, he couldn't let out a complete breath.

In his final moment, he saw another of the eight remaining guards bring his rifle up to his eye, firing a shot that took out the left side of Chanin's head. She hit the ground quickly, unmoving.

Falling down, a hand on his chest, futilely trying to stop the blood from pouring out in between his fingers, Dreden hit the floor, which was already painted well red from his first wound.

The last thing he felt were his lungs filling with his own warm blood.

***

They followed the sounds of the alarm bells easily for the first fifteen minutes. After that, Renny and Honja figured the police had lost track of the escaping prisoners. Parking the horse, the two of them had watched from a distance to see if the officers caught them. They didn't. Since the police had failed to keep up with the escapees, the two of them didn't know what to do.

Renny had a plan. He knew there was no chance the police would know who he was. To them, he would just be any other random citizen, with the exception of his strange, robe-like clothes. He told Honja to stay by the horse as he asked the police about what had happened.

"What's going on?" he had asked.

"I'm sure you've heard of the three visitors from beyond the Sea?"

"I've heard. Why? Did they get into trouble?"

The officer chuckled. "Yeah, and now they're gone. You didn't see anything, did you?"

"No." Renny had shaken his head. "I've been in my workshop all day. Anything I can do to help?"

"Tell us if you see Morell Edland. Word has it he's the one who broke them out."

The professor nodded, telling him he would, pretending that he knew who Morell Edland was.

Later he remembered he was a lot of the reason for his son leaving him.

To avoid suspicion, he didn't ask the officer any other questions. Renny caught a random person on the street down the block to ask him about Morell. Apparently he was a young, wealthy socialite who had a face no one could forget.

And his estate was twenty minutes down the road.

"Why don't the police go there?" Honja asked.

"From what I'm told," Renny said, getting back on the horse, behind the aveho. "the Edlands and the police have a bit of a complicated relationship."

"How so?"

"It sounds like the Edlands own the police."

Honja rolled his eyes, taking the reins in his hands. "Why would anyone want to live in a place like this?"

Kicking the side of the horse, the human and the aveho went dashing down the street. Renny feared they would be stopped by police for how fast they were going on the horse, but never saw any, even when they were going so fast that people had to dive out from the middle of the street to avoid being trampled.

"Did that man say how we would know we made it?"

"He said it was the tallest building around, that it was impossible to miss."

And it was. A long way before they arrived, Renny could make out the estate in the distance. It was tall, thin, and looked like a giant needle. It was right on the edge of the peninsula. In another circumstance, Renny knew he would have thought it was an impressive sight.

The gate and the front door were unguarded, wide open like a carnival ride

"You think that's strange?" Renny asked.

"Yes. A place like this should have patrolmen. Where did they go?" The aveho said, hopping off the horse.

He parked the stallion against a post along a wooden fence. The fence acted almost like a border between the rest of the world and the eerie feeling that being in the estate's presence gave the professor. Honja helped him off the horse, and the professor landed awkwardly on his feet.

Renny's face went white as he saw the top of the building.

"Holy…"

It looked as if meteor had pummeled through the top floor. The entire roof was like a crumbling wet cookie. Debris decorated the side lawn. Large, unbroken chunks of the roof were littered along the ground behind the building.

As the two of them approached the disaster area, Honja was the first to see him.

The aveho's hand caught Renny on the shoulder, his claws making holes in the professor's clothes.

"Ow! What are you doing?"

Honja paused, staring the human through the eyes. Straight through. Renny felt a shudder wash down his back as the aveho's pupils shrank.

"What is it?" he asked.

Letting him go, Honja sprang into a dash, running faster than Renny's body, even in perfect shape, would have permitted.

Chasing after him, Renny saw it. A tightness constricted in his throat as his mind tried not to convince him that he was actually seeing what his eyes were telling him.

Honja took a knee, surrounded by the mess of bricks and glass that hid his son's body.

Gerrika was still recognizable, but Renny knew there was no chance he was still alive. Broken white bones jutted out where his elbows and knees used to be. His yellow beak was broken into multiple pieces, and his body rested in a pool of fresh dark blood.

Renny collapsed next to Gerrika's father. Putting a hand on his shoulder as the professor fought every part of him that was telling him to burst out sobbing.

"I shouldn't have let him leave." Honja said, slowly. "I shouldn't have let him leave."

He felt the aveho's breathing quicken, then slow, as Honja pinched the base of his beak with a talon. With his other hand he brushed the top of his son's head, putting his fingers affectionately through the uneven feathers, then closing Gerrika's half-open eyes for the last time.

The sound of rushing feet made Renny turn around. He lifted his hand from Honja's shoulder. The aveho stayed on a knee as the guards rounded the corner.

"Hey." One of them said, cocking his gun. "Hey, whoever you are, the two of you aren't supposed to be here!"

The second guard stopped at his side. Both of them had their weapons pointed at the professor.

Renny didn't hear Honja move, or see him put an arrow in his bow, but an arrow was suddenly sailing through the air.

The arrow got the lead guard right between the eyes. His head went back with a snap as blood gashed out of his wound. Renny recoiled with a choked gasp, as Honja jumped in front of him before the second guard could fire a shot.

Honja's next shot got the other guard through the heart, sending him down to the ground next to the one whose brain had been split.

The aveho stood up, looking at the two dead humans. He paused to admire his work.

Honja put his boot on the bodies, plucking out the arrows and putting them back in his bag as he reloaded a fresh one. "I'm going to kill everyone."

***

"Fuck!" Keeting shouted as he stomped his feet in rage. "I told you not to shoot! We *needed* them!"

He grabbed a lamp from one of the tables and hurled it against the room in a wild fury. Cipre thought he almost looked like a rabid monkey.

She couldn't believe the last few minutes. From Minkompa turning out not to be a real dragon, if the Unmaker was to be believed, and the brutal killing of the Saedians, she felt like clutching her stomach to prevent her from vomiting. Only the fact that the spotlight was no longer on her allowed her to keep herself together. She tried not to look at Dreden and Chanin. The latter's injury had rendered her unrecognizable. Blood was everywhere in the middle of the room like an artistic accident.

Dreden's eyes were closed. He hadn't moved since he hit the ground. Having been shot three times, she didn't think there was any chance he was still alive.

Keeting continued to curse as he threw things against the wall. Janely, Loid, and Skitt, watched him, not looking any less excited with the current state of the situation.

His son, Morell, stood in the corner where he had spent most of the event. He was bent over against a chair, mouth open like a fish out of water as he stared longingly at Dreden's body.

The guards who had shot the two of them were looking everywhere but at their boss or at their kills, like dogs pretending not to notice the mess they made.

"You should have taken the fucking bullets!" He flipped a desk over, sending everything on it to the floor, shattering. "They were about to use all their shots! Their lives were worth more than a thousand times yours!"

He approached the guard who had given Dreden his fatal shot. Keeting delivered a quick kick to the man's stomach, knocking him over and taking the gun from his grip.

Keeting but his foot on the back of the man's neck, the barrel of the gun pressed against the base of his head. "Tell me why I shouldn't kill you? Tell me right now!"

The guard tried to reply, but all that came out was a series of gurgles. Keeting was stepping too hard on his neck for him to produce discernible words.

It felt to Cipre as if a minute had passed before the elevator door opened, and two guards entered the room.

"Boss!" The lead man shouted; his weapons tight on his chest. "There are intruders outside. They've taken out Rinding and Ewell!"

"Can't you see I don't give a fuck?" Keeting spat.

"That's not all." said the other. "One of them is an aveho, and it's really pissed off."

"Then you should have led with that." Keeting replied, fixing his tie and easing himself back into civility. "Alright, maybe this isn't over yet."

From around the other side of the room, a door was kicked open. Out from the stairway came what Cipre first thought was Gerrika, but promptly realized wasn't.

The guards moved their guns but weren't fast enough. None of them were fast enough for the enraged aveho.

The new, larger aveho fired a shot through the second guard's neck. She covered her eyes at the struggling man as his hands went to his throat and fell down, but she didn't look away in time to see the aveho rush the first guard.

Dagger in talon, he slashed the man's throat in one motion. The guard's mouth fell open as if it had been cracked like a wishbone. Blood spilled out as the massive bird put both hands on the man's neck, snapping it in one motion with a crack that made her head go light.

She didn't know whether the bird had seen the gun in Keeting's hands, if he thought he could beat them, or just didn't care, but the next sound that came was the blast from Keeting Edland's rifle.

CHAPTER 14

Dreden didn't remember closing his eyes.

He didn't remember opening them either. At first he thought they were still closed, because everything around him was as black as a starless night.

He stretched his arms, feeling the ground around him. There was not much to see anywhere, but he could tell he was lying down on his stomach. Planting his palms on the warm, solidness below him, he pushed himself onto his knees.

"What the...?"

Being on his knees didn't help make anything clearer. Everything was dark, with an intermittent sparkle of light that flashed colors his mind couldn't grasp. He blinked, sniffing the air and feeling his chest.

And he remembered what happened.

"Where am I?"

His senses caught something. There was a quiet sound of footsteps to his right, like stepping on carpet, but there was no echo or a ripple on the ground from motion. Once the sound came, it was as over as soon as it appeared.

"I don't know if I should be happy to see you here or not."

Dreden turned to the voice. In his daze, it took him an extra second to remember its owner. The first real shape of whoever he was took form as he recognized his avian friend's deep green eyes, jet black feathers and a beak stuck in a warm acceptance.

"I was terrified that I was in this place alone." his friend said.

"Gerrika!"

The aveho put out his hand and Dreden took it. As he got onto his feet he slapped his arms around Gerrika's shoulders, squeezing harder than he ever had before.

"Yeow!" he squawked. "Dreden, we may not be alive anymore, but I can still feel pain."

"I'm sorry."

Dreden relaxed his arms and the two of them touched each other's heads with their fingers. He had to fight the urge to kiss his friend on the beak.

"When did you realize you were here?" Dreden asked.

"I just woke up here," Gerrika replied, scratching his head. "It couldn't have been more than a minute before you got here. What happened to you?"

"I…" He had to take a moment to remember. "I got shot. I got shot two more times after you died, and then… Chanin!"

"She's gone too?"

"Yes, definitely." Dreden looked around, seeing nothing but a lot of darkness and hearing nothing but loud silence. "Chanin! Chanin are you here?"

"I'm here!"

They didn't know how they hadn't seen her there, but their first instinct was to leap for joy and grab Chanin in a three-way hug.

"I can't believe you guys are here!" she cheered, wrapping an arm around each of them tight before letting them breathe again. "Do we even know where *here* is?"

The aveho put a talon over his eyes, looking around at the empty vastness as if it were a beautiful canyon. "I think…I think this is the afterlife."

Dreden looked at the two of them. More than one part of the situation didn't make any sense. If they were dead, why did they still have the same appearances as they did when they were alive? He, Chanin, and Gerrika still wore clothes, the very clothes that they were wearing when they died. Besides clothes, why did Chanin still look like a human and Gerrika look like an aveho? Didn't people who believe in the afterlife think that the body was left behind? That the soul was immortal? Did their souls look the same as their physical forms?

"Part of me can't believe it," Dreden replied, feeling up his arms and his legs. Everything felt as it should. "but there's no denying that we're here, and that we're conscious, and…that we were killed."

"But if that's true," Chanin said. "why are we alone? Where are the rest of the dead people?"

"You're not dead. At least not in the way you're probably thinking."

The voice that answered Chanin sounded unowned, like it didn't belong to anything and was produced by some freak motion of the molecules around them, but Dreden still noticed as a bright figure appeared out of nothing, glowing like the first ever light in the universe.

Dreden approached the figure, feeling Gerrika and Chanin shadow him, while blocking his eyes from the intense light. "Who are you?"

"Who am I? I am the second of the two last magical beings in the universe. You have met the Unmaker, so that would make me...the *Maker*."

"You're the Maker?" Dreden blinked.

"You're God?" Chanin asked.

"I'm not God. If I am, that's not a secret I've been let in on. For as long as I've lived, I've existed to oppose the Unmaker."

Dreden put his hand up to block the Maker's light. "So that makes you about a hundred years old?"

"That is right, but time doesn't feel quite the same here."

"And where is *here*?" Gerrika asked. "What did you mean when you said we're not really dead?"

"You're not dead because you can't be. You were never truly alive in the first place."

Despite the fact they couldn't make out any of the Maker's features, Dreden imagined it having a blank look on its face after its pause, as it sensed they still didn't know what it was talking about.

"The three of you come from an Unmade realm," it continued. **"Because of Mickeel Jowns's spell, your ancestors were made nonexistent. When you left that realm, you joined the world of the *Made*. But that didn't fix you. Because you don't exist in their world, and you died in their world, your consciousness can't move on, which brings you here: to the end of all that has been Undone. The Realm of the Unmade."**

"Yay?" Dreden tried to smile.

"Wait," Chanin shook her head, confused. "If that's where we are, then why aren't we home? Is there more than one Unmade Realm?"

None of them could see the Maker's face, if it had a face, but they sensed it was nodding. **"Maybe one day you will learn more about the wonders of** magic. **This is the end for everything Unmade, where only consciousness remains.**"

"What about everyone back home?" Dreden asked. "What happened to them when they died? Are they here?"

"**No, they've moved on. Don't confuse what's happening here. Everything here is still a part of the material world. Magic is not a supernatural force that many have perceived it to be. It is as material as atoms and supernovas. You've noticed I've not referred to your presence here as your 'souls'. It is your consciousness. It is because of your status in the real material world that you are here.**"

"What are you saying?" Gerrika's eyes widened. "Is there no God? No gods?"

"**The answer to that question is not one I have the privilege of knowing. I am the Maker, but everything in my domain is only what exists in Creation. If there is anything beyond Creation, I have nothing to do with it.**"

"If you have so much power, why are you here?" Dreden asked. "The Unmaker is out there in the real world, already having killed thousands of people. Is there nothing you can do?"

"**I'm afraid I'm not nearly as powerful as the Unmaker. It gets its power from the passage of time. The more lost possibilities for everything and every creature in existence, it becomes that lost possibility. I, in turn, gradually get weaker. As time goes on, things die. Things are born too, but one day, if I still exist, will be no better than a frail old man. The Unmaker has an advantage. It was long dormant, unaware, but now that the three of you pose a threat to it. After you found yourselves in the real world, it was made sentient, better able to fight now, and in my growing weakness, my hold on it has grown softer.**"

"There must be something we can do to help." the aveho begged. "There must be a reason that the three of us were brought to the real world."

"**Indeed, there is, dear boy, but before I tell you everything I know, I have someone here who wants to say something to you. He's been waiting here for hours now, hoping you would show up.**"

Gerrika furrowed his eyes, focusing on the Maker's light. He tried to find something in there, as he looked around, unsure who the Maker could have been talking about.

Like Chanin had before, a shape formed on the aveho's right. It started as a tiny light, like a star in the sky trillions of miles away, and out of the light, a head formed, and the body below it fell down like water soaking a desert for the first time.

When the figure finished forming, Dreden had no idea who the man was, but turning to Chanin, he knew she did.

"Hello, kid." The man said, putting a hand on Gerrika's shoulder.

Gerrika's beak almost snapped and fell to the unmade ground below their feet.

"Winds!"

Winds Wilk's hands flew up as Gerrika buried himself against the man's chest, almost shoving him down on his back.

"It's a pleasure to see you again." Winds laughed. "If only it were under better circumstances."

"That be damned! I'm just happy I get to talk to you again!" Gerrika let go of his body, leaving his talons on Winds's shoulders as he looked at him, almost in reverence. "I'm...I'm so sorry your life ended the way it did. Did you intend to kill yourself?"

The man stared at Gerrika for a few seconds, looking like he didn't want to do him a disservice by not looking him in the eyes. "I did. My memory of it is hazy. Memories of booze and hard drugs don't clear up even after you've died. I haven't been well for many years. I'm afraid I wasn't strong enough to continue. I felt too sick of myself."

Winds's consciousness allowed himself to breathe a moment, before returning to Gerrika's glowing eyes. "What you saw was the worst version of myself, kid. Drunk, high, and no will beyond what his addictions had planned for me. I wasn't always like that. I always loved laughing, and making people laugh. I was never the smartest or prettiest in the room, so I defined myself with my humor."

"You did more than that," Chanin said, stepping in front of Gerrika and Winds. "I read what they wrote about you in the afternoon paper after you died. You always made time for fans, you visited sick and dying children in hospitals dressed as characters from your plays. You were selfless."

"I was," he smiled at her, even with his eyes. "once upon a time, I was better. I owned all that pain, from seeing people dying to what the critics would write about me. I owned it, even though I spent so much of it alone."

"You left everything behind when you left Kroonsaed," Gerrika sniffed. "you gave your life to finding success in Brunswald. Did you ever feel you had any?"

"It depends on how you define success. Sure, I won some awards and made some good money, but I was never happy."

"You made so many people happy." the aveho replied. "You made me happy. That night, before I came to this world, I fell in love with your work. I couldn't believe that someone who would write about the humor and positivity of the world around him would do what you did."

"It's a sad truth, kid, that sometimes the ones that smile the brightest are the ones most in need of joy."

Dreden felt himself wipe his eye at Winds's words. He had gotten so focused on their conversation that he had forgotten that, even mostly dead, he could still feel pain.

"How do you feel now?" Gerrika asked. "This is the real you, isn't it? Do you feel okay right now?"

"I wouldn't exactly say that, either."

"**You see,**" The Maker said, returning from its silence with a flash of light. "**It's a tricky business trying to find out who we really are. There is only so much control we have over our own environments. Are we any more than the sum of our actions and experiences? The sum of what we've felt and what has happened to us?**"

"We can play guessing games all we want." Winds said. "We can wonder maybe if we'd gone to a different university, married a different woman, or chose different friends, would we be the same person we are today, but of course, we wouldn't be. That person could be as different as me and you."

"I see…" Gerrika said, tucking his arms at his sides. "You're saying you wouldn't be like this if you were still alive."

He nodded. "Being in this place for a few hours does something to you. It makes you lose yourself, your ego. I am so happy I got to talk to you again and apologize, but you never would have gotten these words out of me if I didn't die. Embrace whatever you're feeling right now. Try to love it. Love everything that has ever happened to you. Because that's who you are. You have so much growing left to do, and I think you will become a wonderful little aveho."

"Thank you." The aveho cleared his throat. "Thank you so much." Gerrika turned to Chanin and Dreden, whose consciousnesses were watching him and

Winds with eyes that could hold galaxies. "Winds, these are my best friends. This is Chanin Adderfoth, the sweetest, kindest person I've ever known, and Dreden Sharpstand, the only man I know who can turn philosophy about the meaninglessness of life into something wonderful, and is so full of love as he does it."

Winds approached Chanin first, putting out his hand and taking hers in a firm shake. "It's lovely to meet you. Thank you for those things you said about me. I'm happy I can still feel grateful for them."

"You've earned it." She smiled at him. "You've earned it, good man."

Dreden almost couldn't bring himself to look the man in the eyes. He had made a complete ass of himself when he told Gerrika that there were better things he could have been reading instead of Winds's plays. And now, with a spirit gleaming in front of the Maker, the playwright was smiling at him with his hand outstretched.

"It's great to meet you, Dreden."

Dreden took the man's hand as if he were holding onto a ledge. "It's an honor, Winds. It truly is."

The Maker's light beamed again. **"Winds is right, and that's the Unmaker's weakness. If you know yourselves, it can't fool you, and if you know the people around you, it will have no power over you."**

"What's the Unmaker's plan?" Chanin asked. "Why is it killing all those people? What was it doing to the dragon?"

"As the Unmaker is not a natural part of the world of the Made, I don't have the answer. Only the Unmaker knows its own intentions. As far as the poor dragon, I think I can help you with that."

To the Maker's right, a new sphere of light appeared. It wasn't nearly as big, but it looked to be full of action. Its light flickered like moonlight against the skin of a jumping dolphin.

"Minkompa, are you there?"

"Yes," the sphere replied. "I am here, but I'm not sure where that is."

"This is the Realm of the Unmade. Your mind is here because you're in a battle for control of your own body with the Unmaker. I assume you've realized that you're not a real living creature?"

"I've realized, once the Unmaker took back control of me. I will not lie: the truth is quite painful."

"What's happening?" Dreden asked.

121

The dragon's light blinked. "Who's there?"

"The three young ones from the room. They're here because they were killed, but it's not over for them. Minkompa, in order to have a chance to win, you must fight for who you want to be. Friends, when the Unmaker was first created, it was almost defeated by Jowns. The Unmaker suffered serious injury, and had to cut a part of itself off, like an amputation, in order to heal itself. That part, eventually growing into a self-aware being, forgot what it was, and suddenly what it *wanted* to be became its reality."

Dreden remembered one of the final lines he read from Jowns's Testaments, the line about Jowns's feeling like he was battling a dragon. Apparently, in an effort to save itself, stole that image from the mind of the man trying to kill it.

"You've fought hard before." Dreden said. "You didn't win the first time, but you didn't lose either. You can hold on again."

"I'm trying. I'm doing everything in my power to fight it off, but it's a lot stronger than me. I can already feel myself being absorbed back into it."

"Do not fear, noble reptile, I'm going to send help. I may not have a lot of power, but I will send these three creatures back to their bodies. They will fight for you."

"What did you say?" Gerrika asked.

The Maker's light filled their eyes again. This time, none of them put up their hands in shield. **"The three of you have never been Made. I can Make you, and you'll finally be real. All the empty space between and inside all the molecules in your bodies will be restored with magic. You will no longer be victims of Jowns's evil."**

"Wait!" the aveho raised a talon. "What about Winds? Why isn't he coming back with us?"

Gerrika turned back to the playwright, whose still gaze with sorry eyes told him all he needed to know.

"No..." Gerrika shook his head, not believing. "This wasn't the first time you died, was it?"

Winds didn't need to nod. "Alcohol poisoning took me the first time two years ago. That's when I first met the Maker. Though he didn't tell me all this stuff about Jowns and everything back then. I think he's gone soft."

"Maybe, Winds, but I oppose you referring to me as 'he'. I'm an interdimensional being who has no evolutionary need or interest in gender or sex. For the same reason, I've always thought it strange that people can refer to God or gods with that language. Perhaps it's just

animal arrogance." The light beamed and blinked at the aveho. "**I'm sorry, dear boy, but Winds needs to move on. Because of my first connection with him, I was able to hold on to his consciousness long enough for him to see you here, but now I need to let him go, so I can focus the rest of my energy on holding the Unmaker back.**"

Gerrika turned back to Winds, grabbing him tight by the shoulders. "I'm not going to let anyone forget about you. I'm going to keep your work alive. I promise."

"That's very sweet, Gerrika," Winds said, patting him on the head. "but don't forget to live your own life. Be who you want to be. Live for yourselves."

"How did you know Gerrika would end up here?" Dreden asked. "Do you know what's going to happen? Do you know if we win?"

"**I'm afraid that that's knowledge I'm not going to give you. If I do, it could change the outcome.**"

"Can't you give us any clues?" Gerrika asked.

"**I'll do you better than that, young aveho. I'm going to give you something that you'll need. I'm going to give back to you what has been taken away.**"

The three of them became bathed in light. This time, they had to shut their eyes tight, but even that wasn't enough to stop the insides of their heads from looking like a sunny sky. Dreden's hands rushed to his eyes, covering them up to give them extra shielding, but that didn't work.

It seemed like a conversation between Winds and the Maker was the only thing in all of the universe.

"Tell me a joke, Maker," He heard Winds say. "Tell me a joke, before I pass on to whatever comes next."

There was a pause, as the Maker thought to itself. "**Don't you think it's a shame, Mister Wilk, how dishonest some people are? It seems like the only thing that keeps certain people from telling barefaced lies is a mustache.**"

The playwright's laughter echoed through the realm. Either because they were being sent back down to their bodies or because Winds's consciousness was moving on, the laughter faded away like ink in water. Dreden wasn't sure which one it was.

CHAPTER 15

"What going on?" Allin asked. "I can't see anything!"

"I'm sitting a foot away from you." His wife replied, trying her best to swat away the smoke clouding the inside of their vehicle. "My vision isn't any better than yours right now."

They had never taken the motor-carriage out for a distance longer than just down the road, so now that they were fifteen minutes gone from their garage, the weight of their situation was intimidating. The added reality of everyone taking notice of them didn't do them any favors either.

The Gumarys heard a few screams here and there, with many of them shouting for the police to come and intervene. None ever came. There wasn't even a hint of emergency sirens in the distance, as if something else were keeping all of the city's police occupied.

"We're never going to catch up to them at this speed." Sidra said. "Isn't there anything we can do? Maybe a shortcut somewhere?"

"I don't think so. Even if there's a slight chance, I don't think our machine here can fit anywhere speedy without the risk of trampling multiple people to death."

The fact that smog was filling their lungs quicker than water under the sea wasn't what was inhibiting them the most. With the wind blowing from ahead, all the smoke was clouding their windows, making it difficult to see. They couldn't bring themselves to go quicker than fifteen miles per hour. Even with Sidra sticking her head out the window for a clear view, they didn't want to risk anything.

The heavy, spitting sound of the engine being pumped was loud enough to give them both headaches. After going down the streets for as long as they were, its most useful function so far was drowning out the screams of startled onlookers.

"Aw, damnit, Allin," Sidra sighed, covering her mouth after another cough. "there's nothing we can do. There's no chance we can catch up to the police now."

Allin bit his lip, looking like he wanted to argue. "I know. I know, but I still refuse to just stop after how far we've gone."

"I have nothing else up my sleeve, and we have no idea where they went."

They continued down the road, braving a left turn at an intersection. Allin had to pull back on the steering-reins, pushing his whole body back against the seat as far as it would go in order to succeed without their left wheels getting more than even an inch off the ground.

As they continued for another few minutes, they noticed the screams getting louder. The rumbling of the engine was no longer keeping the sounds at bay.

"What's going on?"

Sidra grabbed onto the side of the door, putting her head out the window. "I can't see anything. I think all the action is on your side."

Allin fanned the smoke away. He got some soot in his eyes, forcing him to squint in order to make out even the shapes of buildings around them. "I can't tell. Maybe if-"

The pounding of two fists against Allin's side of the carriage caused Sidra to scream. Allin jumped up in his seat, leaning himself away from the window to avoid the wrath of whoever it was that had jumped against their machine.

"What is this?" a man's voice came. "Who's in there? Answer me!"

"Alright!" Allin raised his arms against the roof. "Just the two of us!"

Out of the windy smoke came a man's face. He leaned into the vehicle, taking a look at the two of them.

The Gumarys recognized him. They had met a couple times on less-than-pleasant circumstances. It was the man's frown-like mustache that gave away who he was. It was the same man that Chanin told them interviewed her and her friends at the police station after they first appeared in the city.

"Chief Milbrey?" Sidra breathed easy. "What are you doing here?"

"Do the two of you not know what's going on?"

They both shook their heads.

"If I didn't know better, I'd say it was the end of the world." The police chief rested his arms against the window, defeated. "We get a terrible earthquake last week, and now a fucking dragon is laying waste to the city."

"A what?" Allin asked.

"You heard me right. A *dragon*. The military has been called into the city, but their attacks aren't doing a damn thing. It's like the animal is absorbing all our bullets."

The Gumarys looked at each other, showing each other their teeth in complete confusion and discomfort.

"Wait a minute." Milbrey pointed to Allin, then to Sidra. "You two are the Gumarys, aren't you?"

"Yep." Allin said, sheepishly.

"Yeah, I remember you two. You two make the papers sometimes. You make things that blow up, right?"

Sidra winced. "We do, but usually we don't intend that to happen."

"What are you two doing out here?"

"We're trying to save our friends, the visitors."

"Allin!"

"Did you not hear what he said about a dragon?" he asked his wife. "I think they have more important problems now than a few delinquents."

Milbrey blinked. "You know the visitors?" They both nodded again. "Just my luck. You know, after they escaped, I found some things littered in their cell. Some things called 'Jowns's Final Testaments'. Was curious, so I picked up a couple. *Fascinating* stuff."

"I'm afraid we don't know anything about that." Allin said.

"Jowns?" Sidra asked. "Mick Jowns?"

The police chief wiped his brow, sighing. "There's too much going on here. Earthquakes, people and a bird-man come out of the Sea, they escape, then dragons suddenly exist. After what I've read of the real Jowns, there's no chance these events aren't connected."

Milbrey's head disappeared. They heard the back door of the carriage open, the police chief leaped into the back seat.

"What are you doing?" Sidra demanded.

"The dragon scared my horses away. I need a ride. We're going to find the visitors."

"But we don't know where they are." Allin said.

"I think I do." Milbrey adjusted himself in his seat. "Last we had sight of them, they were going to the Edland Estate."

"Are you kidding?" Sidra's eyes went wide.

Milbrey shook his head. "For the first time in our nation's history, if I have anything to say about it, we're going to raid that fucking place. The dragon came from the peninsula, so some serious stuff must be going down there."

"What about backup?" Allin asked. "The three of us are powerless."

"Drive around the corner. I'll let all my men know the new plan. This infernal new device of yours could actually be useful." Milbrey paused, putting his hands on the upholstery, fingering it as if there were a swimming piranha around him. "Wait, is this thing an explosion hazard?"

"If you really think about it," Sidra smiled. "everything is an explosion hazard to some degree."

"Just drive." Milbrey sighed. "And let me tell you about a place I just learned a lot about. The story of Kroonsaed."

***

Renny heard the shot, but there was nothing he could do about it.

Honja had left him on the first floor of the building. After killing the guards down there, the aveho rushed up the stairs, heading for the top where all the destruction had occurred. The professor wasn't fast enough, so he barely made it a third of the way when the aveho had been struck.

It wasn't fatal. Honja was left with a wide gash on the left of his abdomen. No one would tell him why, but they proceeded to cover up his wound to stop the bleeding. The aveho had tried to continue fighting, but a few kicks to the stomach from Keeting Edland after his wound were enough to immobilize any creature.

The way they got *him* was a less interesting story. Renny had no weapons, no training in physical combat, so after he successfully delivered a punch to a short, mousy man's face, an armed guard got his forehead with the butt of his gun.

With the action over, Renny and Honja were sitting down, their arms tied behind their backs on their chairs. Their captors had moved them down to the sixth floor, for the sake of the estate's structural integrity being challenged from whatever had happened on the top floor.

"Easy…easy." Janely Edland said, after slapping Honja across the face. "Stay with me. We may need you, so don't go dying on us."

"Leave him alone!" Renny shouted, almost falling back in his seat in fury.

"That's enough out of you." Loid warned. "We're all civilized here, aren't we? No reason to bite. Let's talk like men."

Honja shook his head, as if trying to rattle something inside him. "Like you talked to my son?"

"That was unfortunate, I won't lie, but the sooner you help us, the sooner you can get home. How did you get here?"

"My son told us how to get to this place." the professor answered. "Where is he? Where's Dreden?"

The leading man ignored him. "Is that true, bird?"

"A man named Jowns." Honja answered. "He let us through."

"I like the sound of that." Janely turned to Loid, flaring her nose.

Before they could interrogate the two of them any longer, the man that Renny had punched in the face came racing down the stairs. He held a cloth to his nose, covering the wound.

"What is it, Skitt?" Janely asked.

"I think we're running out of time." His voice was muffled from the bloody handkerchief. "We can see flashing lights from the upper floors. Not only is the Unmaker trashing the city, but the police are on their way here."

"No." Loid punched a fist through the air. "Damnit! Why?"

"Could be a number of reasons." Skitt said. "We can argue all day, or one of us can get down there and handle them. They'll probably only be another few minutes."

Loid and Janely looked back at Honja and Renny. "Very well." said the latter. "These two aren't going anywhere."

The three of them, including a couple guards by the door, went down the stairs. A few moments after the sound of their feet going down the stairs vanished, someone came out softly from the door.

It was a young man, couldn't have been more than twenty-four. One hand was in his pocket, as the other ran through his hair, making most of it droop over his eyes, as if that were an attempt to not let Renny or Honja see them.

The aveho, groggy from blood loss, looked at him as he entered, before shaking himself up in his restraints. Renny, awake and alert from everything, could nearly count the man's eyelashes.

"Is it true?" asked the young man. "Are you Dreden's father?"

"I am." Renny answered. "You know him? Where is he?"

The man approached the professor, getting down on a knee at his chair. "I know him. I'm... I'm Morell Edland. My parents are behind everything happening here."

"What are you doing, then? It doesn't seem as if you approve of what's happening." Morell looked down at Renny's feet, ignoring another one of his questions. "Fine, keep it to yourself. You're close to Dreden, isn't that so?"

"We were...basically a couple." Renny wasn't sure what he was doing with his face, but he could feel his eyes almost touch his hairline. Even Honja to his side raised his brow at the man's words. "After what's happened, I don't think you will care to see my face again, but," He took the professor's tied-up hand in his, closing his eyes. "I failed him. I failed all of them. I'm just not built the way you people are. I can't do it. I just wanted to see you and apologize."

Morell turned away and got back on his feet. As he went back to the door and headed down the stairs, Renny shouted for him.

"Answer my question! Where is he?" The professor kicked the floor in anger. "He wouldn't tell me. Why wouldn't he tell me where my son is?"

After the condition that Gerrika was in, the possibilities for his son and Chanin terrified him. He didn't want to think about it, but there was no way he could relax being tied up and powerless.

Honja tried to sit up, grunting in pain as a bit of blood dripped through the gauze on his belly. Sitting as straight as he could, he looked to Renny. "You know...if it was going to turn out that one of our sons was crooked, I would have bet on it being Gerrika."

The aveho lowered his eyes, unable to hide the pain as his chest moved with laughter, a crazed smile on his beak.

Renny closed his eyes, sharing the laughter with the aveho. Even after seeing his son dead, he couldn't believe that Honja would make a joke, let alone smile. He didn't know what would happen when the Edlands and their gang returned to the room, so Renny let himself have the moment with Gerrika's father, because there was a good chance they wouldn't have another one.

Once Honja's laughing was over, he cleared his throat, using it to hide a series of pained moans produced by laughing with his stomach wound. "Shit, Renny, everything is over for me. My son is gone, my life's purpose now ceased.

There is nothing left for me anywhere. My son...he hated me. He hated me because I could never be his mother and father at the same time."

The professor let himself have a second, remembering Gerrika's body. "Gerrika did *not* hate you. Don't think like that, Honja. Your son might have been the biggest thing in your life, but that doesn't mean you no longer have purpose."

"Doesn't it? Isn't it not the duty of the father to protect his progeny?" The aveho winced, as more blood seeped out of his side. "I don't live like you. I don't even *feel* like you. I don't even feel as avehos are supposed to. I've been emotionally empty for so long. Now I'm feeling everything at once and I don't know what to do."

"No one, human or aveho, can maintain themselves after what you've gone through." Renny said. "You've lost your son, and the pain from being shot is definitely getting to your head, but I don't think you should fight it. Just breathe. Breathe and talk to me."

"Since Gerrika hatched," Honja said, after a few deep breaths. "I thought all I needed to do to be a proper father was to act like one. When he...when he came out of his egg, he came out earlier than expected. Just these big, beady eyes so ready to see the world. Tridienne and I were very young, but we knew we could provide for him."

Renny nodded, realizing that was the first time he ever heard the name of Gerrika's mother.

"You say you don't think my life is over? Let me ask you, how would you cope if Dreden died?"

With what was happening around them, Renny didn't even want to entertain the thought. "Honestly, I would probably be saying exactly what you are. I've always had my love of books and learning to help keep me level, but it has always been my son's presence that had kept me from becoming an alcoholic again."

Honja paused. Renny could see him trying to fight the pain in his stomach. "What should I do?"

"You're asking me for help?"

"Yes, Renny, please! It's your job, isn't it? Asking big questions? Analyzing characters? I can admit that this is an area you are surely more adept in, so please tell me what you think I should do."

The professor didn't know what to say. Reading a character in a novel and talking to an actual suffering person were two very different things. "Right now,

I say don't think about later or tomorrow. Think about where you are right now, and what you'll immediately do next. For now, don't think ten steps ahead."

"Is that the moral thing to do too? Trying not to think about it?"

"I would argue, yes. If you can keep yourself focused, you won't have certain distractions inhibiting you. We may not completely know what's going on here, but it's safe to say that taking these bastards out would be the good thing to do. Doing whatever preserves your ability to kick their asses would be the moral thing to do."

"I like what I hear." Honja replied. "Even though part of me isn't convinced I'm feeling things properly."

Renny wished he could have put a hand on his friend's shoulder. "If it's true you haven't had many feelings in a long time, I'd bet that the weight of our situation is debilitating."

"Maybe morality doesn't come from emotion." the aveho said. "I've never considered myself amoral, I've just never *felt* much. Have you ever wondered if morality actually comes from reason? From rationality?"

"I have." the professor smiled. "I don't think it's what I believe, but there have been philosophers, human and aveho, who have argued that case."

"And that idea just came from me." Honja coughed, smiling as a bit of blood came out of his beak. "Surprised?"

"Of course not."

CHAPTER 16

As he opened his eyes, feeling his face against the cold, dry floor, Dreden couldn't even remember the pain of being shot. There wasn't the warmth of his own blood on his chest and his knees. Looking around, there was no blood anywhere.

"We're back. We're back!"

He could hear Chanin moan from several feet away, where she had been shot. Having one's mind put back in their body was a lot like waking up. Dreden had a sudden craving for bitter coffee.

"How about that?" Chanin got to her feet before Dreden. She fixed her pants. "We are!"

She rushed over to him, hugging him again, since doing it while they were all just floating consciousness in the Unmade Realm just didn't feel the same.

"How do you feel?" she asked.

Dreden felt his arms, chest and down his legs. "I feel the same. Maybe being 'Made' is just a metaphysical thing. Perhaps we're not supposed to feel different."

"Probably. I don't feel different either."

"*I* do."

The two humans turned around to see their friend in the corner of the room. Dreden didn't even think to look for him, since he had died on the ground outside.

Dreden had to rub his eyes to make sure his senses weren't playing tricks on him. "Oh…MY GOD!"

Gerrika raised his arms up, both so he could get a good look at himself and so his friends could continue staring agape at what was hanging under his arms.

Sharp, black feathers lined the new muscles added to his body. His arms looked to be the same length as before, but crow-like wings now were the pride of his frame.

The aveho spun around, showing his friends every inch of his new upper body. "I can't believe it. My wings tore my shirt! Crap, none of my shirts will fit me anymore."

"You look majestic!" Chanin cheered, rushing to wrap her arms around him.

Dreden followed her. Gerrika laughed as he embraced them with his wings. To Dreden, his friend's new wings were like a soft down blanket. He couldn't imagine what having them would feel like, but he guessed it might be something like a warm coat that you could never take off.

"I guess that bastard Keeting Edland wasn't lying." Dreden said, smiling to his ears. "Avehos have wings."

"Getting used to these is going to be really hard," he whined. "but I'm not about to complain. We're all alive and right now I feel like I'm seriously high on something. Suddenly I have the urge to swoop down and dig my toes into some poor animal."

"I'm sure you'll have plenty of time for that later." Chanin laughed. "The Maker said you'll need the wings, so somehow they must be what helps us win."

"Okay. Okay, let's take a moment." Dreden put his hands around his friends, burying their heads in a huddle. "We're alone on the top floor, no one knows we're alive, Gerrika suddenly has wings, and there's apparently a rampaging dragon, what's our first move?"

"The book." Chanin answered. "That magical book that they tried to get us to write inside. Something needs to be done about it."

"Think we should destroy it?" Gerrika asked.

"Impossible to say." Dreden answered. "The last wizard died a hundred years ago. None of those people knows how it works. For all we know, destroying it will just keep things the way they are forever."

None of them liked the sound of that. Even if it meant that all the neighboring countries were safe from the same fate as Kroonsaed, it would also mean no hope for their own homeland.

"If there's anyone that might have answers," he continued. "it's the Unmaker. It's very powerful, and the only magical being in this world."

"I guess this is it, boys." Chanin tightened her grip on their necks for measure. "First it was just about our own survival, but I guess we're fighting for billions of lives now."

"The three of us against the world." the aveho remembered. "I guess it's now the three of us *for* the world. So, the Unmaker is fighting the dragon right now for control. I guess I need to find it and help the poor guy out."

Dreden agreed. "Sounds like it's going to involve flying, buddy."

"You guys won't let me do it alone, will you? I can't go out fighting a big scary monster by myself!"

"Neither of us want to." Chanin turned to Dreden, who looked as confused as she did. "But we can't fly."

"Don't worry. One of you can grab onto my legs."

Gerrika lowered himself, trying not to accidentally tumble over from the additional weight his wings gave him. He untied his boots and kicked them into the corner, leaving him with just his pants.

"I hope that's all you're taking off." Dreden said.

The aveho was ready to unbutton his pants but stood back up after Dreden's advice. "This already feels much better. Come on, Dreden, I'll do the flying and you can, like, shoot or whatever. I'll use my feet to hold onto you, like a real bird."

"That is absolutely not going to happen."

"*Someone* is sassy since coming back to life." Gerrika sighed, jumping up and down on his feet to get his wings loose. "I'm going to do it. We're going to be heroes."

The aveho slowly approached the broken corner of the floor, where just minutes ago he was dropped to his death. He stopped as his feet touched the corner of the room, tightening all six of his yellow toes as he perched himself over, with his wings spread out like a waving flag.

For several tense seconds he just stood there, with Dreden and Chanin being too scared to move or say anything. Their friend's wings hung in the air like a gliding eagle's already in flight, with nothing but the openness all around him and the wind blowing his feathers back.

Gerrika stepped off the perch, as if just realizing where he was. "No. Absolutely not. Can't do it. I'm *afraid.* If I fall and die, I'm dead for good this time."

"Probably." Chanin said. "I would be really concerned if you weren't afraid. I think...I think that the Maker wouldn't have given you your wings if you were just going to instantly plummet to your death."

"True." Gerrika put his hand on his beak pensively, unable to stop his whole wing from coming up too. "Or maybe that's part of it. I just have to die right away for us to win."

Dreden approached his friend, lowering his wing off his head. "Remember what Winds said. Try to forget yourself. You're not Gerrika. You're the air and the sky around you, and you're no better or worse for it. You just *are*."

The aveho closed his eyes, clenching his beak as he turned around and faced the open air around him. "Or maybe I'm a Sky Man, and if there's something that that song taught me, it's that the Sky Man doesn't die before he can soar."

Dreden tightened his fists, raising them to his head in powerless terror as he and Chanin grabbed onto each other. Black wings spread out like a starfish as he slowly tipped himself over the edge.

***

"Don't say anything." The guard whispered in Cipre's ear. "Don't scream."

She was being held inside on the first floor as the first wave of police carriages arrived on the scene. Their horses almost overran the estate with their speed. Cipre knew it wasn't just the beatings from the reins of the drivers. Something else was causing havoc.

Someone else.

After settling their horses down, the officers hopped out of the carriages. Half of them had their guns in their hands, but none of them were pointed at any of the guards or the other men in the Edland gang who had congregated outside.

"A bit far away from the library, aren't you, Loid?" asked one of the officers.

"I don't live there, if that's what you're implying." From the side, Cipre could see he was trying to play it friendly. "Besides, the library has been closed since it was ransacked."

"Never got the guys who did it?"

"Not yet."

"Shame."

Cipre felt the guard's grip tighten on her neck. She felt he wasn't concerned about her trying anything funny. That was probably just who he was. "Why are you doing this?"

"I serve the Edlands, woman."

"You know what they're doing! What kind of sensible person would protect them?"

"The kind that has studied history. The *real* history." The man relaxed a bit, as if soothed by his own voice. "You heard what they said as clearly as I did. There can only be peace when the supreme culture rules. The supreme man. Our people have suffered long enough."

"If you think that you need to constantly be at war in order to have peace, then maybe it isn't really the 'inferiors' that are the problem."

The tip of the blade tightened against Cipre's throat, telling her the man wasn't in a debating mood. If things came to worst, she needed to be ready. She needed to think of something to do in order to stop everything. Even if only to avenge the deaths of the Saedians.

"What are you even doing here?" Loid shouted at them. Now his arms were flailing in the air. "Isn't there a monster wrecking downtown right now?"

Another officer came forward, showing a smile to combat the large man's body language. "How do you know about that? That's many miles from here."

"Where's the chief? Milbrey? I'd very much like to see him and get this ridiculousness over with."

"He'll be here soon." replied the first officer. He pointed up to the top floor, noticing the trail of carnage that had led to debris on the ground, easily visible to everyone. "Say, how did that happen? Someone forget to take their biscuits out of the oven?"

Loid snorted. "That's none of your business. Unless my colleagues or I am under arrest, I'm afraid I need to remind you all that this is private property."

"That's right." Came a call.

Cipre could see Keeting and Janely Edland come from the other side of the estate. With Janely's hat and Keeting's new shirt and tie, it looked like they had done a good quick job freshening up after the chaos. Even Keeting's nose looked back to normal.

"You have no right to be here." Janely told them all. "Go back to the city. We have everything under control here. Unless I see an order from a judge or from the chief himself, we're going to have to order all of you out of here."

"The military is currently trying to save thousands from a giant rampaging beast." replied a new officer, as several more behind her exited their carriages. "Civility has flown the coop. Clearly something's happening here. Either we could do this easily, or not."

"You little…" Keeting spat. "Do you know who we are, woman? Do you know how much of your pitiful paycheck comes from us? Do you realize-?"

Cipre didn't hear him finish the sentence. In the next moment everyone's eyes went to the sky.

From her angle, she could see the shadow of what looked like a giant bird cast itself over everyone.

***

"YeeeeeaaaaaaHOOOOOOOOO!"

Dreden felt as if he were the one with wings as he watched Gerrika soar back to the top floor after leaping off the edge. He and Chanin let go of themselves, throwing their fists in the air in cheer at the sight of his flapping, as he settled into a steady glide and circled the top of the estate.

The aveho flapped his wings a few more times before kicking his legs in the air. As Gerrika dipped to the left, returning to the top floor, suddenly any steady momentum he had in flight was no more.

"Waaaaaahh!"

Dreden gasped. "Oh shit."

He and Chanin dove out of the way as Gerrika came crashing against the floor. If the room hadn't already become a complete mess, the aveho's tumbling and crashing would have trashed the place from the desks to the bookcases.

When their flying friend was no longer skidding like a stone on the floor, they rushed over to him. Wings and loose feathers littered the floor around him.

"Are you okay?" Chanin bent over, unable to hide her amusement. "If it makes you feel any better, you made some incredible airtime."

"Nnnngg." Gerrika grunted. Chanin put her hand out for him, helping him up. "Landing is a lot harder than taking off."

"How long do you think you can keep the flying up?" Dreden asked. "You think you can make it to the city?"

"I do, but there's only one way to know for sure, right? What are you guys going to do?"

He and Chanin looked at each other. "I think we need to get the book." she said. "Even if what they're trying to do could work, everyone is a lot safer with that thing far away and out of these monsters' hands."

"There are fifteen floors to this place." Dreden remembered. "I think trying to find it will take as long as it'll take you to deal with the dragon."

Gerrika let out a breath, shaking himself loose again. "Alright. Hope everyone realizes I'm on their side. Last thing I need is to get blown out of the sky right away." He winked, giving the humans a thumbs up. "Godspeed."

He dashed into a sprint, leveling his wings like the arms of a dashing penguin. Even his black tail sticking out of his pants seemed to flap on its own.

The two humans had to grab onto each other again as they watched their friend take a small dip in the air before flapping into the sky, slowly becoming a dot, indistinguishable from any other bird in the air.

"I hope he can do it." Chanin tugged on Dreden's arm.

"For not having wings for a hundred years, I have hope for his species." Dreden replied.

The room around them was silent. There was no doubt that the Edlands and their group were still in the estate somewhere. It was hard to hear, but it sounded like there was some commotion going on outside the building. The loudest sound was the ringing of emergency bells as police carriages rushed to the estate.

Their weapons were still on the floor. Neither of them knew much about guns, but there wasn't anything else to use. The downed, dead guards that they killed most likely had bullets left, so Dreden and Chanin helped themselves to those.

"How many shots you think we can get from these?" Dreden asked.

Chanin raised the weapon to her eyes, turning it around and looking for the magazine slot. "Guessing…five or six. We're just going to have to make them count, if needed."

"We're splitting up?"

That wasn't what she wanted. That much was clear as she tightened the weapon to her chest. "I think so. When one of us finds the book, let's meet back here."

Dreden smiled, raising his rifle to meet Chanin's. They clinked the barrels together like shot glasses. "See you later, Chanin."

***

"What the…" Loid covered his eyes with his hand, blocking the sun as he watched Gerrika soar way overhead, flapping faster as he approached the Brunswald skyline. "That bird… it was shot!"

Janely grabbed him by the collar like an angry parent. "You had him tied up! How did that bird escape?"

"I don't know! I don't…"

They knew they couldn't make too much of a scene. Dozens of police officers were paused, watching them. More than half of them had their guns in their hands.

"Get back in there." she ordered. "Get to work on the man, at least. Get him before we lose anyone else."

Cipre was confused. There were so many questions she wanted answered as Loid retreated out of the spotlight, leaving Janely and her husband with a handful of armed guards in the front to deal with the increasing number of officers.

Stepping back into the estate, Loid kicked the wall twice, his thinning, curly hair getting frizzy at the top.

He looked over to the guard holding her, wiping sweat from his brow. "If anyone tries to come in here, police or not, blow them away."

CHAPTER 17

"I'm afraid, Renny." Honja said. "I don't think I can go back home without my son."

The professor sympathized. As sad as their conversation made him, he knew he had to be the person the aveho thought he was: the person who knew what kind of thoughtful responses to say to any problem.

"I understand. Suffering an incredible loss can make even the most normal activities seem impossible." Renny sniffed, wishing he was free to wipe his eyes. "Maybe you shouldn't. I don't think that people ever truly get over losing someone. I think they just learn to ignore it, and it gets easier over time."

"Did it with you? Have you gotten over your wife?"

"No." Renny smiled bitterly, closing his eyes and turning his head away. "The worst part? I only knew her for three years. She died eighteen years ago. Six times as many years as she was in my life."

"You know what I think?" Honja asked, fixing himself up in his seat. The blood soaking through his bandage had come to a stop. "I think that we accept the deaths of everyone we know the moment they walk out the door for the night or when they leave for work or university. We don't tell it to ourselves, but we know there's a chance that that's the last time we'll ever see them."

The professor turned back to Honja. "Some people might say that it's healthy to already consider everything in our life gone, and everyone dead. If I have a book, I know I won't have it forever. I'll lose it, it'll get stolen, thrown away, burned or anything that proves that its presence in my life is impermanent. When the day finally comes that it's gone, I can just nod my head and say, 'Of course'."

A rushing came from the stairway. They were loud, but just one set of feet. He had only heard the man rush once before, but Renny knew who it was.

Loid entered the room, out of breath. With the way he was looking at Honja, it was as if the aveho were the only thing left in existence.

"How did you do that?"

Honja threw his head forward, dully looking at the man. "How did I do what?"

"You were just outside! You were just flying in the sky!"

"I thought I was the one in pain here." the aveho replied. "Why are you the one talking nonsense?"

Honja's answer sated the man. Loid bent over, putting his hands on his knees as he tried to get his breath back. There was a table in the middle of the room, so he took a seat, fixing his hair and his coat.

"Can I have some water?" Honja asked, eyeing his bag in the far corner of the room.

Loid dried his palms against his thighs, having enough of his breath back to laugh at the aveho's request. "No, but I hope you don't mind if I do."

Taking note from where Honja's eyes were pointed, the large man got back to his feet and retrieved the bag from its corner. Loid plopped it on the table, digging through it as if he were a kid on his birthday.

"This is some impressive stuff." Loid showed Honja his teeth. "In another life, maybe I could have been an ornithologist."

"Get your hands out of there." Honja ordered. "You'll poke yourself with something then pop like a balloon."

Loid took out the canteen, opening it up but finding it empty. Renny remembered that he had finished all the water on the way to the estate.

"Empty." Loid tossed it away. "I'm sure you knew that. You wouldn't have asked for water if there wasn't any left."

"We've got a detective among us." Renny laughed.

The man burrowed further, shifting around the treasure of big and small weapons in the bag. A smile appeared on his face as he extracted a new bottle from the bag, the perspiration on his forehead adding to his glowing face.

"Here we are." Loid twisted the cap off the bottle.

Renny's mouth hung agape as he watched Loid take the cap off. He remembered the bottle from earlier. When they first arrived in the city, Honja had rushed out of the visitor's center to stop him from taking a sip from that bottle. He looked to the avian, who was watching Loid with the same dead expression.

Loid took several gulps from the bottle, wiping his mouth. "Interesting. Water tastes the same where you come from."

"What's more interesting to me," Honja said, sitting up, a new fire in him as he planted his boots on the floor. "is that a fat, weak, pig of a human can think he could beat me."

"You're forgetting the most important detail." Loid smirked, tapping the side of his head. "You are *not* smarter than me."

"Maybe, maybe not, but I'm not the one that just poisoned myself."

Renny saw it. Loid was going to reply, but he couldn't. Eyes wide, as if he were being squeezed like a doll, his hand flew to his throat and he fell on his knees.

Honja lifted himself up, standing on his two feet as his hands were still locked around the back. "Untie me. Untie me and my friend and I will give you the antidote."

In his choking fit, Loid managed to throw himself over to Honja, his head high and his neck straight up as he tried everything he could for air. With a blade from the aveho's bag, he cut the ropes behind him, rushing over and doing the same to Renny.

Now the two of them were free.

Honja rushed over to his bag and grabbed a smaller bottle from inside. Renny couldn't believe that the aveho was honoring his word, but he didn't want to say anything. It was clear that the human was not the one in charge of the scene.

Loid downed the dose of the antidote in a second. As the aveho took the bottle away, the large man let out a heavy breath, as if he were trying get a whole rabbit out of his throat. He dropped to his hands and knees; his fingers splayed on the ground until he had recovered his normal breathing.

The aveho didn't let him have the moment for too long. Honja grabbed Loid by the collar and shoved him against the ground. He easily grabbed the blade out of Loid's sweating hand, and now held it against the man's throat.

"Now," Honja lowered his face to Loid's, his beak right up against the human's nose. "you're going to tell me what's going on. Make it fast."

***

Gerrika could already see the carnage. He was still miles from the center of the destruction, but smoke was pouring out of the tallest buildings, and the screams of people and the rushing of carriages could not be ignored.

The smell of fire hit him in the next minute. If he weren't so high above the city, he wouldn't have been able to see everything so clearly. It made the aveho feel a knot in his throat, but he knew he couldn't lose focus. If he wobbled too much, he would have to force himself back up before he hit the ground, and he wasn't confident enough yet in his ability not to panic from falling.

Okay, he thought. *What am I going to do?*

He could feel people watching him as he passed over into the downtown area. As hard as it was, he fought his urge to wave to them. If he had, he would have gone spinning like a top in the sky. Part of him envied those watching him. Where they were, they were safe from destruction, and they didn't have any power to help anyone, unlike him. Therefore, they didn't have his terrifying obligation. Besides, Gerrika wanted to know what he looked like from the ground.

As he crossed over the city, seeing how quickly the buildings disappeared under him, he was reminded of his speed. He had built himself into a steady velocity, going stretches without flapping and just gliding under the clouds. He didn't know how to land yet, and he didn't really know how to slow down either, which was a problem when he was only getting faster.

When Gerrika saw Minkompa, he almost stopped dead in the sky. The dragon didn't look anything like it had when it had broken through the Edland Estate. A blackness was being washed over its body, and where the black became stained, new creature was growing.

It was bigger, louder, and it looked like Minkompa was losing its struggle with the Unmaker. Losing its struggle with itself.

"That's ugly." He said to himself, the wind and his speed almost making his words imperceptible to himself. "Hang on! I don't know what to do, but I'm going to try to help you!"

If I can't, maybe I can at least distract him. I don't know how many people have died because of him, but maybe I can lessen the blows.

***

When is the chief going to be here? Cipre wondered, the guard's blade still against her neck. *Something needs to happen. Anything needs to happen.*

A couple more carriages had pulled up to the estate. Cipre couldn't tell who was currently in charge of all of them, but a few had formed in the center of the commotion, forming a circle with Keeting and Janely Edland. They had their weapons drawn, but were just talking with them, still in their heated arguments.

It didn't look like they were getting anywhere.

She yipped as the guard grabbed her, tucking her back against the wall. The sound of unidentified footsteps spooked the guard. He shoved himself into the corner, using her as a shield.

"Who's there?" the man called. "No one is supposed to come in that way!"

The footsteps stopped. For several long seconds, Cipre tried to suck in her throat to ease the pain of the blade against her neck. She wasn't sure if it was just her imagination, but she thought she felt the warmth of blood going down to her chest.

The sight of the young woman with a rifle didn't do anything to ease the guard.

"You!" he screamed, loud enough to turn some heads that were outside. "How…you were shot! You and the others are dead!"

"We were." Chanin answered. "Not anymore. Interesting story about magic and makers."

For a moment, no one said anything. Cipre was trying to do all the communicating with the bulging of her pupils.

"Are you okay?" she asked Cipre.

Remembering their situation, the guard returned his force to Cipre. "Put the gun down, girl. Put it down or she's going to bleed some more."

Cipre knew what the guard was doing. With now just one arm around her neck, squeezing as tight as he could, he was going to use his free hand to get his pistol. Chanin was just standing at the doorway, unable to have any less cover.

She tried to tell Chanin, but the man's arm was too tight against her throat. She had to do something different.

Cipre remembered what Chanin had done on the top floor to escape a guard's grip, before she and Dreden died.

She relaxed herself. The shift in her posture put the guard on instant alert. He drew his hand away from his gun to stop her. He bent his head forward, as he tightened his grip on her.

The back of Cipre's head made clean contact with his face.

The crack of his nose followed. She felt his other arm go over her shoulder. He was trying to fight the pain in his face while keeping a grip on her, but he couldn't do it. His hand flew to his wound, letting Cipre go.

Relaxing herself, slipping out of his arm, she spun around and delivered a punch to his stomach with her elbow. He reeled back, bending over, as his other hand went to his side.

Now that he wasn't using Cipre as a shield anymore, Chanin saw him reach for his gun. She raised her weapon quickly, leveling it to the man's chest before letting loose the blast.

***

"Shots fired!" Screamed one of the officers. "Shots fired!"

Any civility in the tension building outside ceased. The group of the Edlands and several others in their gang that were arguing with the lead officers immediately dispersed at the sound of the gunshot.

Dozens of officers dashed behind their carriages for cover, drawing their weapons as they prepared for the next shot to come.

No one could tell which side fired the second shot, but it caused the estate to be lit up like a holiday ornament.

***

Chanin and Cipre rushed down the hallway. They crouched down low as the thundering of bullets sounded from outside. Several rogue bullets peppered the windows and the doorway, burying themselves in the first-floor walls.

"Are you okay?" Chanin asked. "Your name is Cipre, right?"

She nodded, wiping a little trail of blood off her neck. "I should be asking you that! How are you alive? Is Dreden okay? And Gerrika?"

"They're fine. At least they were the last time I saw them. Gerrika has wings now. He took off to help your friend."

Cipre remembered the shadow of the giant bird being cast over the then peaceful crowd. "That is simply incredible. You will have to tell me all about that later."

"I hope we survive to be able to." Chanin said. "Dreden and I are looking for the book. I went low while he stayed high. Do you know where they put it?"

She gave herself a second to regain her breath, making sure they were out of harm's way of the outside firefight. "No. I'm sorry, I don't remember where they took the book. What do you plan on doing with it?"

"That's a problem for our future selves," she smiled. "but we hope, assuming everything the Edlands told us was true, to reverse everything Mick Jowns did in the past. We want to bring our home back, and to make sure nothing like this ever happens again, if possible. Whether that means destroying it, tearing pages, or even risking our lives to try to write in it, we're going to do it."

Cipre fought the urge to hug her. The young woman was incredible. She was selfless, brave, and already knew how to handle a gun. It was a humbling contrast to the person she had been over the last week.

"I should be ashamed of myself." Cipre said.

"There's nothing you could have done." Chanin replied. "You were completely helpless up there. Just like we were."

"That's not what I'm talking about." They ducked down for cover behind a toppled table, blocking themselves from the outside view. "I was almost a victim of the earthquake days ago, the first appearance of the Unmaker. I could have spent my time helping people. But no. I didn't. What did I do?" She shook her head with a critical smirk. "I encountered a fucking dragon, and it turns out it, Minkompa wasn't even real."

Chanin inhaled. "Well, I don't know you too well, but if there's something I've come to understand over the last few days, it's selfishness in the face of trauma. It can happen to the best of us. When we all finally get out of here, maybe I can tell you about the story of me and my friends."

"It would all be off-record, obviously," Cipre smiled. "no way I'd be comfortable making money off this."

"Deal." They shook each other's hand. "You have more power than you realize right now. I suspect your presence here will have great benefit to many people in Kroonsaed."

The two of them, leaping into action, found the stairway entrance on the far side of the hall. Now that Cipre was with Chanin, she knew she needed to find a weapon too.

Neither of them had seen a shadow watching them from the other side. Morell Edland, after hearing everything that they said, rushed up the opposite staircase.

CHAPTER 18

Dreden heard the shooting. He could tell that it was all coming from outside, so he knew he was probably safe as he slowly went down the stairs, passing by the twelfth floor.

He couldn't find anything on any of the floors in between the wrecked fifteenth and the eleventh. As big as the estate was, there wasn't as much area on the top half as the bottom half. Dreden was able to circle himself through a bunch of empty rooms, from a kitchen to a guest room and everything in between but couldn't find a place where the most powerful object in the universe would be stored.

The eleventh floor looked wider than the others. Hopping off the stairway, Dreden could spot entrances to at least ten rooms. The first one on the left looked like another bedroom. He knew it would probably be another bust, but he had to be sure.

Stepping into the room, he immediately drew his gun at the figure sitting on the bed.

"It's true." Morell said, with an expression like a hungry hawk. "It's really fucking true. You're all alive."

"Yes, we are." Seeing that Morell didn't have a weapon, he lowered his rifle.

"How did you do it? I really want to know."

"I don't think a man like you would believe it."

Morell put his hands together on his lap. "I'm happy. I'm glad that the three of you aren't dead. I meant what I said earlier. I didn't know that my parents were going to throw Gerrika out the window."

"You led us to our deaths." Dreden replied. "And *I* meant what *I* said earlier, when we were in jail. We're done, so I don't know what you're hoping to accomplish right now."

"This was my childhood bedroom." Morell ignored him, looking around at the walls. "My parents' bedroom is on the second floor. How's that for delightful childhood memories? If I ever needed them and tried to yell, they would never hear me. I imagine it wasn't like that for you, was it?"

"Never have I slept more than a room's length from my father." Dreden said. "If you want pity, you're not going to get it from me. Not now."

Morell sighed, looking down disappointedly at the floor to his left. "Hmmm. I didn't think so. Anyway," He reached behind his back, pulling a large book off the comforter behind him. "you're looking for this, aren't you?"

Dreden raised his rifle back to the sitting Morell. *The Century* was in his hands. "Give it to me."

"Cut the act, Dreden, I know that you're not going to shoot me."

"I could. I killed two people when I went out in that blaze of glory. That was something I never thought I would do."

"Fair, but I'm not just a nameless gunman to you, sweetheart." Morell opened the book, leafing around to random pages. "My parents wanted you to write in this, but they don't know anything about magic. No one does. Maybe something interesting will happen if I start tearing out pages."

"Don't!" Dreden tightened his finger on the trigger.

He watched Morell's fingers slip through several pages, not even watching what he was doing. He was just watching for Dreden's reaction.

"Who knows what could happen?" Morell smiled. "Maybe Kroonsaed would be stuck forever. Maybe all Jowns's work would be undone, maybe the Unmaker would grow more powerful, maybe absolutely nothing at all would happen. Neither of us knows what would happen, but I'm willing to bet you're less eager to know for sure than I am."

"Don't be an idiot." Dreden spat. "Take your hands off it."

"Put the gun down. Let's talk like civilized people."

He didn't know what else to do. He was right. There was no way he was going to shoot him. Pretending that the possibility existed would make Morell keep his fingers on the pages, increasing the chances of him doing damage.

Dreden lowered the rifle, dropping it to the ground.

"There we go." Morell rose from the bed, the book still in his hands. "Dreden, you're a fool if you expect me to think that you're not conflicted about what you're doing."

"You mean about deciding which jail your parents will be spending the rest of their lives in?"

He snorted. "I don't think you want to do this. I haven't forgotten about those lovely days we spent with each other. I don't believe that you love your friends, at least not as much as you love how being with me made you feel."

"You're ridiculous. You're incapable of understanding how someone wouldn't want your life."

"Come on. I see it in you. What you wouldn't give to go back a few days, huh? Before you knew the truth about everything. Maybe if you could, you would stop your friends from finding out, so you could still be with me."

Morell raised the book up, causing Dreden to shrink away. Turning around, he dashed out of the bedroom, into one of the adjacent rooms. Morell was on the move, not wanting Dreden to get away from him.

"Because what's the alternative?" Dreden could hear enjoyment in his voice as he raised it, looking around for him. "That you couldn't make it with me? You couldn't make it in real society? You couldn't even emulate the best in Brunswald, the culture capital of the world. And now, since you couldn't make it, you have to ruin it for everyone!"

"Morell?"

"Yeah?"

"Shut the fuck up."

Dreden dashed through the small library on the corner of the floor. Dropping his weapon was a bad idea. Now Morell had the upper hand. He didn't believe he would try to do anything with the book without having Dreden's face to watch, so he looked around for him, seeing if there was any way he could get his gun back without Morell anticipating it.

"You're just stalling." he laughed. "You know, the longer you hide, the more likely it becomes that one of your friends has died. You need to hurry up and make a move, Dreden. You need to decide who you're going to choose, because even if you fail, I believe part of it will be because you wanted to fail."

Dreden paused behind a table in the library as he listened for Morell's movements. He might have sensed what he was trying to do, because Dreden couldn't hear anything.

He looked around the corner, as he heard a light creak coming from the ground just behind the door.

Dreden's blood went cold as someone tapped him on the shoulder.

Spinning around, his hand in a fist preparing to strike, he recognized the face behind him. It was the short, baby-faced young man who had raised his hand up to the dragon on the top floor. It was the man the Edlands had called 'Mister Bair'.

The Unmaker smiled down at Dreden.

"That Morell is a hell of a charmer, isn't he?"

The Unmaker raised a finger and held it above Dreden's head.

"Let's talk."

Its finger made contact with Dreden's forehead, and his vision left him.

***

Gerrika crashed several times. As much as it hurt, there was no way he could have avoided it. From needing to slow down, to having to help people on the ground, he knew he needed to be more useful than just being some pretty thing flying in the sky.

Amidst a flurry of dragon fire, he tried landing on the street. His attempt resulted in being a painful victim of a series of summersaults.

"OW!" He groaned as he picked himself back up, after ending up leaning against a broken bakery, upside down.

Minkompa was just around the corner. He had swooped down low to survey the street and couldn't find anyone there. On his street, next to the destroyed bakery, there was an overturned carriage. He could hear people shuffling inside and screaming for help.

There was no one else around. If he didn't help them, no one would.

Crashing into the abandoned bakery was the fourth time he'd crashed. His elbows felt like they were on fire, and he had lost skin on his soles from awful attempts at landing, but he was still too high on his wings and peril to be inhibited.

Leaping onto the carriage, he pulled the door open with ease. Of the benefits of his new body, Gerrika was continually impressed with how much strength his wings had given him.

There was a family of three trapped inside, and the driver looked like he was unconscious. It would be a challenge, but he wasn't about to give himself a moment to calculate the odds of survival.

"Are you people alright?" he asked.

The two adults looked up at him. Their child even stopped crying.

"I don't think so." The mother said. She grabbed onto her daughter and her husband. The man winced as she tried to take his hand. "We were thrown through the air. It's a miracle our daughter didn't break anything."

"Can you stand? Can either of you stand?"

The looks on their faces told him no, but since someone had come to save them, they wanted to make another effort. The man couldn't even get off his side, and his leg was bending a way it definitely shouldn't have been. The woman didn't look a lot better.

"Take Enzie first. Please take our daughter."

The aveho bent himself over, ignoring the sound of the approaching dragon as he shoved himself into the carriage enough to get his hands under their daughter's arms. She couldn't have been more than three years old. Gerrika intentionally didn't look at her eyes, not wanting her frightened look to be something that he would remember forever.

But he had to. When he did, he saw that she wasn't scared. Her little eyes were wide, as if wanting to swallow everything around them, even the sights of destruction. Gerrika couldn't imagine what was swimming through her head as he raised her out of the carriage. There was a time in his life, a time he couldn't remember, where he saw a human for the first time. He didn't know if he had been scared or impressed, but he knew that he was the first aveho Enzie had ever seen. In the future, she might not remember it, but *he* would remember.

She wasn't afraid, and that made him forget his pain for a second.

"Thank you, mister." she said to him, as if he had just given her a cookie.

The aveho put her down on the ground, unable to stop smiling. "Thank you, Enzie."

Her parents were a lot harder to help. They both had broken legs, so he had to be more careful. Even with his added strength, he didn't trust himself to get them out without hurting them.

He tried grabbing ahold of the carriage's rear wheel. With enough force, he was able to make it right-side up again. The wheels still looked like they were strong, and with his weight it was a slow process to get it back up. It was the most painless thing he could think about doing to help, and it worked.

The driver was okay. It took a few shoves and a short explanation about what was going on, but the man didn't seem to be in bad physical pain or have a concussion. After their discussion, the man agreed that he would pull the carriage to safety, since he was the strongest and most able-bodied of them all.

Opening the door, Gerrika raised Enzie up, tucking her snug in the back seat next to her mother. Considering the state of the city, it would probably be a while before the two of them could get medical help, but the aveho let himself feel good about what he had done in the meantime.

"There is no way we can repay you." said Enzie's father.

"There is." Gerrika told them. "Be good to each other."

He left them with a smile before closing the door. He slapped the rump of the carriage, letting the driver know that they were ready to go.

"Where are you taking them?"

"I've driven through this area many times." replied the driver. "I know where the nearest hospital is."

"Good luck. Be safe."

He watched for a minute as the man dashed down the street, with easily less than half the strength of a single horse. It wasn't going very quickly, but with the heat of fire and the stomping of the monster behind him, every second was precious.

"Okay, Minkompa," Gerrika said, panting to get his energy back. "please go easy on me."

Leaping off the ground and taking to the air again, he could see that the struggle between the dragon and the Unmaker was still going the same. The blackness that had taken over Minkompa's body had halted around his chest, while his eyes flickered from a light blue to black like a flame in the wind.

All around the block were tipped-over military vehicles and abandoned state carriages. Gerrika hoped that didn't mean they had given up on fighting the beast. Hopefully it was just a retreat or that they were waiting for reinforcements. Otherwise, that meant the aveho was flying solo.

The giant beast had already wrecked the street. Half of the buildings were on fire. The redness of the dragon's scales molded perfectly with the background; with the black traces of the thing he was fighting along the right side of his body giving a proper burnt appearance.

"Are you there, buddy?" Gerrika asked sheepishly.

Minkompa's only response was looking him straight in the eyes and opening his maw wide enough for the aveho to see down his throat.

"Oh no."

He got out of the way just in time. A rushing of flames barely missed the feathers on his legs. Taking back to the sky, Gerrika wobbled with his wings in the air, flapping around like someone trying not to slip on a wet floor. He used all his strength not to fall back into the inferno below him.

Kicking against the crumbling building's wall behind him, he leaped higher into the air.

"I guess you're not in control now. If it makes you feel any better, it looks as if you're showing a lot of restraint."

His compliment didn't do anything to sate Minkompa. The dragon reared himself up on his back legs, looking at the soaring aveho as if he were an annoying fly.

The dragon snapped his teeth at him. Gerrika didn't have time to scream, but he had the reflexes to swoop down in time, missing being chomped in half while feeling the beast's hot breath on his wings.

Taking another look at Minkompa, Gerrika could only find one vulnerable spot. His eyes. They were being lit up with the struggle between the two beings.

Then a new noise began to come from all around him. The sound of gunshots littered the air.

The military, Gerrika realized. *It's about time. I can't do this by myself.*

The aveho could hear the bullets pounding against the dragon's skin. It didn't look as if anything was happening, and any bullet that hit the blackness on his body didn't seem to recoil off. They just seemed to *become* part of the Unmaker.

For all he knew, he would end up getting shot out of the air, either intentionally or accidentally, so he had to act fast. Gerrika swooped low, picking up a downed, broken streetlamp with his feet. It was broken from the middle, and on the bottom side it looked to be sharp enough to pierce through the toughest leather.

Gerrika transferred the large beam to his hands as he dove for the dragon's eye.

***

"What do we do? What do we do!"

Allin shouted to his wife as they both got low at the wheels of their motor-carriage. They had gotten to the border of the estate just as the parade of bullets had commenced.

"How should I know?" Sidra asked, covering her head in her hands. "I've never been in a shootout before!"

Chief Milbrey, using the front of the carriage for cover, bolted upright and shot at the guards in front of the building. "Don't worry. Once you've been in a few it gets easier."

"I don't want to get comfortable with this." Allin replied. "I think we're going to need something to help us."

Milbrey ducked back down behind the vehicle, digging into his pocket to reload. "Got one! The jackass didn't see it coming. That's what you get for firing on my men and women!"

"I *really* don't think we should be using the motor-carriage for cover." Sidra said, after another bullet pounded into the front of the vehicle. "The damn thing could explode at any second."

The Chief paused, taking his hand out of his coat, smiling like a manic toddler. "You just gave me a wonderful idea."

CHAPTER 19

Everything was black. Dreden found himself alone in a darkness that seemed to go on forever. It reminded him a lot of the Realm of the Unmade.

Did I die again? he asked himself. *Is the Maker here?*

It was just as silent and empty. The only thing he could hear was the sound of his breathing, which sounded more like thunder in the nothingness.

"Feeling okay, Dreden?"

The voice sounded like it was coming from everywhere. He recognized it. It was lifeless but commanding, without a shred of compassion.

"Wouldn't you know? You're the one that did this to me, Unmaker."

"That's true, but I just want to get you in a good mind before we begin."

Dreden turned around. There was still no sight of anything or anyone else around.

"Where am I?" he asked.

"You're in my head. You're inside me."

"It's quite empty in here. I thought with someone as seemingly smart as you there would at least be a desk and maybe a bookshelf."

The Unmaker's voice sounded like it would have tossed its head back in laughter. "Funny. I was going to say something similar about you. You're a bright man, Dreden. I know that you've been wondering the big question about me: Why? Why am I doing this? Why have I killed thousands of people and why do I seem like I just can't stop? Do you know the answer?"

Dreden paused, not loving being in a position where someone was baiting him to talk. "I don't. Shouldn't you know that? Are you not 'Everything That Isn't'?"

"Let me ask you something," the Unmaker's shape began to manifest in front of him. It moved like a dark cloud, turning into a human-looking form. As it grew into its features, from the tip of its boots to the hair on top of its head, Dreden recognized the Unmaker's new image.

Dreden was looking back at himself.

"Am I supposed to be impressed?"

"Do you not see it?" the Unmaker asked.

"What am I supposed to see?"

"I can't actually become you. I can't take the form of anything real." the other Dreden blinked. "Tell me, what's different about me? What's not the same as you?"

Dreden approached his other self. He circled him, while the Unmaker stood watching him with an eager smile on his face. He had seen himself in mirrors and reflections countless times in his life, but he hadn't seen himself as much as Gerrika, Chanin, and his own father had seen him every day since they met. One of them would be more likely to notice what was off about the Unmaker than him.

"Have you done this to many people? How often do they get the answer right?"

"They never do."

"And you think, for some reason, I'll be different?"

"I'm *hoping* that you'll be different." the other Dreden put his hands on his hips. "Maybe this was too hard. I think I need to start you off with something easier. I know what to do!"

With a wave of its hand, the Unmaker created a crowd around them. Looking at the formation of people around him, it only took him a second to realize that everyone in the crowd was only two people.

Clones of Chanin and Gerrika surrounded them, spreading out into infinity.

"If you don't know yourself," the Unmaker smiled. "let's see if you know your friends. Your challenge, Dreden: find which one is the real one here, or even better, which one *isn't* real."

The silence of the area, previously only interrupted by Dreden and the Unmaker's dialogue, became extinct when all of the figures of Chanin and Gerrika erupted into immeasurable conversations. It was impossible for Dreden to hear all of them, and the sound itself was enough to make him raise his hands to his ears. It didn't help. The look on his other self's face showed that he was going to make sure he heard as much as possible.

"Why does he talk like that?" one of the Gerrikas said. "I mean, he knows we don't really care right? I've never read anything he likes to talk about. I think he's just doing it to hear himself talk."

One of the Chanins on his right said: "He's unhappy. Everyone knows he is. He was raised by Renfield Sharpstand, how else would he turn out? He turns to philosophy for consolation. Don't you see the problem with that?"

A Gerrika laughed. "Because so much of the philosophy he reads is depressing!"

"And the way he talks about it." Another Chanin continued. "The way he tries to make us have an interest in it. What would that solve? You know how he sometimes says that he doesn't believe a happy philosopher ever existed? Yet he tries to tell it all to us. Why would he want the two of us to be as miserable as he is? Doesn't he see that we'd be happy if we didn't have to hear any of that?"

"If it's going to make us unhappy," Gerrika laughed. "why the hell would he tell it to us?"

A new figure appeared in front of him, in between all the Gerrikas and Chanins around him. It was his father; he knew that much. Easily fifteen years younger than he was now. He was seated at a desk, a glass in his hand and two empty bottles of whisky next to him.

The illusion of his father raised a glass, downing the rest of the alcohol.

"Dreden!" His father shouted. "Dreden, come back! Your mother left me with you. That wasn't very fair, was it?" He grabbed one of the empty bottles and chucked it away. The sound of a shattering glass bottle came from nowhere and everywhere. "Because of her, you're all I have! Come back!"

"This is what you did, Dreden." The Unmaker said, coming out of the illusions. "You left your father alone, all by himself. Sure, you've mostly had fun here, but what do you think poor Renfield has been dealing with? You can argue that you should just go out and live your life, since you're young and it is indeed *your* life, but no one's life is ever just their own. It belongs to everyone they know. It's an awful condemnation, but it's true."

"Alright, I get it." Dreden growled.

"I don't think you do. This isn't really just an illusion. Do you really think that this wouldn't happen because of your selfishness?"

Dreden looked back to his father. He had thrown another glass against the wall and was gripping a piece of broken glass so tightly that blood was pouring out between his fingers.

"That's not my father." Dreden said. "His birthmark on his wrist is supposed to be on his other arm. He has brown eyes, not green."

The other Dreden shook his head. "That's not the point here. Tell me, which conversation between Gerrika and Chanin was real? Which one actually happened?"

"I think none of them happened." He tried not to show any fear, or any of the building sadness that was causing his head to get heavy, but no doubt the Unmaker could see it all. "I don't think you're capable of showing anything real. You said as much, didn't you? I think you're lying to me."

"Maybe," the Unmaker instantly grew several feet into the air. Now Dreden was looking up to his other self. "but that's just what you're supposed to be. The filthy, unpleasant animals that you all are. You're supposed to feel sad, excited, fear, happy, pain, and you're eventually supposed to die. But what about me? It's not fair that I'm sentient. I shouldn't be! Earthquakes aren't, tornados aren't, why am I, a force of nature, the only one condemned to awareness, and even worse, why do I feel emotion? Do you see it now, Dreden? Do you know what I want more than anything in the world?"

"I think I do." Dreden replied. "You want to die, don't you?"

***

Loid had spilled everything that he had to spill. If there was anything he was leaving out, Renny wouldn't have wanted to imagine how outrageous it was.

"I swear to you," A new layer of sweat had formed on his brow, amplified by Honja's intense glare. "I'm telling you the truth. It's completely true."

"The man who led us here," Honja said. "you're saying that he's the one that trapped us?"

"Basically! Though that wasn't actually him. It was magic. It was just his spell going to work."

Over everything else, the professor was surprised at how quickly Honja accepted the man's story. Though the aveho certainly didn't seem new to using fear to get what he wanted. He could probably tell when someone wasn't telling the truth.

"And you thought that my son would be able to help you? To continue the evil that you've done?"

Loid looked like he knew better than to answer the question, but his nervousness told the whole story.

"What about my son?" Renny asked. "And Chanin? Were they part of it? Where are they?"

He saw it. He saw the way Loid blinked. There was something that the man wasn't going to tell them.

"I'm sorry," Loid shook his head. "I don't know. I've never seen them before in my life. Now, before the two of you start making any more trouble, I suggest-"

A quick wet sound of metal burying into flesh came from below, and the man's eyes went wide. Soft gurgling came from his throat as blood quickly began to pour out of his mouth.

Renny looked down. There were already five different entry wounds from Honja's blade, and the aveho didn't look like he was going to stop at seven or eight.

The professor had to back up. Blood was pouring out over every inch of his body. A pool filled under the large man, getting on Honja's boots and his pants, but he didn't look like he cared at all.

The gurgling came to a stop as Loid stretched himself out with his head against the floor, already having taken his last breath.

Getting back up on his feet, Honja wiped his blade against the parts of Loid's clothes that weren't completely drenched red. He raised it to his beak, licking the rest of the blade clean before putting it back into his bag.

The aveho saw the look on the human's face. "*That*, Renny, is me angry."

"You played that man like a violin."

"My years of hunting have taught me that all creatures are most vulnerable when they believe they have the upper hand." Honja threw his bag over his shoulder, as if completely forgetting the wound that was still fresh on his stomach. "Now, let's go find your son and his friend."

"We don't even know that they're here, Honja." Renny replied. "You saw the look in his eyes just like I did. I'm terrified... I don't think I'm going to want to know the truth."

Acknowledging the professor's anxiety with a nod, the aveho walked over to the stairway. Renny followed. "Let's check upstairs. Sounds like there's a war happening outside, so it looks like we're stuck in here."

***

When Morell found Dreden on his knees in the library, he didn't know what to do.

Walking out in front of him, he could see that his eyes were completely white, no trace of colored irises. After checking for breathing and a pulse, it looked like everything was fine with him. And he wasn't alone. One of his parents' guards, Bair, was on the floor in the same position as Dreden. Morell remembered that that wasn't really who the man was.

The Unmaker? Morell wondered.

He knew nothing about magic, but it looked like the Unmaker had him locked in some kind of trance. That couldn't be anything good. From what he witnessed earlier and what his parents told him, the Unmaker and his parents were deeply at odds.

If Dreden and the Unmaker had the same end goals, then it was his job to sever their contact.

Morell hesitated. He had told the truth about being happy Dreden was still alive. He didn't want to hurt him, but he wanted to preserve his family and their status more than anything else.

He turned around, picking up one of the metal stools under the nearest table. He raised it above his head, leveling himself in front of his foe.

"I'm sorry about this, Dreden."

Eyes closed, he swung the stool down.

It never touched Dreden's head. Before he could finish the blow, a bright beam of light shot out of the Unmaker's eyes, hitting Morell square in the chest. He stumbled back; hands raised to try to grab onto anything as he fell onto the ground.

As he lay there, looking at the two people stuck in their trance, a tingling overtook his body. Morell raised his arms up.

All the hair was falling off his body.

All over him, his skin was changing color. A dark brown was being washed up and down his body, smoothly erasing the former paleness. It was painless, but his face felt like it was being tugged from his nose. It began to grow longer and longer, until his new eyes could see that a sharp beak had formed where his lips used to be.

CHAPTER 20

"What was that?" Dreden asked.

The Unmaker reappeared, smiling to the back of his head. "Just taking care of a little distraction. Needless to say, Morell isn't going to be a problem for us anymore." The other Dreden returned to his size, almost hovering over him. "You're right. I want to die. Nothing would make me happier than ceasing to exist."

"You can't kill yourself?"

"I've tried. Many times! It is not something I have the ability to do. When I was created, I was condemned to live out my purpose before offing myself. Something must happen first, in order for me to be able to do it nice and proper."

"And you think I can help you?" Dreden took a breath, still shaken from everything the Unmaker had shown him. "You're trying to get me to kill myself."

"*Very* good!" The other Dreden clapped.

"How would that help you?"

"Because, Jowns let the three of you here for a reason. His spell clearly believes that it's the three of you that have the power to defeat me. I want to use that in the only way I know how to accomplish things. Death."

"Sorry to ruin it for you," Dreden had to smile. "but telling me your plan is going to make it harder to get me to do it."

"You would think that, wouldn't you?" the other Dreden cackled. "But this is magic we're dealing with. You can't just philosophize and outsmart your way out of it. Magic isn't about that. Jowns realized that, and that's what he hated about it so much. He wrote that the physically weak could use it to overpower those stronger than them. It's true. Because magic isn't about strength or intelligence, Dreden, it is a *feeling*. When I have broken every last one of yours, it will be over."

"And that's why you've killed so many people? Does murdering thousands help yourself be okay with your own death?"

"Who do you think you're talking to?" The Unmaker frowned, his lips almost going down to his chest. Dreden had to recoil at the sight. "I *enjoy* taking lives, but it's not my fault, right? It took me many many years to form into what I am now, evolving to my full potential, and a love of killing just came with it. It's just how I was made. No no no no, I'm going to put my pleasure to good use. That's why I want you to kill yourself, even though I also want you to win. You all must die before you win. I want to kill you all. All humans, all avehos, and everything that has any kind of evolutionary potential to one day gain the ability to use magic, because I don't just want to die, I want to make sure that there is no chance that I can *ever* come back and be alive again."

Dreden fell on his back at the Unmaker's raising tone. He had forgotten where he was. Inside the Unmaker. It definitely had complete control over everything around them.

"What's stopping you?" he asked. "What's stopping you from ending everything? From ending all threatening life? What's stopping you from killing me?"

"The Maker." It gave a sound like a snort. "That weak buffoon is serving its purpose well. I'm only so strong with it in existence."

"And *me* too."

It was a new voice. Dreden looked around, but the only thing in sight was still his doppelganger.

"Shut up!"

"Is that Dreden there? I must say, I am quite impressed with the way your bird friend is handling himself."

On hearing the voice a second time, Dreden remembered its owner. "Minkompa?"

"Mmhmm, I'm getting the best of you, aren't I, Unmaker?"

The Unmaker turned around, throwing a fist into the air in rage. "I told you to shut up!"

"Dreden," the dragon's voice continued. "Gerrika is doing excellent. He just stabbed me through the eye. Did you feel that?"

"You know that I did!" His doppelganger looked like it was struggling not to pull its own fake hair out. "You don't have to tell me what I already know. We are the same body, after all!"

A silence followed. Dreden could hear the hesitation in the beast's pause. "Dreden, I don't know if I'll make it, after this is over. I most assuredly won't, but…when you see Cipre, can you give her a message for me?"

"I would love to."

"Tell her…tell her that I never had a friend. Tell her that I only knew her for a very short time, but that it was my friendship with her that helped me understand who I am. Who I really am. I'm no longer part of this monster, I had memories, a personality, and a life, and in the end, I think it is her that is giving me the strength to beat this thing. I'm forever glad I got to show someone my real self."

"Then how about I kill her first?" The Unmaker bellowed.

"I will!" Dreden called. Minkompa's voice had started to fade during his speech. He feared that the connection was being lost, so he knew he had to rush his words. "I will tell her! I promise!"

"You'll never get to." His other self put its fists together, closing its eyes tight. "If I have to do this the quick way, then that's how I'll have to do it."

A crippling pain out of nowhere enveloped Dreden, starting from his head all the way down to his toes. He wasn't on fire, and he didn't feel like he was being crushed. It was like he was feeling every bit of pain, anger, and sadness he had ever felt all in one go. His throat became heavy from the pressure, making it hard for him to speak.

"This shouldn't take long," the other Dreden laughed. "and you know it too, don't you? Out of you, Chanin, and Gerrika, you know that it's *you* that would take the least convincing to kill yourself, don't you?"

In the whirl of pain keeping him on the unseen ground, his thoughts went to everything and everyone he had ever seen. He remembered Winds Wilk. He remembered what became of him, and how he was the first Saedian to enter the real world again.

"He was a funny story," said the Unmaker, as if reading his mind. "*I* was actually the one that let Winds through the Sea. He was so sad and pathetic, a lot like you right now. I guess you can say I have a soft spot for your kind."

"No…" Dreden said, tightening his teeth through the pain. "you're lying. You have no power in Kroonsaed."

"Maybe you'll never really know. All you know is that he had the proper sense to kill himself, something you will have in another few moments."

***

Stabbing Minkompa through the eye didn't do a lot, but Gerrika could see the effects.

His concentration was bust. Granted, the presence of a giant dragon was not something to be happy with, considering the circumstances. A clumsy one would probably do a lot more damage.

The military saw what the aveho did and decided to follow suit. They concentrated all of their firing on his good and his damaged eye. They had to get very close to be accurate, and Gerrika was having a lot of fun swooping and soaring around, getting the dragon to spin like a dog chasing its tail. He didn't know how to tell if Minkompa was winning in his struggle with the Unmaker, but the fact that the beast had gone sluggish was definitely a good sign.

Seeing that the dragon had taken several more shots to the eye, Gerrika swooped down to the line of soldiers that had lined the corner of the streets. He tried his best for a soft landing to impress them, but he just ended up falling down on his elbows again.

"Are you alright?"

One of the men, a young man, probably not much older than himself, extended his arm to the aveho.

"You know what?" Gerrika said. "Somehow, I think I am."

"I've seen you before." Came another one, a middle-aged gentleman. "I saw you perform at the Lesting Theater. Wow, wings really suit you."

If he could, Gerrika would have blushed. "It's a long story. I'm glad I could find some use for them, now that I have them."

"We heard you came from the Edland Estate." said a woman his age, after she fired more shots at the dragon. "Is that true?"

"It is. My friends are over there right now."

"I hope they have some weapons with them." the young man said. "I heard that place has become a bloodbath. Police and private guards are going in an all-out war."

"What!"

The older man lowered his weapon, giving the aveho soft eyes. "You've done enough here, son. You're battered like fried fish right now. Go back to where you're needed."

Gerrika knew he had to be off. If anything happened to Dreden and Chanin while he was gone, he didn't think he would have the strength to forgive himself.

"I hope to see you all again." he told them. "If everyone around here were as nice as you, I think this never would have happened."

He raised his talon to them in salute before leaping into the air, flying right past the dazed dragon as he furiously flapped his way back to the Edland Estate.

***

With most of the action downstairs, Honja was having an easy time with his arrows.

Going from room to room, Renny and Honja found several people positioned against the windows, shooting at the police from above. None of them heard the aveho coming, and a quick arrow to their backs took care of them.

Some of them weren't even guards. There were a couple men in suits with rifles up on the seventh floor. Honja told him that he remembered seeing them. They were associates of the mousey man that Renny had punched in the face.

The two of them got arrows just like the guards.

"What if you run out of arrows?"

The aveho looked back to him, raising an eye. "You've seen what I can do with a blade."

"Fair enough."

Renny was getting antsy. The estate was massive. If Dreden was there, they still had a lot of ground to cover.

"Stay behind me!" Honja ordered. "I can't have you going off on your own. We need to stay together."

"I think the upstairs are vacant." Renny said. "I don't hear any shooting from up there. I think it's okay."

Renny moved to pass up Honja in the hallway, and that earned him the aveho's claws. They dug into his shoulder, tearing his shirt.

"Ow!"

"*Please*, Renny. I'm not losing you."

The noise of a pair of rushing feet from the stairway stopped them in the middle of the hallway. Honja had used more than half his arrows, but he still had enough to take out whatever new threat was coming up to their floor.

The aveho motioned in front of Renny, pulling his bow back and leveling it to the open doorway.

A young woman with a rifle entered the floor, with another woman coming in right behind her.

"Chanin!" Renny screamed.

"Mister *Sharpstand?*"

Honja lowered his weapon as Chanin dashed over to them, locking her arms around Dreden's father.

"What are you guys doing here?" She looked to Honja, noticing the bloodied bandages on his stomach. "Oh…are you okay?"

"I've suffered worse." he said. "I'm glad you're alive."

"Me too." One hug wasn't enough. Renny grabbed her another time, hugging her tight with the barrel of her rifle stabbing against his shoulder. "Where's Dreden?"

"He's here! We split up a few minutes ago. He should still be somewhere on the top floors."

The woman behind Chanin tucked her rifle under her arm and raised her hand awkwardly in a wave. "I'm Cipre. We don't have the time for me to explain how I'm connected to all this."

"A pleasure to meet you, I'm sure." Renny smiled. "Chanin… I can't imagine how you're feeling now. Losing someone close to you is a horribly painful thing, and you're too young to have to bear that burden already."

Chanin relaxed her weapon, blinking. "What are you talking about?"

"We found my son." Honja answered. "Looked like he was thrown off the top of the building. Tell me who did it."

"Oh…oh my…" Chanin shook her head with a small laugh. "No, wait! Gerrika is okay. He's alive."

"I assure you, girl," Honja crossed his arms, irritated. "that I know what I saw. I'm sorry you have to find out this way."

"AHHHHHHHHHHHHHHHH!"

A scream came from somewhere off in the distance, its volume dwarfing the gunshots that still went off on the ground below them. The sound grew louder and louder, until a very visible shape of a giant winged creature became discernible.

"What is that?" Honja said, instinctively readying his bow once more.

Chanin smiled, putting her hand on the aveho's arm. "That, sir, is your son."

Gerrika's screaming reached its peak as he busted through the window. Despite his speed and his awful landing, he only rolled a couple times on the ground before finding himself upright on his feet, though he looked dazed enough to not know where he even was.

Chanin rushed over to his aid. Honja just stood still, in awe of the debilitating sight of his still-breathing son.

"Are you okay?" she grabbed his hands, holding him upright.

Gerrika's knees were wobbly. Only Chanin's cradling arms kept him standing. "F…fine. You should have seen me. I saved at least hundreds of people."

"Gerrika," Chanin grabbed the side of his head, which was shaking up and down like a ringing bell as he panted for breath. "your father's here. Look."

"What? No. That's impossible. That must be the Unmaker."

Attracted by Gerrika's screaming, and the crashing that followed, several armed men stormed up the stairs. Four of them were guards, and two of them were part of the Edland gang. One of them had a bandage over his nose.

It was Skitt.

"They're alive!" he shouted at his men. "How is that possible? Can you people not do anything right?"

His people didn't have a chance to reply. Honja had already unleashed two arrows to their chests. The rest of them leveled their guns, but the aveho was faster. Dashing from the center of the hallway, the blade did the rest of the work. With slashes to their necks, the rest of the men went down. Their leader, Skitt, didn't put up a fight. He had opened his mouth, preparing to beg for his life as the blade buried itself in his neck.

"Never mind." Gerrika said. "That's definitely my father."

Once the action was over, and they could hear no one else coming up the stairs, Honja wiped the blade clean and walked over to his son.

Gerrika, still out of breath, bent himself over, dropping his wings. Renny could see that the young aveho wasn't used to the additional weight on his body. He wanted to rush over and wrap his arms around the aveho and lift him up over his shoulders at the joy of seeing him alive, but he knew that Honja and his son needed the moment.

"What happened to you, son?" he asked.

"This was done to me, father." Gerrika said shying away at his father's stare. "Do you know anything about the truth of this place?"

"A fat man told me everything before I killed him."

"It turns out that we're winged birds, father. Mickeel Jowns took our wings from us." Gerrika raised his wings again, looking at them left and right. "They don't feel that bad either. I think if I can buy som-"

The young aveho let out a yelp as his father grabbed him from under his wings, lifting him off his feet and tucking his head at his son's shoulder.

"I'm very happy to see you alive, Gerrika."

"Thank you. I'm glad to see you here, father, but I won't be breathing much longer unless you let go of me."

Honja eased his grip on his son, holding up for another second before letting his feet back on the ground. "I will never stand by and watch you do something so foolish again. At least, I'll never let you do it again without me."

Renny opened his arms for Gerrika as the winged bird approached him, now free of his father's embrace. "I guess the only thing my wings are better for than flying is giving hugs. How are you, Mister Sharpstand?"

"Wonderful, Gerrika."

He dabbed a tear from the corner of his eye as Gerrika wrapped his wings around his friend's father. Renny made sure not to hold him as tightly as Honja had.

"What's the situation now, Chanin?"

"There's still shooting downstairs. It sounds like it's slowed down a bit, but it's not over yet."

"Where's Dreden?" Gerrika asked.

"I think he's still upstairs."

"Let's find him!" Renny beamed. "We need to get him, and we need to get ourselves out of here."

*****

Dreden couldn't scream. He didn't have the energy to do it, and there was no chance that the Unmaker was going to let up any time soon.

"Why fight it, Dreden?" his other self asked. "So much pain, and for what? It can be over in a second if you just will it.'

He didn't look up. He wouldn't give the Unmaker the small satisfaction of acknowledging his words.

"Isn't life mostly suffering? Sure, you may be happy some of the time, but it doesn't last very long? You're just a naturally unhappy person, Dreden. For you, there is no happiness. There are just moments where you forget that you're unhappy, but they won't last. Don't you think the most utilitarian thing you can do is to cut your life short? Haven't you said something like this before, when you were talking philosophy that nobody asked for? Do as you say, Dreden."

***

"Slow down!" Gerrika called, as his party rushed up the stairway. "My feet are in a lot of pain."

Honja, Chanin and Cipre stopped for him, but Renny was in a dash and didn't want to stop for anyone.

He got to the eleventh floor. Honja and the others called for him, but he was too on the move. There was a bedroom to the left, and several rooms past it. A bathroom and a utility closet were the first things on the right. Their doors were open, and there was nothing interesting there.

The library was the next door on the right. He slipped between a series of small tables and a counter, knocking over a couple stools along the way.

There he was.

His son was on his knees, facing someone who Renny had never seen before.

The man's eyes weren't right. They were completely without color.

"Dreden!"

***

"Ugh…" The Unmaker threw his head around, grunting like a child. "*Another* distraction. You're going to love this one, Dreden. It's your father. He's found you."

"Stop!" Dreden raised himself up, barely holding himself with the skin of his knuckles. "Are you at all capable of telling the truth?"

"You should see him right now." laughed his doppelganger. "He looks so sad and pathetic. Honja has found his son, and now he's desperate. Desperate for the biggest thing in his life that gives himself purpose. The thing that ran away from him in pursuit of a pretty boy who never really gave a damn about him in the first place. Should I do to him what I did to Morell? I think he would look good as a bird, or maybe something else? Maybe killing him would break the last spark inside you."

Dreden wouldn't make a sound. The whirlwind of anger and sadness put in him by the Unmaker wouldn't stop. The only thing keeping him up was the thought that the Unmaker was lying, and that maybe everything inside himself was just another illusion by the magical being.

But he knew that wasn't true.

He was no stranger to pain. A part of Dreden feared that the day would come when he would grow numb to his emotional pain. But wouldn't that make him happier? Wasn't unfeeling better than feeling some of the time?

Not all the time. He loved his father. Loving something always meant accepting the inevitability it would hurt you. And of all the things he loved, his father had hurt him the least.

Dreden bit down so hard he could feel veins in his mouth pop.

"What the…" The Unmaker blinked, it tried to move its arms and its head around but couldn't do it. "How…how are you doing that?"

He shook his head. It didn't do much, but he needed every tiny break to get the best of the Unmaker.

"We're inside you, aren't we?" Dreden showed the thing some teeth. "If you were inside me, you would kick my brain around or try pulling my spinal cord, but you're not like me. I don't need to do any real fighting. I just need to feel. I need to remember how I felt at the times where you have no power over me. You're strengthened by what *can* be but are weakened by what *is*. If you can't fool me, then there is nothing you can do. You shouldn't have let me in here. I'm impressed you didn't know better than that."

Dreden planted a boot firmly on the non-ground, gaining strength. "This pain is an illusion. It's so familiar, so intimate, but not real. I'm *remembering*. I'm reminding myself what the real pain, real loneliness feels like. It's not always been easy, but every time, every fucking time I've ever felt like I couldn't be any sadder, I've survived. I'm reliving everything I've ever chosen to survive, and you know what? It feels a lot easier. Your fake pain can't beat real pain."

His doppelganger became frozen in place. Its movements grew static, as if it were moving so fast that reality couldn't even register it. At first he thought that he wasn't fighting hard enough, that the Unmaker was once again getting the best of him, but the pained expression locked on the thing's face told him another story.

"This isn't over." The Unmaker's form evaporated, leaving Dreden alone in the nothingness. "I'm not done. If I can't stop you, then I'll take a thousand more lives. You'll have to live with yourself, and we'll be reunited again one day in the nothingness. We're not done."

The blackness left him, and his vision came back.

The Unmaker was gone. There was no longer the form of Mister Bair kneeling in front of him.

"Dreden!"

He turned around, his mouth agape at the sight of his father.

Dreden looked at his father's wrist and his eyes. His eyes were brown, and his birthmark was back where it should be.

"You're real." Dreden said, getting back on his feet. "You're really here."

"I'm am already tired of doing this," his father hid his smile behind his hands. "but can we hug?"

"Absolutely."

Dreden wrapped his arms around his father. Suddenly he missed his home horribly.

CHAPTER 21

"We need to do it now!" Milbrey ordered. "Time is running out!"

"I know I know!" Allin replied. "I just…I need some time to say goodbye to it."

The shooting had become less frequent. The motor-carriage wasn't taking as many hits as it was a few minutes ago, but there was still a lot of shooting going on, and if they were lucky, they had what it took to bring it all to a halt.

Sidra took her head out of the engine, slamming the lid shut. "If you want my professional opinion, it looks like this thing is about to go off like a volcano."

Milbrey sprang out from behind the vehicle, unleashing several more shots into the estate before getting back to cover.

"Okay," he said. "I'm ready when you guys are."

Allin gave the hood of the carriage a couple affectionate pats. "Alright, friend. Now is your time. Go out and be free."

The three of them got behind the vehicle and put their hands on the back. From where they were, there was a long downhill trail to the front of the estate. If they positioned the motor-carriage at the right angle, the dip in the land would take it straight to the estate's front door.

"Ready?" Allin asked.

"Ready." His wife answered, a fire in her eyes that rivaled the engine's heat.

They lifted themselves to the tips of their toes, shoving as hard as they could. With the help of Chief Milbrey, they were able to get the front wheels rolling.

The back wheels began to move, slowly picking up speed from the downhill trajectory.

"Get out of the way!" Milbrey shouted to his officers. "Get out! Watch out for the carriage!"

***

After being reunited with his father, he was rushed back down to the others. Not before finding *The Century* sitting on the floor next to him. Whatever happened to Morell, he left it right there, unclaimed.

He was happy to see Chanin and Gerrika still in one piece, and even more surprised that Gerrika's father had come to get him. It turned out to be a pleasant surprise, as he was told what the aveho had been doing.

It sounded like they all owed their lives to Honja.

"What do we do with it?" Renny asked.

"I'm not sure." Dreden replied. "It's great that we have it, but not even the Edlands knew what to do with it. Jowns didn't include an instruction manual."

"Give it to me." Honja said.

Dreden didn't want to argue with him. He was armed and definitely high on the blood he had spilled, so he gave the massive book to Gerrika's father.

Honja took it and flipped through the pages. He wasn't sure what the aveho was looking for. If he remembered correctly, Honja couldn't read.

"This thing?" he snorted. "This is the thing that all those humans were fighting to have?"

"Apparently." Cipre replied. "I had been the one in possession of it for a few days. I didn't know what it really was. But now it makes so much sense. I guess magic can be an intriguing author. It told a strange history I never thought was real."

"I can't blame you." the aveho replied. "Just looks like any other book to me."

The group was heading down the stairway, passing the fifth and fourth floors as quickly as they could. The shooting outside had become less frequent, so if there was a time to make a run for it, it was now.

They all came to a stop as three voices began screaming from outside.

"What is that?" Chanin asked.

"GET OUT OF THE WAY!"

"OUR CARRIAGE IS GOING TO BLOW UP!"

Chanin and Gerrika looked at each other. They realized who two of the voices belonged to.

"Allin and Sidra?" they asked each other.

"How did-?" Chanin thought. "How would they even-?"

She didn't get to finish her train of thought. A massive bang sounded from below that rocked the estate to its foundation. As they paused on the stairs, it felt as if a giant were pulling the rug out from under their feet.

Everyone's hands went to the railings. Gerrika and Dreden couldn't grab onto it in time, so the two of them took a fall down a couple of stairs. When it was over, the whole building still vibrated, as if every molecule in every wall was fighting to get out.

"Ugh..." Gerrika rubbed his injured side as he helped Dreden back up to his feet. "Something definitely just blew up."

Continuing down the stairs, the smell of smoke became obvious. After they passed down the third floor, the entire stairway was clouded in a haze. They all had to cover their mouths and hold their breaths, as the walls and the metal railings to their sides began to get hotter.

The front of the estate was completely engulfed in flames. As they got down to the first floor, they knew there was no way they would be able to exit the same way they came. They went back around the main hallway and elevators, finding their way to the back half of the bottom of the estate before ending up in the back yard, where there was a lot less smoke and destruction.

Honja, bow drawn, let himself out first as the leader of the group.

They only took a few steps outside before a blast from a rifle stopped everyone where they stood.

The aveho's hand went to his chest, and he fell to his knees.

"Father!"

Gerrika rushed in front of him, holding him up by his shoulder.

"Get away from him!"

The gang turned to the two figures hiding out by the corner of the wall.

Keeting and Janely Edland approached them, rifles pointed and fingers on their triggers.

"Not so tough now, are you?" Janely asked. "Your fighter is down. You have nothing."

Dreden felt his knees start to buckle as Gerrika dashed to hold his father. The wound in his chest looked worse than the shot to his stomach. From its location, there was no doubt that his heart was hit. Without immediate help, he wouldn't have a chance.

"We asked you for a very simple request." Keeting barked. He and his wife paused ten feet in front of the group, guns pointed to Dreden and Gerrika. "Don't try anything, or you'll get what he got."

"There isn't much time left," Janely said. "but there is still time to fix what you have done. Open the book and get to writing. The moment we see an officer approaching, we'll start picking more of you off."

As Honja was shot, he dropped *The Century* onto the ground. Its spine hit the ground, opening to a random page in the middle of the book.

As much as he and Gerrika tried to stop the bleeding, Honja's blood slipped between his fingers, pouring like a broken fountain.

His blood landed on the page, soaking into the text and becoming one with the words.

It glowed red on the page, as it merged with the text that had been written by Jowns.

"What the...?"

Gerrika picked the book up. In the heat of the moment, he didn't know what to do with it. The text was changing right before their eyes.

"What's happening?" Chanin asked, her voice cracking in emotion.

"Nnng..." Honja grunted, holding his wound tight in his talon. "I...I'm here. I'm in. My blood is in the book."

"Father..." Gerrika tried to push Honja back, but it was no use. "Please stop. This is making the bleeding worse."

Dreden looked around. No one, especially Keeting and Janely, knew what to make of the scene. Seeing the blood in the book reminded him of one of the Jowns passages he had read while he and his friends were still in jail. Jowns wrote the book in a blood spell.

Maybe blood was the only way to undo it.

"The contingency..." Janely said, her eyes wide, marveling at the sight of the aveho's blood swirling in the book. "Of course...the spell was cast and sealed in blood. The blood of the Unmade. It's letting him in."

Honja's breathing quickened. His hand fell from his chest, letting as much blood pour out onto the page as possible.

He reached over to his left arm and plucked out one of his own feathers.

And began to write.

His hand was moving through a page a second. The text manifesting on the page was going too fast to read, but that didn't stop everyone from looking over the aveho's shoulder, trying to see what was happening.

"How is this possible?" Gerrika asked. His eyes darted to everyone around him for help, but no one was any wiser. "My father never learned how to write. How is he doing this?"

Dreden remembered what the Unmaker had told him while it had him in its trance. He remembered what it said about magic and how it was used.

It didn't make a difference how smart or how educated one was.

"Magic is a feeling." Dreden said. "I think your father is just feeling it inside, and the magic is taking over."

In the way the aveho moved, there was no sign he had suffered two bullets. Keeting and Janely Edland, getting their wits back together and realizing what was happening, tensed up and lowered their guns to the kneeling Honja.

Their rifles never went off. With a flick of his finger, magic coursing through every cell in his body, Honja flicked his wrist at them. A bright beam shot soundlessly from the book. It hit their weapons. Their rifles sank in their fingers and turned to a dark powder, like black sugar.

Keeting and Janely looked at the mess in their hands, as the dust slipped out of their fingers and onto the ground. There was a deep look of pure belief in their eyes. Everything in their faces from their pulsing veins to their glazed eyes admitted defeat.

Honja swatted his hand again, and two arrows soared out of his bag. With two thumps, they were buried in the Edlands' chests.

They let out their last breaths softly, without fight. As they both fell and hit the grass under them, the force of their bodies hitting the ground sent the arrows the rest of the way through their chests and out their backs.

The gang didn't need to check their pulses to know they were gone.

"I'm not going to let you do this alone, Honja." Renny dug into the aveho's bag and picked out one of his arrows. He stabbed a small hole in the palm of his hand. "I'm going to help you."

The professor raised his hand over the book, letting his blood drip onto the pages as they turned and turned.

Dreden took the arrow from his father's hand, pricking himself below his fingers and passed it to Chanin. Chanin gave it to Cipre, who was already motioning her hand to the book.

"You can't do this alone." Cipre put her hand on Honja's back. "It's sucking everything out of you."

"Listen to her, father." Gerrika begged.

With all their palms pricked, they hovered their hands over the book. Honja weakly tried to fight them, but the force of the magic compelling their bodies forward was stronger. Their blood mixed in a swirling cocktail.

Chanin screamed.

Her hand, beginning with her open wound, began to turn black. Before Dreden could do anything, the same pain had struck him and Gerrika. Cipre clenched her hand as quickly as she could, and the pain forced a cry out of her too.

"What's happening?" Gerrika stumbled back.

Renny shoved his son out of the way as Dreden screamed. His son stopped for a moment, looking at the blackness building on his hand. It was the same charred blackness that had taken the people in the photographs the Edlands had shown them.

They weren't allowed to help.

"We've been *Made*." Dreden said. "I don't think we have any power over the book anymore."

To their collective relief, it looked like they had taken their hands out just in time. The blackness on their palms was receding into a soft warmth until it vanished into a smoke that dissipated instantly.

Now it was just Honja and Renny in control.

Renny was being sucked dry. With each turn of the page, it was demanding more of his blood. His wound didn't have the same severe steady flow as the aveho's, so the magical book had to forcefully extract it if he wanted to continue writing.

Dreden knew what was happening. He knew what would happen to his father and to Honja. He was stuck, glued to the grass under his boots.

Honja knew it too. In his weakened state, tethered to the book, he knocked the professor over with his shoulder, sending him onto his elbow.

"There is no need, Renny." he said. "I am already dying. There is no reason for you to take your life as well."

Renny got back on his knees, forcefully trying to send his hand back to the book. "I'm not letting you go."

"It's already happened." Honja smiled. "Earlier you told me the things you still want to do with your life. I'm not letting you forget."

Honja's feathers seemed to grow pale, as if the magic were taking all the color out of him and turning him into a black and white photograph.

Gerrika grabbed onto his father, holding him up as the last drop of blood poured out of his chest and the book closed by itself.

One moment of vibrant silence passed before it happened.

A roaring earthquake, like the sound of a continent-sized monster waking up from the depths of the sea, seemed even to come from the stars above them. A bright light beamed out from the cover of the closed book, shooting up in the sky like a speeding comet, and exploded into a million little pieces. In the brightness of the new creation, everything had been swept into invisibility like a puddle in an ocean. The lights were already halfway across the world.

A force pulled Honja's arms up. Everyone around him had to back away as he spread out his arms, and a powerful mass sprang out from his armpits. It was like his arms were melting. A bright light surrounded him as massive feathers formed on the tips of his arms.

In his final moments upright, Honja extended his big black wings as far as they would go.

But his new wings couldn't keep him up. Everyone stopped to marvel at the metamorphosis of his arms. To Dreden, they were just as wonderful as Gerrika's.

The aveho fell on his back. Blood had stopped pouring out of his chest quickly, settling into a soft rhythm like a draughting creek, in sync with the hole in his stomach. Dreden watched Honja's chest rise and fall in forced, uncomfortable breathing.

Dreden couldn't see Gerrika's face. His friend was bent over, holding the back of his father's head in his wings.

Renny took a knee next to both avehos. Honja looked up at him, his beak open and his eyes lit up in wonder like a summer sky.

"Honja," he said slowly. "do you know what you've done?"

"Know?" His chest rose and fell quickly in laughter. "No. I don't know. I feel. I *feel* what I've done."

"Keep your head up, father." Gerrika sniffed. "Please, this isn't over. This wasn't how it was supposed to happen."

Honja looked up at his son, as if just noticing he was there. "Gerrika… I'm sorry."

"No. No no no." His son bit the end of his beak. "Don't start. You don't start that with me. That's not what's happening."

"I wasn't always good. Most of the time I wasn't good. Now... now, there's nothing that I'm not feeling. The book...it's making me feel everything."

"How do you feel, Honja?" Renny asked. "How do you feel, friend?"

"I feel. I *feel*." He stopped letting out another breath as his chest rose for the last time. "I feel... I can feel the ground under my wings. I feel full. I feel well."

"Please..." Gerrika raised his father's hand to his forehead. "This isn't fair. You don't deserve this."

"I have taken many lives in my lifetime, son. It's been my job. Dying doesn't anger me."

Blood began to pour out from the sides of his beak. It was quiet, with no struggling. He didn't have anything more to say when he closed his eyes.

"It's not over." Gerrika said, fighting a sob. "The Maker...the Maker can bring him back!"

Dreden took a knee next to his friend, not wanting to look Gerrika in the eyes. "I...I don't think that the Maker exists anymore. Your father got his wings back. I think everyone and our home has been Made again."

"I want to go home..." The aveho sniffed, tightening his fists. "I want to go home!"

Chanin plopped herself down next to them, her face shiny with tears. "Our home is thousands of miles away, buddy."

Dreden looked to his father. He looked to him for any hint of anything to say that could possibly make his friend feel any better. The countless hours he and his father had spent discussing philosophy and the meaning of life all felt so worthless now. There was no feeling like being forced to confront the ideas that you had the luxury of entertaining in such an academic way.

No one said anything. Even Cipre approached and fell to her knees, putting her hand on Gerrika in consolation, who was no longer the only aveho in the world.

***

"Gerrika!" Chanin called out, as the aveho stormed back into the estate. "Come back! Where are you going?"

"Stay back." he shouted. "Don't follow me."

He didn't want to tell them what he was planning on doing. No doubt they all would restrain him if they knew. He was so full of emotion, anger, grief, that he couldn't think straight. He knew it but, with the events of the last day swirling in his mind, he didn't care.

A rifle sat next to a dead guard's body on the still-smoking second floor. Eyeing the magazine, Gerrika could see there were at least five bullets left in the gun.

Good, thought the aveho. *That's four more than I'll need.*

He searched all around the second floor, but no sign of his prey. At some point he was going to find him. The farther up you climbed the estate, the smaller the floors were. He had to be up there somewhere. There was no way an unarmed man would try to escape the estate alone with all the fighting going on.

Morell was hiding somewhere.

If I were a rich, back-stabbing piece of shit, where would I hide?

Gerrika expected to calm down, the longer the search took, but he was still seething. He could almost feel steam coming out of the feathers on his head. Morell deserved to die. Of course he did. He had led him, Chanin, and Dreden to their deaths, resulting in the permanent death of his father. There was no way Morell would ever get jail time for his role in the action. At best he'd have to pay a fine. Gerrika couldn't live in a world where that happened.

He tightened his grip on the trigger.

Kicking down door after door only excited his fury. He felt like a starved animal released from its cage, on the hunt for the first time in its life. Saliva almost dripped down his beak. Every little nook and cranny where a human could hide was met with the force of his kicks or the butt of the rifle. After manically searching five floors, thrashing everything in sight, there wasn't any sign of a hiding human.

"Where the fuck are you?" he shouted, having long stopped caring about being sneaky. "Show yourself, Morell! You're responsible for this!"

As he touched his bare feet on the top step, he caught a faint sound from the corner room. A bedroom, holding nothing but a guest bed and a dresser. A closet was tucked on the dresser's corner.

He could hear something scratching against the inside.

It could only be one person.

Gerrika dashed into the room, using his wings to gain momentum. Over the sound of his own running, he could no longer hear anything coming from inside the closet, but it didn't matter. Morell had already revealed himself.

The aveho turned the knob, swinging the door open.

The gun almost slipped out of his fingers.

It wasn't Morell, but it was. Gerrika could tell by his eyes. Even though they now were owned by a different creature, the former human's arrogant, helpless glare couldn't be mistaken.

"Morell?"

The creature sitting in front of him had fallen out of his clothes. His thinner waist could no longer hold up his pants, and his wings had busted his shirt open. His feet were too big for his shoes, so the new Morell looked about as helpless as a newly hatched chick.

"Help me…" Morell showed Gerrika his arms. His bare skin was bloody from all the frantic scratching.

"You're…you're not human anymore." Gerrika couldn't breathe. "You're an aveho."

The new aveho tapped his head softly against the wall, wincing in pain. "The Unmaker did this to me. Please help me."

Everything seemed to wash out of him. The anger, the hate, the murderous rage, it all fell off of him like an old skin. He could almost feel his emotions clump together in his head and swirl down a drain, to a place deep in his subconscious, to be found one day if he ever needed to protect himself again.

Not for killing helpless creatures.

"I was going to kill you. I was really going to go through with it, Morell."

The former human covered his eyes with his talons, tucking himself into a feathery protective ball. "I don't blame you. I would have done the same if I were you."

Gerrika collapsed to his knees, overcome with shame.

***

The explosion caused by the Gumarys' motor-carriage had taken out the rest of the guards on the first floor. After that, it was only a few more minutes before the remaining ones threw up their arms in surrender.

All the injured officers had been rushed to the hospital safely. A chunk of them had been shot, but none of them had suffered fatal wounds.

For the next hour, the police had to take statements from everyone there. As outrageous as everyone's story was, they had to accept it. Chief Milbrey, being the only officer who had read any of Jowns's Final Testaments, ended up clearing everything.

And if they needed any further proof, the Sunitian Sea had inexplicably vanished. Where it had previously been the mysterious pride of the city was now a long piece of grassland. It was not nearly as interesting.

About an hour after Honja's death, the police were searching every inch of the estate. Despite the explosion, most of the foundation was still strong enough to not make it unsafe to enter the building. Gerrika finally showed himself again, as he was followed by two policemen out the front door.

Dreden's jaw dropped when he saw what two officers were holding.

"Oh...MY."

They were holding an aveho by the arms. It was almost completely unclothed, with only a pair of pants hanging loose from the creature's thin waist. Brown feathers with splotches of white on his belly and shoulders colored his body.

"This guy," one of the officers smiled. "this guy is claiming that he's Morell Edland."

At the sound of his name, Chanin turned around, stepping to Dreden's side.

Gerrika paused in front of his friends, head hung low at the spectacle.

"What...?" Dreden had to take a moment to remember what the Unmaker had told him when he was inside him. "The Unmaker did that to you?"

The aveho nodded. Even with new avian eyes, the human Morell was still visible in them. "Dreden...please help me."

Patches of Morell's arms and legs were featherless, as if he had tried to pluck them all off to stop the transformation.

"I say that he looks fine." Gerrika said. "Heck, if we put a fresh coat of feathers on him, he could end up being a real looker."

"Gerrika..."

"No," the aveho gave him a hard stare. "I'm going to enjoy this."

Dreden didn't know if it would work. There was no way to know for sure. With magic back in the world, it seemed like anything was possible.

He picked up *The Century*. Flipping through it, there was only one page left in it with text. Whatever it said was impossible to read, but if it didn't contain the last work of the Unmaker, then there was probably nothing to be done.

Dreden hovered his sleeve above the text. It had caught some of Honja's blood as he and his friends lowered their bleeding palms to the book in an attempt to help. The blood, crusty and dried over the last hour, regained its liquid instantly as if the book were a hot stove. It settled on the final text, spreading out until there was only an indiscernible splotch left.

Morell's skin turned back to its normal human color, and all the man's features came back.

The new man raised his hand, feeling his face for a beak and feathers, and finding none. "Thank you."

"Why did you do that?" Chanin asked.

"Because," Dreden answered. "I think that the changes around here are going to be punishment enough for him."

Seemingly content now that his human form had returned, the officers snapped cuffs behind the half-naked man's back and ushered him to their carriage.

Gerrika grunted. The three of them were alone.

"It's okay." Dreden said. "None of us can blame you for how you're feeling."

"I went in there to find him." the aveho said. "I was armed and ready to kill him. When I found him in the closet, all feathered and pathetic-looking, I couldn't do it."

"Because he looked like you?" Chanin asked.

He nodded, thoughtfully. "I remember what you said about having selective empathy. It seems I'm not immune to it." Gerrika shook his head, scrunching his beak. "Damnit, guys, I beat myself up saving people from Minkompa. I must have saved hundreds of humans, and it was only selective empathy that stopped me from murdering a helpless man."

Chanin crossed her arms. "I probably would have done the same in your position."

"I just don't get it," Gerrika sighed. "it doesn't make any sense. Why would Jowns give my father the ability to reverse what he did? He was an aveho. Why would that genocidal lunatic do that?"

"If I were to guess," Dreden began. "it's because Jowns never doubted himself. He spent his life attempting to prove that the strong will always conquer the weak, that humans were the future and avehos were the past. I think that, once realizing he created the Unmaker, he had to accept that, while he may lose the battle, he will not lose the war. I believe he thought that even if his life's work were reversed and Kroonsaed and avehos returned, it would one day happen again, and again, as long as it will need to happen until the superior species reigns forever."

"I hope that's not true." Gerrika said. "I really hope that's not true."

The aveho stopped, staring out to the massive exodus of police carriages. He hadn't yet spilled everything that was on his mind, but he clearly just had to give himself a moment.

"My father didn't care for humans for most his life. With magic in his hand in his last moment, he could have done anything. Yet, even knowing that it was humans that condemned us to our lives back home, he chose not to take revenge, or any kind of rogue justice. He just reversed everything."

"He was clearly deeply changed in the last day of his life." Chanin said.

Gerrika put his hand against his head in frustration. "But that never would have happened if not for my death. He would have lived with his prejudice forever. It seems he was doomed to die because of his newfound feelings."

"We can never know how things would have happened if things went slightly different." Dreden crossed his arms. "There's no way to know if your father ever would have come around and found his emotions if not for today. The real point is that he did. In the end your father was selfless, and that will never be Unmade."

CHAPTER 22

Mirthinout was back in business.

In the week that followed, everyone was asking questions. Most commonly, passing ships had discovered that the Deadlands were no longer the Deadlands. There were people, and there were a ton of avehos.

Everyone wanted the truth, and Cipre was determined to give it to everyone.

"You really want to do this?" Radoff asked.

Cipre's hands were tight at her sides. "Everyone impacted by what Jowns did deserves the truth. I believe that we are no better than he was if we attempt to cover it up."

"You realize what this will do?" her boss asked. "This will forever change our nation. There will be no going back from this. This could end up doing more harm than good."

"That is a risk I'm willing to take. Telling the true story of millions that died at the hands of an evil man is not the wrong thing to do."

With the full support of Chief Milbrey, he had given Cipre every bit of Jowns's final work that had been left in the Saedians' cell. Even knowing what she intended to do with it, he gave her everything.

"Alright," Radoff said, forcing a smile. "if word gets out, Prime Minister Dowlepot is going to hit us with everything he has."

"Let him try."

Leaving his office, she walked down the hallway. Her friend Matry was hard at work at his desk, but seeing her pass by, he jumped out of his seat.

"Cipre!"

She paused as he rushed into the hallway. She couldn't help but remember that that was the first time she was seeing him in almost two weeks.

"Is it all true?" he asked. "Everything I've heard? It's all true?"

"Yes. It is all true."

"You were friends with the dragon? You kept that from me? Why did you do it?"

She bit her lip. She knew the answer to that question, and it didn't make her feel good about herself. "I just wanted to do something *bold*. I wanted to do something that Morell Edland's novel wasn't going to do. I encountered Minkompa on a freak chance."

"You didn't tell me." he beamed. "We agreed that we would never keep things from each other around here."

"I wanted to have something for myself." she answered, lowering her eyes guiltily. "It was wrong, and I was a fool, but I felt that I needed it. I wanted to be the discoverer of a great work of art, but look what happened. I've had an easy life. A lot of us have been so comfortable that it's become easy to ignore the suffering people around us. Despite my priveledge, I've never done anything to help others in need. All I've done is read crappy books and edit them so they can be sold to upper-class readers. I want this place to change. Publications like Mirthinout are going to need to if we're going to survive."

Matry put his hands in his pockets, considering her words. "No way for me to say with certainty that I wouldn't have done the same. I understand."

"Do you forgive me?"

Matry smiled, opening his arms for her. She gladly accepted his hug. "Always. You're a good person, Cipre. Everything you've just told me only reinforces it."

With Matry bringing him up, she couldn't help but think about Minkompa. A part of herself knew that she would never get over what happened. Once everything was over, after Honja had died, word had quickly spread that the dragon attacking the city had simply ceased to exist.

Even though it meant that the threat of the Unmaker was over, Cipre began to cry. It meant that a soft soul had been taken from the world.

Dreden had told her Minkompa's last message. She couldn't keep herself together after hearing it.

"I don't know why I'm crying so hard." she had told him. "he wasn't even real."

"He was." Dreden replied. "I really think he was."

***

After the publication of Jowns's Final Testaments in the next week, the entire world was sent into mayhem. Once the truth about the Edlands had also gotten out and what they had tried to do, there wasn't a nation in the world that didn't suddenly point its guns at Skaltbard.

Andayt, Borgetta, and Gontland were the quickest to action. Allying up, they all sent their best armadas to the coast.

***

It was the worst day of Charles Dowlepot's political career. It was easily the worst because it was the one that would finally decide that his life in politics was over.

The Prime Minister got a fatal sense of déjà vu. Once again, as he had been on that day before Dreden, Chanin, and Gerrika had first arrived in the city, he was meeting with representatives of the other three most powerful countries in the world.

Only this time it wasn't some political courtesy. It was, quite literally, to save the country's ass.

"I think all of you need to keep your ships off our shores." Dowlepot warned, knowing he had no real power. "This isn't how modern people should work out their problems."

"Is that something your first Prime Minister ever gave consideration to?"

The man speaking to him was Mister Pulk, the youthful representative from Gontland who had nearly made a foreign old man have a stroke the last time they met. He sat smugly, chair pulled up too close to Charles's mahogany desk for comfort.

The other two in the room with him were from Andayt and Borgetta. The Andaytian was a middle-aged woman named Jacky with a purple dress and her coffee brown hair everywhere but on her shoulders, as if meeting the Prime Minster weren't an important enough event to fix her hair for. The Borgettan was a man who couldn't have been much older than Pulk. His name was Stottard. He neglected to provide a first name.

"That's unfair, and you know it is. I can't speak for someone who lived a hundred years ago."

"Would it be fair to allow a nation such as yours to keep the Edland fortune?" Jacky asked. "After everything that's come out? You don't deserve it."

Charles knew that's what they would want. Firstly, to ease anti-government sentiment, he began an initiative to dissolve the Edland fortune, as well as the fortunes of those who perished, also part of the Jowns conspiracy. It was all going back into the community, to rebuild the hardest hit areas of the earthquake and the rampaging dragon, along with providing homes for those who had found themselves employed by the Edlands after the family's faux charitable outreach.

But now, other countries wanted a piece of it too.

"We lost millions of our people a hundred years ago." said the Borgettan Stottard. "Birds or not, they were our people. They worked and were tax paying citizens. We need payment."

"Do you? Your economy is booming right now." Charles turned to Jacky. "Yours as well. Why do you need it?"

"It's about more than just what we lost." said the woman. "Believe it or not, it's also about making you look good. How is your government supposed to earn back the trust of the people if it looks like you're trying to inconvenience yourself as little as possible?"

"Do you know how much money this government's lost?" Charles had to catch himself, almost accidentally saying 'I've lost'. "Don't you know everything I'm trying to do? Putting all the money to good causes and making sure avehos feel welcomed? Can't you see it?"

It didn't matter if they did. Charles knew it. This whole thing was just a morality circus. Looking around at the three representatives, anyone could tell they didn't really care about avehos or the humans of the former Deadlands. They just wanted to see Skaltbard embarrassed. They just wanted to see *him* embarrassed.

He rested his fists on the top of his desk. This all could have gone better. If he had chosen to help the Saedians, then the public might have seen him as a hero. Maybe someone who, even though they didn't do the best at every turn, realized that there were bigger things than Skaltbard's highest office. Now that the truth was published, all he did was look spineless. A coward on a national scale.

"What do you want from me?" Charles nearly whined. "What can I do to make this end quickly?"

The young Mister Pulk looked at his two peers. The three of them shared a predatory, toothy smile.

"We want a full surrender. Immediately."

***

Kroonsaed, now back in the real world, wasn't about to be ignored. As part of the surrender agreement, Skaltbard would be forced to pay billions in reparations. The humans and avehos of Kroonsaed and every other part of the former Deadlands finally had ways to get their resources back.

In the months that followed, another problem began to hit Skaltbard, and it seemed as if there was a piece in the paper every day about them.

Avehos.

They weren't staying in Kroonsaed. They wanted to see the world and get out. After the first month of being Made again, thousands of avehos had made their way to Skaltbard, most of them even coming to Brunswald. Their courage to leave their homes was eased by the new coalition government being formed in Skaltbard. Radical activity of avehos and humans fighting in the streets and taking flames to buildings with the Edland name still on them caused the need for immediate action.

Kirriel, a female aveho who had been a law professor in Kroonsaed, was appointed to interim Prime Minister to help ease radical activity.

In a piece published by the Brunswald Herald, one of their journalists had invited a man from the Skaltbard Weekly, the most popular paper in the country.

Their conversation went:

BH: The topic today: avehos. Look, it's not an understatement to say that the world we live in now is vastly different than it was a few months ago. Personally, I think, considering the great evil that it turns out Jowns inflicted on the world, we are moving in the right direction. Would you agree?

SW: Well, yes, but it's important to not lose our heads over this. Mickeel Jowns, not a great guy, but we have to look at this from a pragmatic perspective. Should we feel bad about being the most powerful nation on earth?

BH: Umm, that's not exactly true anymore. You've heard about the surrender?

SW: Yes, but it's not always about winning wars. It's about having the best people. Having the best culture, and that's really what's at stake here. Look, I'm sure most of these avehos are well-meaning, but you can't just toss them into a society like ours and expect a smooth transition.

BH: I agree, but who does that burden fall on? Us. I believe we need to adapt.

SW: No, they do. No reason they should be here if that's the case.

BH: You realize that our country completely screwed them over a hundred years ago?

SW: It's awful what happened, but what, you expect me to feel bad about it? I wasn't alive at that time. I never killed any of them. Look, I don't want to get off topic, but all I meant to say was that you can't have so much of new, non-humans in our society and expect them to fall in line so quickly. They're not us, why should we expect them to be?

BH: According to the Kroonsaed records, crime there has been almost nonexistent for as long as it has been Unmade. That includes human on aveho crime and the other way around. Not just that, but in the new Kroonsaed and the surrounding states and countries, it's still humans that greatly outnumber avehos. By the numbers, more humans from there are coming to this country, why aren't you concerned about them? Why are you only choosing to focus on avehos?

SW: And another thing, I don't like seeing the young Morell Edland's name being dragged through the mud at every turn. The guy clearly didn't know that his parents were involved in horrible things, and the papers are tearing him apart as if he killed millions of avehos himself! It's too much. It's sickening.

BH: I think there are many people out there more deserving of our sympathy than a former billionaire.

SW: But getting back to the real question: surely you must admit that the whole thing is a little unfair? Avehos go away for a hundred years, humans make incredible advancements in science and technology, and suddenly they're owed our modern commodities? They didn't make them. We did. Don't you think it's unfair that they get to reap the rewards of what humans have toiled for in the last hundred years?

BH: You cannot be serious.

CHAPTER 23

It had been two months since magic returned to the world. The thing was: most of the world seemed exactly the same.

"Isn't it weird?" Dreden asked Chanin. "There are no sorcerers popping up. No potion stores anywhere."

"Maybe, as a species, we are done with magic." Chanin mused. "Just because it's back doesn't mean that people are going to use it. Besides, I think maybe most things that magic can do can be accomplished with modern technology and medicine anyway."

"Fine by me. Besides, if magic was going to be used for more evil in the world, it's no great loss that it's gone from our lives. But we'll have to see, won't we?"

"We'll have to see." echoed Chanin.

"Have you heard from your parents lately?" he asked. "How have they been doing?"

"I sent them a letter." she replied, hesitation in her eyes. "That's how we've been communicating for a while. Of course, I haven't seen them since the day I told them that Brunswald existed."

"If they were my parents, I think I would hate them."

"But I don't." she told him. "I'll see them again. Hopefully soon, but right now, I am not going to forgive them for ignoring me like they have."

They were sitting on the roof of the Gumarys' garage. It was just after noon on a Tuesday. The sun was shining. Not a hot summer sun, but more of a crisp fall kind of sun, even though there was still a month and a half left of summer.

"Get any new letters from Gerrika since Friday?"

"I did. Did you? I hear he has some kind of big surprise for us." Chanin checked her watch. "He'll probably be here soon."

They only had to wait five minutes for Gerrika to show up.

"I'm here, guys!" They heard him call from the street.

The aveho climbed up the ladder. Dreden and Chanin watched the ledge of the roof for him as the sound of talon on metal grew louder.

Gerrika's hand and boot gripped the top, stepping out onto the roof.

Dreden and Chanin instantly realized what the surprise was.

"No…" Chanin said, trying to keep her jaw from touching the floor.

Dreden's eyes widened as he looked at what his friend was wearing. He was wearing his normal clothes, tight sleeves and all. The aveho raised his arms up, spinning around like a runway model so his friends could see how his body looked.

"Your wings…your wings are gone!" Dreden exclaimed.

Gerrika took a seat next to Chanin, his beak opened in a shy smile as he put his talons together on his lap. "It was a big decision, and I still had some money from my time singing. My wings were wonderful for what they were for."

"They were magnificent." Chanin said.

"Not going to argue with that." the aveho laughed. "I used them to save people. Flying, soaring through the sky was the most incredible feeling I'll ever feel. Feeling the cool air through your feathers and between your toes…it's something on another level. But…" He let himself have a breath, exhaling. "If I'm being true, I didn't trust myself with them. I didn't trust myself not to one day just fly away. Just take a leap into the sky and keep flapping and never land. I didn't trust myself not to become a Sky Man."

"That's very poetic." Dreden said.

"Right? I don't want you guys to feel bad for me. I had a lot of time to think about it, and I think what I did was right. I found a sympathetic aveho doctor and he removed them safely. I'll be happy to permanently ground myself. Grounded with you guys." The aveho paused, suddenly becoming pensive. "I'm nervous. I remember what I did with my wings and the way those military people looked at me. They loved me. Now that more and more avehos are coming to the city, it's hard to keep convincing myself that those good people might not feel differently about me."

Dreden understood. "It's a whole new situation. One aveho is interesting. It's a novelty. It's new, but thousands of them…"

"Is an unwanted invasion." Gerrika finished. "I should stop. It's all current events, but hopefully in the near future it won't be. Anyway, I don't want to think about it too much. I want to focus on this moment, here and now."

"That's really sweet!" called a voice from down below. "I'm proud of you, Gerrika!"

Two people began climbing up the ladder. Right on time, Allin and Sidra Gumary stepped out onto the roof.

Allin had a pair of six packs in his hand. His wife had to hold him so he wouldn't fall off the ladder. "Hope you guys don't mind, I brought the party with me."

"Not at all." Chanin said. "God, thank you so much. I would kill for a beer right now."

The Gumarys sat down next to the trio, distributing bottles of beer to every one of them.

"As much as I liked your wings," Sidra popped the cap off her bottle. "I think you made a good choice. Anything you feel that strongly about must be the right choice."

Gerrika plucked the cap off with the tip of his beak. "I'm glad in other ways too. I missed my old clothes, and those things were sometimes exhausting to carry around."

"I've got to hand it to you," Dreden said, patting the aveho on the back. "as far as surprises go, that one was a big one."

"Oh no," Gerrika shook his head. "no, that wasn't the surprise."

"*That* wasn't the surprise?" Chanin almost spat her beer out.

"Nope!" Gerrika crossed his legs, relishing the suspense. "You know how you guys haven't been seeing a lot of me lately?"

"I just assumed you were cheating on us with your new aveho friends." Dreden joked.

"He doesn't have any." Chanin said.

Gerrika dismissed them with a swat of a talon. "The truth is I've been hard at work on a masterpiece. I wrote a play."

"You wrote a play?" Dreden asked. "*Wrote?* Past tense?"

"Yep. I finished it and I submitted it to the Lesting Theater for review."

"Wait, but didn't they denounce you?" Sidra asked. "Weren't you done with them after you assaulted that other theater owner?"

"Yeeeeaaaahh." Gerrika scratched his head. "I didn't use my real name."

"You have a stage name now?" Allin sipped from his glass.

"Can I guess what it is?" Chanin asked.

"You can try."

"Ham."

The aveho frowned mirthfully. "No."

"Hamuel."

"No."

"Ham Hammond Hammington."

"I really need new friends."

"No!" Dreden laughed, suppressing a belch from his beer. "I promise we can be enough for you. Just give us a chance!"

Chanin pointed at the aveho with a free finger on her beer-holding hand. "I think Gerrika's on to something. I think we need a new member of the gang."

"The gang?" Dreden asked. "We're not a gang. We're a trio."

"Hey!" Allin recoiled, a hand to his chest. "Just what do you think we are? Screws and bolts?"

"Correction, maybe we are a gang. But look, we have a rigorous application process, and it could be months before an applicant gets to the interviewing stage."

"I can solve this." Gerrika took a gulp of beer. "They need to be an aveho. That much is certain. And they need to be a girl."

Sidra hesitated. "This might be an awkward question, but how do you tell the difference between a male and female aveho?"

Dreden and Chanin looked to Gerrika. Even though they knew the answer, avehos were much more his territory. "Females are brighter colored. They also have higher vocal tones for the same evolutionary reasons that human females do."

The sound of flapping forced their heads to the sky. Dreden pointed to the fast approaching figure. "Why don't we ask *her* to join our gang?"

Gerrika rose to his feet. An aveho was quickly approaching. "Great, I think this is for me."

The aveho landed on the roof of the garage. She was red and had a bit of black along her collar, her brow, and on her shoulders. She looked a lot like a cardinal, if a cardinal could ever replicate the kind of exhausted look on her expressive face as she reached into the mail bag on her shoulder.

"Parcel!"

She took out a white envelope from her bag, looking at the name printed on the front. "Is one of you Gerard Olyver Winder?"

Gerrika approached her. "Right here."

The red aveho raised her bushy black brow, as if to say 'Really?'. "You sure that's you?"

"It's me."

She extended the envelope to Gerrika, tucking her yellow toes against the ledge of the garage for traction. "Wait," she narrowed her eyes upon seeing his clothing. "where are your wings?"

"It's a long story." He took his mail from her. "But don't worry. I'm okay."

"I wasn't worried, guy. Just making an observation."

Dreden watched Gerrika's expression change. None of them were expecting her to have such a response to a total stranger. She didn't say her words in a mean way. She said them in a way that invited an honest competitive verbal battle.

"Great, anyway, catch you later, Gerard."

He raised his arm, stopping her as she was about to take off. "Wait!"

She turned around, her red tail swishing in the air. "Yes?"

"Umm." Gerrika looked down at his boots shyly. "What's your name?"

"Dezoran, but my friends call me Dezi."

"It's nice to meet you, Dezi."

"I said my *friends* call me that." she smiled.

Dreden had to forcefully suppress his smile. He, Chanin, and the Gumarys were paused, beers stuck halfway to their mouths as they watched the avehos' interaction.

"Okay, Dezoran, do you like being a mail carrier?"

She shrugged her wings. "It's okay. I enjoy flying, and it's one of the easiest jobs an aveho can get in the city. At the end of the week, I like to reward myself for my exercise. I go to Pebillon's on Third Street and get myself a three-plate buffet."

"I love that place!" Allin said. "Their baked potatoes are to die for!"

Dezoran pointed at him, her amused eyes as sharp as the tip of her beak. "This guy has the right idea."

"Were you a student back home?" Gerrika asked.

She nodded. "I'm from Billuway. I was a biology student at Nimman University before coming to this city." She pumped her fist in the air. "Go lemurs!"

"I went to Faeriebridge." He turned around, pointing to Dreden and Chanin. "The three of us did, but I think we're technically drop-outs now."

"Nothing wrong with that. Are you doing what you love?"

"I think I'm starting to."

"Good! That's all that matters then. Anyway, I have a lot more mail to deliver before the end of the day. Later, loser."

Dezoran took off, flapping her wings hard before getting herself into a steady rhythm.

When she was gone, Gerrika turned back to his friends with eyes the size of the sun.

"Can you believe her?" he asked. "The…just the *audacity* of her to talk to a stranger like that."

"She liked you." Chanin told him.

Gerrika's expression instantly changed. "You really think so?"

"I'm having fun." Dreden laughed. "This whole get-together has just turned into watching Gerard crash and burn while talking to a girl."

"You want to kiss her," Chanin teased, extending her lips. "don't you?"

"No. No I don't! Kissing is disgusting! It's an appalling human thing. Avehos have the good sense to know better than to do anything so unsanitary."

As Gerrika took his seat back in the group, Dreden lunged over to him. His lips caught the tip of Gerrika's beak, instantly making the aveho recoil.

"Oh my God!" Gerrika turned around, spitting in disgust over the ledge of the roof.

"That's what you get, boy!" Dreden settled back in his seat. "Wow, how much beer have I had?"

The aveho wiped his beak with his sleeve. "I keep telling you guys mammals are disgusting. You sweat, have the worst diseases, your organs are in all the wrong places, and have off-putting romantic tendencies, but none of you believe me."

"So," Allin said, laughing and resuming his drinking. "Gerard Olyver Winder?"

"I like the name Olyver." the aveho replied. "Gerard is kind of like my name anyway, and Winder of course…"

"Is for Winds Wilk." Chanin answered.

"He was a good man, and he helped me realize what I wanted to do with my life. I feel much less aimless now. My play, *The Down-and-Out*, is very much inspired by my favorite works of his."

Tearing open the envelope, Gerrika took out the letter from the Lesting Theater. He read it to himself, keeping his eyes steady as he digested every word. After going through it a couple times, he gave it to the group to read.

Dreden looked at what it said:

To Gerard Olyver Winder,

Thank you so much for your submission. After reviewing all our plays for the next season, we regret to inform you that we will not be accepting your play. However, we do see a lot of potential in your work. We invite you to come down to the theater at your convenience during the next few weeks to see if we may have a creative contributing position for you. Of course, feel free to submit again next time our submissions are open.

Errick Lesting

"I'm sorry, bud." Chanin said.

"It's okay. It is." Gerrika folded the paper and put it in his pocket. "They had some nice things to say."

"The fact that you wrote a play as quickly as you did, and the theater had something good to say about it says a lot." Dreden said. "I'm honestly impressed. I think this is great news. I wish I had the discipline to do that."

"That's actually what I wanted to mention to you, Dreden."

"Oh?"

"I was hoping you would help me rewrite the play."

"Honestly?"

A twinkle showed in his avian eyes. "You're like the most imaginative person I know. Not to mention you're the most well-read in literature of anyone I know. If anyone can help me make this play the best it can be, it's you."

"I'm honored, Gerard. I'm honored. Hopefully I won't end up like Morell Edland."

"What do you mean?" Gerrika asked.

"You don't know? *A Mad Past* was published yesterday."

Chanin and the Gumarys almost choked on their drinks.

"Why would the publisher still release it?" Sidra asked. "After everything that that family has done?"

"I don't know." Dreden answered. "I think enough people who still believed in Morell were demanding it be published. Apparently Cipre Lane refused to do any more work on it, so it wasn't even the complete project when it was released. And indeed it was…to poor critical reception."

"I'll drink to that!" Gerrika cheered. "Another reason to be happy I didn't shoot him that day."

"Dreden's one of the best shots around." Chanin said, turning to the Gumarys. "Guys, you should have seen the way the two of us handled ourselves in the Edland Estate."

Dreden raised his beer above his head. "Never let it be said that a crooked man can't shoot."

"Speaking of which." Gerrika shuffled his feet nervously. "I'm curious, Dreden, why did you wait so long to tell us? And I'm not hurt or anything, but why did you tell Chanin first?"

"Firstly, I actually didn't tell Chanin. She figured it out on her own." He turned to Chanin, who held her glass smugly in her hand. "To answer your question, it's because people take the label too seriously. If I told you I was a homosexual, then that would forever be one of the first things you think of when you think of me. I don't want that, and I don't think about it that way. I just think about it like anything else about myself: I like toasted bread with butter, I like spending time alone sometimes with coffee and a good book, I like men. It's just another thing about me."

He paused, looking to his four friends who were staring at him blankly.

"You're thinking about it right now," Dreden smiled. "aren't you?"

"You're *right*." Chanin said. "It's something that we can't help. Wow, I have never thought of it that way."

"It's okay." Dreden said. "I know you can't help it. It's just the way things are."

"I don't mean to be the one to ask this question," Sidra said. "but out of curiosity, where have the three of you been living?"

"Right, now's the time." Gerrika answered. "You see, the government has been letting us live in designated housing for the past couple months, but that time is about to expire and…you see."

"We're poor." Dreden answered for him. "We are very poor."

"I see." Allin said. "You guys want to know if it's okay if you stay here for a little while?"

"If it's not too much trouble." Chanin said.

"Not at all!" Allin said. "We love you guys, but this will bring up an awkward question: the question about rent. I'm thinking one hundred."

"One hundred dollars a month?" Chanin asked.

"Right. The two of us will pay you a hundred dollars a month."

The trio broke into laughter. They clinked their glasses together in cheers, as Allin seemed to be the one laughing the hardest at his own joke.

"We have the money too." Sidra said. "After the fiasco that was the motor-carriage, we realized that we were probably not going to get much better with it. We ended up selling the patent."

"Wow," Gerrika said. "so, what's your guys' plan now?"

"We hope to devote a lot of time to improving public transportation. Can you imagine it? A bunch of motor-carriages on the street? All that smoke and noise? Eeghh... Oh! Chanin, did you end up telling the guys the news?"

"Mmm!" she paused downing the rest of her beer. "You guys remember that camera that I was working on? The one that takes rapid-fire photographs? I ended up making it work!"

The group ended up hanging out on the roof for another hour, finishing off all the beer that the Gumarys had provided. They were up there until the sun began to go down.

"Hey!" Chanin cheered. "I just realized something. This is the first time we've all shared a beer together since before coming to Brunswald."

"Are you serious?" Dreden asked.

"Remember? It was at the campus pub, the night before we got here."

"That's right. Shit, I can't believe it."

As they were getting ready to call it a day, and the Gumarys and Dreden were going down the ladder, Gerrika pulled Chanin aside.

"Chanin?" he asked. "This is probably a really stupid question, but I'm going to ask it anyway."

"My favorite type of question." she said. "What is it?"

"That camera. The one you made that takes photos really quickly. Just how quickly do you think it can take them?"

EPILOGUE

"This is really stupid." Dreden said, his cheeks going red with his smile. "I can't believe we're going to try this."

"We need to make this quick, guys!" Allin called from around the corner. "I've only got the street reserved until 3. After that, they're dead serious about us leaving."

It was another bright day, this time in the winter. It was cold. It was hot coffee weather. Dreden's favorite time of year. They were out in the street in central Brunswald. Since the earthquake and the rampaging dragon, the city had done a lot to put itself back together. There was still a mess here and there, but it was fine. It would fit in well with what they had planned.

Chanin came around the corner, taking her large camera out of the back of their production carriage.

The fabled camera. When the trio's ambitions for the camera went public, many bright minds across the country wanted to chip in, in exchange for a portion of the profits. Considering the kind of success they were likely to have, the guys didn't mind agreeing to sharing the profits.

With so many geniuses at their side, coupled with their admiration of Dreden, Chanin, and Gerrika's roles in improving the world, they were more than happy to put all other projects aside for them.

And with everyone's help, held together by the mechanical ingenuity of Chanin and the Gumarys, it looked like their investment was finally going to pay off.

"Okay," she said, positioning the camera in the middle of the street. "welcome all, to the first and potentially last day on set of The Down-and-Out!"

"Did you end up reading the rewrite that Gerard and I did?" Dreden asked.

"I didn't!" She bent herself over, adjusting the device. "I'm sure it's good, but I wanted to be surprised when I saw the thing for myself."

"I'm so excited!" Sidra beamed. "I really am!"

The Gumarys were hard at work covering the entrance of the street from the busy intersection. A lot of people shouted curses at them and screamed at them to get out of the way, but both Allin and Sidra were just as well-versed with salty words.

"Okay!" Dreden clapped his hands. "Where is he? Where's our star?"

"Almost done! I'm still getting dressed!"

A minute later, Gerrika came out from the corner of an alleyway in the middle of the street. He was buttoning his collar and adjusting his pants. "Sorry, I needed privacy while changing. One of these days, I hope we have our own personal carriages on set at all times."

Chanin threw her hands down against her knees, bursting into laughter at the sight of Gerrika in costume.

He was dressed in a light brown coat and pants that had dozens of different kinds of stains on them. He had a ratty, light grey cap on his head, and a black walking cane touching the ground next to his old, worn-out boots.

The aveho put out his arms, smiling at her. "What do you think?"

"You look homeless! You look like a tramp!"

"I *am*! The Down-and-Out is a story about a vagrant aveho. A comedy about a young dreamer fallen on hard, modern times. A budding star in his own mind under the city lights. Sure, it's silly, but it's good, and it might even be smart too."

"Is that true, Dreden?" She asked after she stopped laughing. "Would you say it's smart?"

"Smart?" He rolled his eyes up, putting a finger on his chin in thought. "I don't know if it's smart. How would you describe it, G?"

"I would say it's sweet."

"Sweet…that's right. And it's kind. It's sweet and kind and kind of sweet."

"I think we need to get this rolling." Chanin said, playing with some buttons on the camera. "This thing seems like it's starting to have a mind of its own. If we don't start now, it might not work."

"Then let's not waste another moment!" The dressed-up aveho declared. "Let's get this failure on the road, literally!"

"Once again, I can't promise that this will be any good." Chanin reminded them. "The idea is just too brilliant not to attempt." She looked through the camera lens, raising a hand in the air. "Ohhhhhkay, we're ready."

"We're ready?" Dreden turned around, getting behind the camera too make sure he wasn't in the shot. "I'm so excited. I wish my father were here."

"By the way," Gerrika said. "where is your father? I haven't seen him in a while."

"He decided to obey your father's request." Dreden smiled warmly. "He's going around and seeing the world for the first time in his life."

"I'm so happy for him." Chanin said, relaxing her grip on her camera. "Okay, it's now or never, guys."

"Ready?" Dreden asked Gerrika.

Gerrika stretched his arms, jumping up and down and shaking his limbs loose as if he were getting ready to fly again. "Ready."

Chanin clicked a button on the camera, putting her hand on a side lever and swirling it around as if she were winding up a toy bird. "Aaaaaaaaand action!"

ABOUT THE AUTHOR

Brendan Walsh is currently a grad student at Cal State Northridge. He is also the author of the *Noble Animals* series and *Immortale*. When he's not writing he is either drinking coffee, reading comics, or thinking about what to write next. He is only a philosopher and a recreational madman.

NOTE FROM THE AUTHOR

Word-of-mouth is crucial for any author to succeed. If you enjoyed *The Century's Last Word*, please leave a review online—anywhere you are able. Even if it's just a sentence or two. It would make all the difference and would be very much appreciated.

Thanks!
Brendan Walsh

Thank you so much for reading one of **Brendan Walsh's** novels. If you enjoyed the experience, please check out our recommended title for your next great read!

The Century's Scribe by Brendan Walsh

"If *Harry Potter* had grown up and gone to the university in Lev Grossman's *Magician's* Trilogy, the result might look something like this."

–James Rollins, #1 *New York Times* bestseller of *The Last Odyssey*

View other Black Rose Writing titles at www.blackrosewriting.com/books and use promo code **PRINT** to receive a **20% discount** when purchasing.

www.ingramcontent.com/pod-product-compliance
Lightning Source LLC
Chambersburg PA
CBHW010735100726
47899CB00009B/3066